PRAISE FOR *ARMSTRONG*
BOOK I OF THE CUSTER OF THE WEST SERIES

"The world has a new hero—actually an old hero reimagined—George Armstrong Custer, in this delightfully funny alternative history that's better, or at least happier, than the real thing."
> —**Winston Groom,** bestselling author of *Forrest Gump* and *El Paso*

"Droll satire, this is the West as it might have been if the Sioux hadn't saved us."
> —**Stephen Coonts,** bestselling author of *Flight of the Intruder* and *Liberty's Last Stand*

"If Custer died for our sins, Armstrong resurrects him for our delight. Not just the funniest book ever written about an Indian massacre, but laugh-out-loud funny, period. The best historical comic adventure since George MacDonald Fraser's *Flashman*."
> —**Phillip Jennings,** author of *Nam-A-Rama* and *Goodbye Mexico*

"If you like learning history while laughing, you'll like this book... marvelous satire."
> —**David Limbaugh,** nationally syndicated columnist and bestselling author of *Guilty by Reason of Insanity* and *Jesus on Trial*

"Crocker has created a hilarious hero for the ages. Armstrong rides through the Old West setting right the wrongs and setting wrong the rights, in a very funny cascade of satire, history, and even patriotism."
> —**Rob Long,** Emmy- and Golden Globe–nominated screenwriter and co-executive producer of *Cheers*

"Sly and funny."
> —*City Journal*

"Crocker's Custer, a milk-drinking, sharp-shooting master of disguises, takes us on a series of uproarious adventures in the persona of Armstrong.... Armstrong is an extraordinary hero—a military strategist, a courageous fighter, and some sort of dog whisperer to boot. He's also a dashing romantic with a knack for making women swoon.... I'll look forward to finding out where duty calls Armstrong next."
—*Washington Examiner*

"The conservative novel of the year...*Armstrong* is a rollicking work of alternative history that doesn't sacrifice accurate details or historical nuance for the sake of your entertainment.... *Armstrong*'s Custer is a hero to love and admire."
—**The Conservative Book Club**

"A good read with a wonderful premise.... It does make one think that George Armstrong Custer was a very good man in command during a horrific battlefield defeat."
—**Defense.info**

"Action-packed and great for laughs.... Fathers will love reading this book with their sons. Patriots will love it, too.... Prepare to delight in American history and heroism, unencumbered by trigger warnings."
—**The American Thinker**

"This is the kind of book young people should want to read, which will challenge them and widen their horizons. It is part history, part humor, part drama, and all-around entertainment."
—**Eagle Action Report**

"Crocker knows his history, so his anti-history is knock-down, pain-in-the-stomach hilarious."
—*American Conservative*

Armstrong Rides Again!

Also by H. W. Crocker III

Novels

The Old Limey

Armstrong

Armstrong Rides Again!

Armstrong and the Mexican Mystery (coming 2022)

History

Robert E. Lee on Leadership: Executive Lessons in Character, Courage, and Vision

Triumph: The Power and the Glory of the Catholic Church, a 2,000-Year History

Don't Tread on Me: A 400-Year History of America at War, from Indian Fighting to Terrorist Hunting

The Politically Incorrect Guide to the Civil War

The Politically Incorrect Guide to the British Empire

Yanks: The Heroes Who Won the First World War and Made the American Century

Contributor

The Maxims of Robert E. Lee for Young Gentlemen (foreword)

Bigly: Donald Trump in Verse (foreword and afterword)

THE CUSTER OF THE WEST SERIES

ARMSTRONG
RIDES AGAIN!

H.W. CROCKER III

REGNERY
PUBLISHING
A Division of Salem Media Group
Washington, D.C.

Regnery® is a registered trademark of Salem Communications Holding Corporation

ISBN: 978-1-68451-169-3
eISBN: 978-1-68451-216-4

Library of Congress Control Number: 2021933895

Published in the United States by
Regnery Publishing
A division of Salem Media Group
Washington, D.C.
www.Regnery.com

Manufactured in the United States of America

10 9 8 7 6 5 4 3 2 1

Books are available in quantity for promotional or premium use. For information on discounts and terms, please visit our website: www.Regnery.com.

For the Crocker Boys

Numquam Concedere

CHAPTER ONE

In Which I Am Introduced to a Mystery

D ear Libbie,
 Greetings from San Francisco! I write this from a study with a window overlooking the ships in San Francisco Bay. Beside me, smoking a cigar and criticizing my every word, is Major Ambrose Bierce, the journalist. He would rather tell this tale himself—he is the professional writer after all—but as you know, dearest Libbie, I can turn a handsome phrase myself, and this is our tale, Bierce's and mine, and would not have happened had we not crossed paths (and swords), and I can tell it plainly, unadorned by journalistic exaggeration.

My last letter chronicled how I liberated Bloody Gulch, Montana— and a fine, rousing story it was. But it left you hanging precipitously wondering what happened next. Now I can tell you.

I had to flee. The U.S. Cavalry was on its way—and much as I love the Cavalry, I had to preserve my anonymity. A sorrowing world believes I am dead, and I cannot disabuse it of that mournful conclusion until I can prove that my men and I were betrayed into catastrophe at the Little Big Horn. I now had some clues—it was just possible that Major Reno and Captain Benteen had been suborned by that villainous Indian trader Seth Larsen—but I was still a long way from proving my innocence.

I had to remain incognito, and I reckoned my best chance was to hightail it west. I looked at a map and placed my forefinger on San

Francisco. Named after a Catholic saint, it seemed the perfect destination for a man who has sworn off alcohol and gambling and who has eyes only for his wife—though she's half a continent or more away—a city where a man could commune with his thoughts and with the beasts of the field, with brother sun, sister moon, brother ass, and perhaps Sister Rachel.

But I'm getting ahead of myself.

It also held, I could see, an admirable harbor from which I could flee the country, if necessary. It was just possible that someone linked to my last adventure might track me down, penetrate my clever alias of U.S. Marshal Armstrong Armstrong, and expose me for who I really am: the late Lieutenant-Colonel George Armstrong Custer, former Boy General of the Union Army and husband of the most famous alleged widow in America.

I was left to embark on a long and arduous trail, as you can trace on a map, to get from Bloody Gulch, Montana, to San Francisco. I was obliged to begin the journey on my own. Beauregard Gillette, my Confederate ally, I had sent to you. My Indian scout Billy Jack I had assigned as an escort to take Rachel, both heroine and villainess of my previous dispatch, to a nunnery. Miss Sallie Saint-Jean and her Chinese acrobats had decided to remain in Bloody Gulch, at least for a while, before resuming their perambulations as a touring theatrical company.

I had for companions, then, only my horses, Edward and Marshal Ney, and the large and fearsome-looking black dog Bad Boy, who was both ferocious to my enemies and, I will confess, one of the most loyal and intelligent Lieutenants it has ever been my privilege to command. The four of us got on splendidly as we traveled west. Over the campfire I would hold them—Bad Boy anyway—in rapt attention as I recounted stories of my days at West Point or in the great war or during Reconstruction or in the Indian wars. I had assumed that Bad Boy spoke German, as dogs do. So our fireside chats were a way to instruct him in English—and to break him of one bad habit. Bad Boy, unfortunately, had been trained to hate Indians. I have worked diligently to convince him that not all Indians are evil, and that many, like my old Ree scout, Bloody Knife, or like Billy Jack, a Crow whom Bad Boy knew from our adventure in Bloody Gulch, are some of the best company a man can have.

I suppose it was inevitable, but our happy critter company was eventually disturbed, some miles west of Bozeman, by a lone rider arriving in the night. Bad Boy heard him first, alerting me with a low growl, and then disappearing into the brush as the horseman drew closer. I had a Winchester on the stranger when he approached—and noticed that his black boots matched the black of his face. He raised his hands and said, "You don't need that, sir. I was just passin' through. Saw your campfire."

"Those are Cavalry boots, aren't they?"

He gave me a strange look. "You an officer?"

"U.S. Marshal—was in the war, though."

"Marshal? Well, I'll be. Always took this for a lawless territory."

"I don't know how to take that—and you haven't answered my question."

"Yes, sir, they is Cavalry sure enough: 10th Cavalry Regiment. Indians down south calls us 'Buffalo Soldiers.' I reckon that's what I was. Kept the boots—if you treat 'em proper, they last forever."

"I was a Cavalryman during the war."

"You don't say?"

"You didn't notice my own boots."

"Well, howdy-do, sir—I see 'em now. No wonder you was an officer—you sure is observant."

"And I'm obliged, as a U.S. Marshal, to ask you if you're a deserter."

"Deserter? No sir, not me. Did my time, got mustered out, and moved up here with an Indian woman. Live in a cabin about five miles farther southwest. Just rode into Bozeman for a visit—by which I mean to a saloon. My wife, bein' an Indian and all, don't like me drinking at home. I was hopin', in fact, you might have some coffee to share. My woman don't even like the smell of alcohol."

"Neither do I. Alcohol I have foresworn. As for coffee—I do have some on the fire if you have your own tin cup."

"Oh, yes sir, I surely do. Might I dismount—and might you point that Winchester somewhere else?"

I nodded and lowered the rifle. "Dangerous to be traveling alone—Sioux and Cheyenne on the warpath; you heard about that?"

"You mean, Custer and the 7th getting wiped out—yeah, I heard about that. Amateurs, that's what I calls 'em. Would never have happened to the 10th."

"Is that so?"

"Oh, hell yeah. That's what we did—fought Indians down south—Texas and all. You gotta be a whole lot more clever than to charge right into 'em. They was just asking for it."

"You do realize that Custer was the most celebrated Indian fighter in the Army."

"Pfft—celebrated for his golden curls most likely. I heard about him all right. He was a fancy pants."

"A fancy pants? Do you know who I am?"

"A U.S. Marshal—at least you told me so. I don't see no star."

"That's right—a U.S. Marshal; and I could arrest you right now."

"For what?"

"For slandering an officer of the United States Cavalry!"

"What?"

"You heard me."

"That ain't illegal."

"If you think you're getting coffee after slandering one of America's greatest soldiers—well, you're wrong."

"Now hold on there, sir."

"You hold on there. You are under arrest for desertion."

"Before you go arrestin' anyone—before you go callin' me a deserter—I want to see a badge."

"Very well," and I made the incredible mistake of laying the Winchester by my saddle (which I also use for a pillow) while I ferreted the theatrical old tin star from my saddle bags. When I turned round, I'll be darned if that darky didn't have a revolver pointed straight at me.

"Well, ain't that pretty?" he said as I held up the star. I folded my fingers over it in frustration and rage. "Never thought I'd bag me a Marshal. I'll be takin' more than that coffee now, if you don't mind. What else you got in those saddle bags?"

"Nothing that would interest you—deserter. Marshals travel light."

"So do men like me, Marshal, and what you got I might need. Now you reach in there nice and slow—don't do anything sudden. I'm not sure what to do with you yet. Might even let you live."

"I'm supposed to trust the word of a deserter, a thief, and a liar?"

"Not all lies, Marshal. I got me an Indian woman all right. Fat as a mammy can be—eats me outta house and home. It's on accounta her I turned to robbin' folks. Gotta keep her fed."

I turned to my saddle bags and glimpsed Bad Boy on the periphery, quietly high-stepping through the brush to get a good angle on his target. His eye caught mine. I knew what he wanted—a distraction.

"Well, Buffalo Soldier, if that's the way it's going to be—I do indeed have something you might want. The money I recovered from a stage robbery."

"You got what?" He stepped forward, completely off his guard, right into Bad Boy's trap. My loyal Lieutenant flew from the darkness, canine jaws clamping on the deserter's wrist. A banshee scream, and the deserter's revolver clattered to the dirt, crimson blood drizzling down his fingers. Bad Boy clamped down even harder, jerked viciously, and threw the villain to the ground. I recovered my Winchester and had it leveled in a trice.

"Well done, good and noble Bad Boy. You can let him go."

The dog released his death grip and backed away a couple of steps, growling a warning that the deserter shouldn't try anything. The Buffalo Soldier got the message.

"All right, deserter, on your feet."

"Marshal, that's the Army's business, not yours."

"You pull a gun on me and it's my business. I've got you on charges of threatening a federal officer and slandering a Colonel of the United States Cavalry. Those are capital offenses in my book."

"What do you mean by that?"

"I mean there's a death sentence attached."

"That ain't so."

"As you said, deserter, this is a lawless territory."

"Now wait a second there, Marshal. Maybe we can make a deal."

"Why should I make a deal with you?"

"You asked about Indians. A lone man's at risk. Two would make it safer."

"Not if one is a darky deserter."

"I knows how to take orders, sir, if I wants to—and I wants to. You can have my gun. You can have my knife. I'll be your guide."

"Guide to where? To the Indians?"

"Wherever you wants to go."

"California."

"California—hell, sir, that's…that's…hell, I don't even know how far away that is."

"Then I can't use you."

"But I reckon it's that way, sir," he said, pointing west. "I could take you into Bozeman and we could find us a real scout."

"Us, deserter?"

"Well, sir, like I said, it's my wife that drove me to robbin'. Maybe I need a fresh start. I can be plenty useful—the Army taught me a lot."

"You cook?"

"Yes, sir."

"If I shot game, you'd know what to do with it?"

"Sure as biscuits and gravy, sir."

"I hate to backtrack—could we find a scout beyond Bozeman?"

"Well, sir, there's a trail to Virginia City, and from there onto the Oregon Trail. I reckon there's some old scouts scattered that-a-way. Trail ain't used much now—they might be looking for work."

"What's your rank, deserter?"

"Private, sir."

"And your name?"

"McCutcheon, sir; they calls me Willie McCutcheon."

"All right, Private McCutcheon, I'll give you a chance to redeem yourself and be worthy of those boots you wear. I don't have a Bible, but here, hold this," I said handing him the tin star, "and repeat after me, 'I,' state your name and rank…"

"I, Private Willie McCutcheon…"

"…do solemnly swear to follow the orders of Marshal Armstrong or have my guts eaten by that dog named Bad Boy." I inclined my head to my noble canine companion.

"Does I have to say that last part?"

"To make it binding, yes."

"I do solemnly swear to follow the orders of Marshal Armstrong or have my guts eaten by a dog named Bad Boy."

"Now give me back that star. You're officially deputized, Private. And I promise you, if you're not worthy of my mercy, you won't get it."

"Yes, sir. One request, sir."

"State it."

"Might I have that coffee, sir? I is awful thirsty."

"Fetch your cup, Private. And if you fetch anything you shouldn't— you know the rules, your guts get eaten. Now hand me that revolver, butt first, and that knife you said you had."

If meeting Private McCutcheon profited me nothing more, I had at least acquired a serviceable Colt revolver, a stash of ammunition, and a handsome Bowie knife—all for a cup of coffee. It wasn't a free trade, but it was a fair trade.

We sat by the fire together, and mused, as soldiers often do, on our women folk at home.

"My Libbie," I said, "is the finest woman ever to come from Michigan; fine figure of a woman, educated too, a judge's daughter, and devoted as the day is long."

"I reckon my woman," said Private McCutcheon, "left the reservation 'cause she couldn't fit in the teepee no more, or maybe her snorin' blowed it down—don't know which. Kinda smells funny too, but you get used to that. Big hands—and I tell you, she don't mind usin' 'em. Slaps me somethin' silly when she gets mad. Sort of hate to think about her. Kinda intimidatin' in her own way. Truth be told, sir, I is on the run from her."

I thought it wise to change the subject. "How's your wrist, Private?"

He raised a fist to display the blood-stained bandana wrapped around the wound. "I reckon it'll be all right, but I'd be obliged if that dog slept next to you, not me. I don't care much for dogs, especially those that got a taste for my blood."

I have to say that with my weapons (and his) and Bad Boy beside me, I felt I had little to fear from Private McCutcheon and slept as soundly as a drunken muskrat. When I awoke—and you know I sleep little—he was already at work, the campfire burning, the coffee ready.

"Here you go, Marshal," he said proffering the pot as I dug out my coffee cup.

"Please, Private, call me General."

"General, sir?"

"Brevet rank from the war. It'll put us on a better footing—not law-man and outlaw, but officer and soldier."

"No more, 'deserter,' sir?"

"No, Private, because you've enlisted in Marshal Armstrong's own personal army; we ride to California…"

"Yes, sir."

"…as soon as you find me a scout."

We found one. He lived in a shack outside of Virginia City, Montana, and his name was Johannes Fetzer. He was grey of beard and hair, but sprightly all the same.

"So, you vahnt to go to California, do you?"

"You've been there?"

"Yeah, sure I've been zair—and back too."

"So I see."

"Long vay."

"Yes, I gather it is."

"An old man like me vood need some motivation to go so far. I got everything I need right here."

As "right here" amounted to a shack that might collapse under the snow of a Montana winter and a pasture of fenced mud, it was apparent that Johannes Fetzer was a man of few needs.

"You're asking for money," I said.

"I don't travel vor my health."

"Well, given the manner of life to which you're accustomed, how would a dollar a day suit you?"

"You can double zat, mister. After all, I gotta travel back home— zat's twice zee journey. Half now; half when we arrive in California— and you're responsible for all our supplies. Zat darky vork for you?"

I nodded, and he said to Private McCutcheon, "I like my coffee strong, my tobaccy smoky, and my biscuits fried in bacon grease, *ja?*" He looked at me and added, "Vohn't charge you for any viskey—I'm dry on the trail, at least most of zee time; and vaht I buy or bring is my own concern."

"How long's the journey?"

"Vell, mister, now zat all depends—but for purposes of our negotiations, I'd be villing to settle on forty dollars now and forty dollars ven vee get zair. Forty days and forty nights—has sort of a ring to it, don't it?"

I suppose it did, though forty days in the company of these two scamps was hardly an inviting prospect. Still, one must make do, and I accepted his offer. I counted out eight coins from my saddle bags.

"Vaht are zese?"

"Gold coins, each worth about five dollars—at least that's what they say. They're from the Delingpoole treasure—I imagine you've heard of that."

"I heard stories—never knew it vas true."

"That gold's true enough. You can take it to the bank."

"I reckon so," he said, holding up a coin to get a better look at it. "Whose face is zat?"

"The man himself—vain as a Roman emperor."

"Ugly feller, but I reckon you can do anything if you've got zee gold."

"You've got yours. Let's get going."

"Vell, you know, mister, Californy's a mighty big place. Vair in California you vant to go?"

"San Francisco, the City of St. Francis, a holy and temperate place, I believe."

"*Ja*, I know San Francisco. That's a helluva place. Once lost a month's vages in a saloon zair; and you know vaht, I got myself shanghaied and had to serve six months at sea to earn it back. I can take you zair, but I ain't stayin' zair, no siree; too dangerous. But zair's a railroad now, you know—transcontinental. Vee could drop down to Promontory—that's Utah Territory—and you could pick it up zair. That's vair zey drove zee golden spike, *ja*? You've heard of zat zing?"

"And how far is that? Surely not forty days' ride from here?"

"Maybe not, but it's still a mighty long vay—close to four hundred miles. And zem's no easy miles either: big mountains, cliffs, hard going. But vhen you hit zee railroad—*ja*, it's nothing zhen, like riding a golden chariot straight to San Francisco. You be zair in twenty-four hours, by golly."

"Well, then, let's be off."

"All in good time, young man. First, your darky, he fetches my supplies, and zhen I map out a route, and zhen..."

"And then you get on with it. I believe in action, Herr Fetzer—action that moves us today, not tomorrow. Now snap to attention and see to your duties immediately!"

And so, dearest Libbie, with my admonition ringing in his ears, Johannes and Willie set to work, and soon my pioneering adventure began. Unfortunately, it proved to be more dangerous and deadly than I expected.

On our second day's ride, I noticed a half dozen mounted Indians following a parallel trail on a high bluff to the east. They would disappear behind the bluff, only to pop up again hours later. They showed no apparent interest in us; we tried to show no apparent interest in them, but of course we were wary. That night in camp, none of us slept, though we heard no Indians, or their signal calls; the night was enlivened only by the most primitive of conversations between Private McCutcheon and Herr Fetzer. They regaled each other with stories such as these:

HERR FETZER: "You know, I vonce killed an Indian mit my bare hands."

PRIVATE MCCUTCHEON: "Really, old-timer—how'd you do that? You knife him?"

HERR FETZER: "No, I haff told you—*mit mein* bare hands; *mit my pet bear Hans.* Very loyal zat bear. He scalp zee Indian before zee Indian scalp me."

Or:

PRIVATE MCCUTCHEON: "You know Dutchy, I's actually grown right fond of takin' orders again—gives a man a purpose, don't it?"

HERR FETZER: "You zink zo? Maybe you should reenlist zhen."

PRIVATE MCCUTCHEON: "Well, that might be difficult, given circumstances."

HERR FETZER: "Zo vaht you like about zee Army? Zee marching? Zee uniforms?"

PRIVATE MCCUTCHEON: "Well you get three square meals a day—no worries there. Pay's guaranteed too."

HERR FETZER: "*Ja,* vell, Villie, personally, I like my freedom, *ja?*

PRIVATE MCCUTCHEON: "Dontchya ever get lonesome?"

HERR FETZER: "Pshaw."

PRIVATE MCCUTCHEON: "I mean, in the Army you always got things to do, and in the barracks there's always a card game."

HERR FETZER: Card game? You take my advice, Villie; don't do zee zings I done. No card games in San Francisco, *ja?* Especially at zee House of zee Rising Sun. Dangerous place, by golly. You vahnt some entertainment—you get yourself a bear. Oh, my pet bear Hans, *ach du lieber,* he could dance. Vaht a bear—as if trained in Vienna."

Or:

PRIVATE MCCUTCHEON: "I just don't get it. I mean, why do Indians love torturin' people? It ain't natural. It's kinda disgustin'. Who likes torturin'? Except for Sergeants, of course, but they got a reason—and limits."

HERR FETZER: "You're a married man, *ja*?"

PRIVATE MCCUTCHEON: "Yeah, I guess right enough—it's what you might call a common law marriage. Ain't no preacher involved or nothin'."

HERR FETZER: "Zee preacher is immaterial; your wife is an Indian, is she not?"

PRIVATE MCCUTCHEON: "Yeah, she's an Indian."

HERR FETZER: "Vell zhen, your answer: vimmin, Indians—torturers. All zee same. In scalping, you lose your hair; in marriage, you lose your life. That's how I see it, Villie. You should get a common law divorce. No woman is as loyal as vas my pet bear Hans."

Such was the philosophy of Herr Fetzer. I need hardly say, dearest Libbie, that I learned little of interest and nothing of profit, and I was content to doze until night gave way to glorious day and I could breathe in, yet again, the wonders of the vast Western landscape, which I do so love. If a Cheyenne raiding party had captured me at a suitable age and raised me as an Indian, I would have been perfectly happy—save for the absence of you, of course, darling Libbie. But putting you aside for a moment, what could be better than a life of riding, hunting, and fighting?

Private McCutcheon prepared a marvelous breakfast, and any worries about Indians and any fatigue we felt from our lack of sleep were quickly dispelled by the crisp air, a gentle breeze, the purposeful sway of the horses beneath us—and, most delightful of all, the absence of any visible Indian scouting party. Our spirits soared.

After our long day's ride we slept the sleep of the just. When I woke the next morning, though, I was surprised to find myself alone. Our horses were all picketed, but there was no fire, no boiling coffee, no biscuits and bacon. I assumed Herr Fetzer and Private McCutcheon had gone to fetch firewood or find a stream to fill our canteens. It was unlikely they would be bathing. I set off in search of them, bidding Bad Boy to stay and watch over the camp.

We had camped on a small plateau set above a brake of thick brush and briar penetrated by thin deer paths. I made my way down and examined the weaving trails nearest me. The signs were ambiguous, but I thought I saw tell-tale boot tracks and trampled vines on the narrow, overgrown trace that led right, so that's the way I went, moving cautiously so as not to get my sleeves and pant legs caught on the briars.

It was a winding, downhill passage. After what seemed like a half-mile's descent it opened into a glade. The sun was shining, the meadow was beautiful, but thirty yards into it was not beauty but brutality: staked to the ground, unspeakably mutilated, and unmistakably dead—his head severed from his body and planted in his chest—was poor Willie McCutcheon.

"Vatch out, Marshal, Indians!" It was less a shout than a croak, and I spun to see Herr Fetzer, pinioned to a tree—crucified by spears. His head lolled. He spat. A horrible red slimy spittle stuck to his chin. His shirt was bright crimson, blood streamed down his face, his lips sputtered, and he gasped an epitaph: "I am nothing vizout Hans."

I should have had a revolver or a Bowie knife in my hand, but before I could think of either, a fearsome blow struck me on the head, and I felt brute fingers seizing at my scalp and gripping my throat; others seized my arms, yanking them behind me, ripping my sleeves in the process. My gun belt and knife were stripped from me. I was forced to kneel—but only for a moment. I mustered every pound of muscle, every ounce of sinew, and exploded to my feet, threw off their holds, and twisted from their clutches. They held my torn sleeves, but not me. I was undaunted—even though my scalp was bleeding, and I was dizzy, and my eyes were blurred. I confronted my assailants—five hardened braves—and they suddenly stepped back, affrighted: Good lord, did they recognize me?

One of them grunted and pointed to my exposed right arm. I looked down and was reminded of the evil Indian tattooist who had affixed your image there, Libbie, and beneath your tattooed portrait, my Cavalryman's motto, "Born to Ride."

The braves' guttural exclamations sounded like a Sioux dialect. They talked animatedly amongst themselves, and though I couldn't make out what was said, I reckoned no good could come of it. Still, I was on my feet—and my attackers were unnerved. One of them eructed an authoritative grunt, ending their palaver. He looked at me, raised his hands, showing that he was unarmed; a sign of peace, I assumed—though Private McCutcheon and Herr Fetzer were bloody contradictions. The brave pushed his hands slightly forward as if asking me to sit down.

"I'd rather stand."

He called out a command. Three more Indians bounded from the brake and charged me. I crouched, bracing for the impact. I got in one punch before crashing to the ground with all three of them. We thrashed around wrestling like caged weasels. At one point a savage hand, as big as a bear's, grabbed the back of my head and shoved my face into the dirt. I managed to spin away, caught a glimpse of white clouds and blue sky, then a huge fist, red and menacing, shot up like the head of a giant cobra. It struck, and all was darkness.

CHAPTER TWO

In Which I Experience a Reunion

W hen I awoke it was still dark—because I was blindfolded. I was astride an Indian pony, with no saddle, and my wrists were bound before me (which was considerate—behind me would have been much more painful). I sensed Indian guards riding to either side. If any man could ride a horse blind—even unconscious—and keep his seat, it is of course your beloved Autie; the Indians must have been impressed.

As the days passed, the blindfold never came off; my hands were never unbound; the sun and wind blistered my face and neck; my wrists chafed at their restraints. When it was time to feed and water me—and my captors weren't generous with either food or drink—I felt a wooden spoon pressed against my parched lips.

Then something of a miracle happened. Behind us, faint but insistent, was the excited barking of a dog. The Indian outriders grunted and hissed. They seized my arms and wrenched off the blindfold. They nudged my horse to make a 180-degree turn. I blinked, my eyes unaccustomed to the glare of the sun. In the distance I saw Bad Boy, speeding towards us like a greyhound. Riding placidly in his wake was my Indian scout from Bloody Gulch, Billy Jack, astride an Indian pony and leading my horses Marshal Ney and Edward. He had an extraordinary companion riding side-saddle on a horse beside him: a nun. Surrounding them was a screen of mounted Indian braves.

Bad Boy was first to meet me. I was in no position to lean over and pet him, but I nodded him a salute. He took a sentry position beside my pony and acted as though the Indians were friendly; perhaps I had taught him too well.

Billy Jack rode up and saluted: "Reporting for duty, sir."

"Your first duty, Sergeant, is to untie me. Thank goodness you've come."

"Was not voluntary; these Indians brought us here—and they are not Crow. They are Meahtuah Sioux, cousins of the Boyanama Sioux. They recognized the markings on your arm—Boyanama work—and they know about her," he nodded to the nun.

"Howdy, Marshal Armstrong, surprised to see me?" And I saw that hidden beneath that nun's habit was the raven-haired villainess of my last adventure, Rachel, looking more wickedly attractive than ever. "I found out from your Indian that a religious vow can't be taken by force. But I liked your idea of becoming a nun—not the vows, but the costume. I figured a disguise like this might come in handy—easy to make and gives me a free pass. No one connects a nun with a dead Indian trader like Larsen."

"No, I suspect not."

"And no white man bothers a nun with an Indian. He'd be afraid of getting roped into mission work."

"I suppose, but what about the Indians?"

"The only Indians that matter are the Sioux—and to them I'm the widow of Bearstalker, daughter-in-law to Chief Linewalker. That merits honor, not trouble. It even merits an Indian escort. So," said Rachel with a bewitching smile, "it seems that you're at my mercy once *again*, Marshal Armstrong."

"You know these Indians?"

"Like your scout says, the Meahtuah are kin to the Boyanama, so they know me. And I have a good reputation—despite knowing you."

"I rescued you, Rachel. And you repaid me by conspiring with Larsen."

"That's in the past, Marshal—and both of us have plenty to regret. You need me now. These Indians will do what I say. As far as they know, you're still my slave…"

"Your what?"

"…awarded to me by Chief Linewalker."

"For goodness sakes, woman."

"I stand between you and a scalping. You had a black scout, didn't you?"

"Yes, Private Willie McCutcheon. He was butchered."

"His wife was avenged; he wronged her; these are her people. Your fate is in my hands. They think you kidnapped me from the Boyanama Sioux: I am to decide whether you live or die."

"But we escaped together."

"If you behave yourself, we might again. I'll have them untie you. They say there's a small stream-fed lake down yonder. You can wash. I like my slaves clean. And we have new clothes for you. I thought ahead; I made a collection for indigent miners. Consider yourself one, because I think you just had a lucky strike."

The minx actually winked at me. I was speechless. She said something to the Indians, the cords that bound my hands were cut, and I was yanked from the Indian pony. After days riding a bareback horse, grass under my boots felt good. Three braves escorted me to the river. I took the Indian medicine pouch that hung from a thong around my neck. It held my foldable toothbrush and a small supply of salt with which to brush my teeth. I completed my dental ablutions, and then gladly discarded my filthy clothes for the bracing cold of the lake. The water was clear and wonderfully reviving. Small fish darted about my feet; I was enlivened enough to try to catch them. Then I saw Billy Jack sitting on his haunches regarding me from the shoreline. He had a saddlebag over his shoulder and a hat box in his hands.

"Training?" he said.

"Training?"

"Yes, in Spanish, *entrenando para una pelea*; in French, *entraînement pour un combat*. You work speed of hand, yes?"

"Speed of hand—yes."

"I brought you clothing: fresh, clean, donated by worthy Christians. I have Christian undergarments, shirts, trousers, socks—even a new Stetson hat. You will be well-dressed Marshal. You still have the star?"

"Yes, I still have the star."

"Good. Think we may need it. Sister Rachel believes you head to San Francisco."

"How the devil does she know that?"

"Nuns know many things."

"She's not a nun, Billy Jack."

"I read somewhere, 'Clothes maketh the man.' Perhaps sanctity comes with costume."

"If she's a nun, then I'm a...."

"Marshal—and General," he said, and not for the first time, I wondered how much Billy Jack knew about me; more than I knew about him, I reckoned. He slid the saddlebag from his shoulder, unlatched it, and reached inside. "I even have a towel for after washing."

"Well, throw it here, you..." I almost said "heathen," but caught myself: "...you papist."

"Ah yes, praise God." He threw me the towel. "Hail Mary."

I will say this: Rachel was an exceedingly clever woman—a woman of daring, dash, and plans, as you remember from my previous adventure, but also a good eye for clothes. She had managed to find me buckskins that fit as though they had been expertly tailored to my broad shoulders, barrel chest, narrow waist, and limber legs. I tilted the white Stetson onto my head and wished I had a mirror.

I had to rely on Billy Jack, who spouted, "*Muy magnífico*; in French, *très magnifique*; in Latin, *valde magnificus*; in Italian, *molto magnifico*."

I affixed my badge to my buckskins and strode boldly to where "Sister" Rachel awaited me. It will not surprise you, dearest Libbie, that when I reappeared, Rachel gasped and clutched at her heart.

"Why, Marshal, those buckskins do you proud."

"I'm obliged to you ma'am."

"I think they're enough to spare you—provided you accompany me to the transcontinental railroad at Promontory, and then see me safely to San Francisco."

"I don't have much choice, do I?"

"You could say no, but then I'd have the Indians kill you. They'd like nothing better."

"I think we'll save that for another time."

"I'll retain the option."

"But why San Francisco?"

"I should think that's obvious—it's where you're going, isn't it?"

"Yes, but..."

"I need a chaperone for a big city like that."

"But Rachel..."

"I saved your life. Your duty now is to protect me."

I couldn't deny that. And so I started on the trail anew, with Bad Boy, Billy Jack, Sister Rachel, my horse Marshal Ney, and my spare mount Edward. The Indians retreated whence they came, and, I assumed, we were not followed.

I grieved, of course, that my previous companions had been so horribly murdered and mutilated, but I gave the Indians credit: they had left our supplies intact. Moreover, Rachel's cooking was such a dramatic improvement over Private McCutcheon's, and Billy Jack was so much better and more affordable as a pathfinder than Herr Fetzer that even I—who, as you know, dearest Libbie, am not much given to theological speculation—had to wonder at how Providence had turned Herr Fetzer's and Private McCutcheon's grisly fates into our good fortune. Their lives had been well spent.

The conversation, too, improved. Rachel believed in self-improvement and spent many an evening conjugating French verbs with Billy Jack, eyeing me as she did so. I, however, took no part in language lessons, and instead sat by the fire, sketching diagrams of old battles in the dirt with a stick, instructing Bad Boy in the proper use of Cavalry. He was an attentive pupil.

These were pleasant days and nights, the weather was crisp and comfortable, the aroma of pines and firs wafted over us, and it seemed as though we traveled without a care. Occasionally I would go hunting to provide fresh meat. Sister Rachel was quite the picture, in her nun's habit, with billowing sleeves retracted so she could stir our evening stews over the campfire. Really, it was almost idyllic, save for your absence, dear; but such things must be endured.

There were, of course, difficulties along the way. Some of the trail was hard, as Herr Fetzer had warned: there were precipitous cliffs and steep mountain ranges; the weather was not always kind; Indians we saw no more, but we noted bear-scratches on tree bark, and at night coyotes serenaded the moon. I will not bore you, though, with the details of that treacherous and exciting journey, which pitted me against the elements and the overbearing rudeness of the stationmaster at Promontory (I had to flash my badge to commandeer a suitable railcar for Bad Boy, Marshal Ney, Edward, and the horses belonging to Rachel and Billy Jack). As challenging as the journey was, it is not germane to my main story, and it might mislead you as to the tenor of our travels, because by the time we reached Promontory, we felt as optimistic as the wide open plains, a trio of titans—Marshal, Indian scout, and nun—on a pilgrimage to the city of Saint Francis.

At Promontory, we took advantage of its modicum of civilization. I bathed and shaved—and even acquired a new set of clothes (shirt, vest, and suit: more suitable, I thought, to a city like San Francisco) and laundered my buckskins. I don't know how she did it—a mystery, perhaps, of the monastic life—but when I rejoined Sister Rachel, she was fragrant and glowing, her nun's habit fresh and finely pressed, her cheeks aglow as from a perfumed bath, her eyes alight with—well, one could say "devilment," but "anticipation" might be a better word—for the exciting journey to San Francisco.

"All aboard!"

Sister Rachel stepped onto the train, I followed, and Billy Jack came bearing our slight luggage—two bags I had bought at Promontory to hold whatever wouldn't fit into our saddlebags. We entered a passenger car—and into a mystery. The entire car, though designed for passengers, had been turned into a baggage car, with boxes and cases resting on nearly every seat. It was as if the passengers had been kidnapped, leaving their voluminous belongings behind.

As a nun, mysteries and miracles were surely part of her daily prayers, but Sister Rachel stopped and gawped. Billy Jack, a red man of practicality, gently eased her aside and cleared two rows of seats for us.

"You and Sister Rachel take front row; I take back row with luggage."

Sister Rachel and I did as we were bidden. The train jerked forward and then rocked gently on its rails.

"Strange," Rachel said, "for a passenger car to be used like this."

"Yes, isn't it? But if it pays the freight—perhaps all this belongs to some millionaire in San Francisco, having it shipped out for his wife or something."

"Oh, Armstrong," Rachel said, grasping my arm in a way that I thought inappropriate for a nun. "San Francisco—civilization: dances, dresses, dinners."

"Yes, my dear, but since you have the window seat, I suggest you enjoy the view. The West, my dear: big, expansive, untamed—I feel at one with it."

My eyes looked beyond her, out the window, and appreciated the passing countryside. I had but a few moments, however, to enjoy it. Billy Jack leaned over the seat and whispered, "Marshal, passenger come."

I turned to see a delightful young lady who had entered our car from the rear entrance. I stood as she approached. She bowed and curtsied, almost like a supplicant—then I realized it was for Rachel's benefit, given her nunly garb.

"Excuse me, señor; sister." She pointed at the aisle seat of our row of three. "May I?"

"Why certainly, ma'am."

She took the seat. As I sat adjacent my sense of duty was immediately aroused. She was quite the exotic character, dark of hair and eye, olive of complexion, and with that Latin intensity that comes perhaps from the promiscuous use of peppers in Spanish cooking. Her black, coal-fired eyes burned—as so many have done in my presence—with a passion that belied her demure fluttering lashes. When she spoke, it was with fiery rapidity, but in a whisper, and with a beguiling trace of Spanish.

"Señor, I am loath to disturb you. I did not expect you to travel with a nun…and with an Indian."

"They were unexpected but most welcome company, as are you, *señorita*." I thought my own touch of Spanish might put her at ease.

"You are most kind. When I entered at the rear of the car, I saw you. You appeared deep in thought. You write in your head?"

"Right in my head?"

"They told me you do such things."

"Really, they did?"

"Wait, señor, before we continue, it is important that I know: you are alone—except for the sister and the Indian, yes?"

"At present, yes; my companions are in a separate car."

"I see. You come with many men?"

"Not men exactly. I sent the men away—if you mean the Indians."

"Indians? Away, señor? Not to Neustraguano?"

"No, señorita, not to…may I help you in some way?"

"I expected to find you in San Francisco."

"You did?"

"Why yes, señor."

"Why?"

"Ah, I understand—you fear being overheard. You suspect hidden ears behind these bags and boxes. But, señor, I assure you, I booked this car for myself; so if you boarded alone with the sister and the Indian, then you are still alone, except for me."

"You booked this entire car for yourself?"

"Yes—I took no chances."

"My dear señorita, a car so large for a woman so petite—but these bags are all yours?"

"Of course, señor, I had to be prepared for many circumstances."

"My apologies, señorita; I didn't realize we were trespassing."

"It is quite all right, señor."

"The stationmaster and I had exchanged words—at length. Perhaps he didn't care what car I took after that. He just wanted me gone."

"And I am content to have you here, señor, with my luggage. It is just most unexpected—like the nun and the Indian. But they told me to expect the unexpected from you."

"They did?"

"Yes—and I have tried to be unexpected too. I thought the docks in San Francisco would be watched. So I traveled to New Orleans to confuse our enemies. They would not expect me to arrive by train across America. You can imagine how difficult my journey has been—all the way from Neustraguano."

"Yes, I can only imagine. Just how far away is Neustraguano?"

"First, I had to cross Mexico; then a week's sailing to New Orleans."

"And yet—you knew I would be in San Francisco?"

"They told me you were there—why aren't you?"

"Actually, I'm on my way."

"Ah, you too are trying to avoid detection, yes?"

"Indeed, I am. And how, señorita, did you detect me?"

"They gave me your description. They said you were tall, blond, fierce, determined, and handsome. These things are true, are they not?"

"Well, yes, I have that reputation."

"I see you now: *un hijo de la estrella de la mañana.*"

"I suppose that might be true, but who told you all this?"

"I think, señor, that perhaps you are right, after all—we should not talk here. One can never be too careful. How well do you know this Indian?"

"That," I conceded, "is a very good question."

"I know him," said Billy Jack, "all is well."

She seemed skeptical—as was I, frankly—but she glanced at Rachel, was reassured, and continued, "They told me to give you this—a token of good faith." She produced a small black purse from which she drew a gold coin, kissed it, and placed it in my palm. On one side was a cross, on the other a queen.

"Your monarch?"

"Mary, the queen of heaven," she explained, bowing her head, and nodding at Rachel.

I smiled indulgently—these Latin royals and their titles. "I'm much obliged, señorita. What am I to do for it?"

She looked puzzled. "Nothing now, señor—just an advance payment."

"Of course—but your name, señorita, what might that be?"

"Consuela Victoria Margarita Monteverde Cristóbal."

"I see. Which one do you prefer?"

"Prefer, señor?"

"Victoria will do, then, will it?"

"Yes, you may call me that. And you, señor, what shall I call you?"

"Ah, a good question. You may call me...*Señor Generalissimo*."

"Is that wise, señor?"

I looked penetratingly into those dark, passionate eyes, which reminded me of boiling coffee. Plumbing their depths, I risked an answer, "Sometimes, señorita, the best disguise is no disguise."

"You are a bold man, señor—of that I was warned—but I hope not imprudent."

My face flushed with irrepressible anger; my teeth gritted in righteous frustration. You can understand, Libbie, how that word—that horrible, horrible word—shook me to my core. I expostulated in my most vigorous manner: "*Imprudent!* Really, señorita, you cannot know how that canard, that calumny, that epithet chases me like an old maid chases the town drunk. *Imprudent, impetuous, reckless,* they say. The fact is that if Benteen and Reno had supported me—as duty demanded—I should never have been killed!"

"Killed, señor?"

"Yes—killed, with all my men—it's something I can never live down."

"You are dead, señor?"

"Up to a point—but even if dead, señorita, I do my duty: I am the hero you take me for."

"But you are a dead hero?"

"Only in name, señorita: if you require a knight errant, I am ready to pledge my troth." And I took her noble, delicate hands in my own, even as Rachel's elbow dug into my ribs.

"You are Señor Bierce?"

"*Bierce?*"

"Yes, Comandante Ambrose Bierce."

"My dear woman, I fear there must be some mistake."

"You have second thoughts?"

"No, señorita, I have no thoughts at all, I assure you."

Just then we bumped over a trestle, our seats rocked, and fearing that she might fall I gripped her shoulders tightly and pulled her to myself, knowing that not all women, my dearest Libbie, have your strength and balance.

A conductor meandered down the aisle and winked his approval of my gallant deed. But I had not reckoned on Victoria's Latin blood. "You take liberties, señor." She pushed me away—with a force that would have done you credit, my dear—and Rachel, taking her cue, gave me a stinging slap across the chops, and said, "Really, sir, I must ask you to behave yourself!"

Rachel's blow and admonition were as nothing to the fire in Victoria's eyes. "Señor Generalissimo, my country needs you. El Caudillo himself sent me to find you. Only you can save us from the republicans. But that gives you no right…"

Suddenly I thought I finally understood. Putting a finger to my lips, I signaled her to silence and wondered at the machinations of fate. Had I not been killed at the Little Big Horn, I might have been the Democratic Party's nominee for president—and now this woman, representing some power broker, someone apparently named Claudio, was asking me to return from the dead and take the party's standard.

"Señorita, I know you are fearful, and you speak in riddles lest anyone overhear us—but state your case plainly, and I will answer in the same fashion."

"I should say no more, Señor Generalissimo, until we reach San Francisco."

"Am I to be unveiled there—as the party's candidate?"

"Señor, you are the one who speaks in riddles."

"If there are Republican spies aboard this train, it is best that we stay together. Perhaps you could pose as my wife. That might throw them off the scent. You don't look like Libbie—and they would never guess."

Her dark eyes rested on mine. Behind those swirling pools of coffee, I sensed the rapid calculations of a mathematician. "Señor, I think we are in danger."

I had been so mesmerized by my duty to the señorita that my normal Indian senses had been blunted; as, indeed, had those of my Indian scout Billy Jack. We were not alone. A revolver cocked at my ear. Its barrel tickled my dangling lobe. I did not turn. I kept my eyes on Victoria, but I intuited a large, dangerous, manly presence behind me. He spoke—not to me, but to my companion—in Spanish-accented English. "Ah, Consuela, all that trouble for this old gringo. And now he is captured. Such a waste."

"I must tell you, señor," I said, turning slowly until the tip of my nose hit the muzzle of his revolver, "that if you think the Republican Party can intimidate me, merely because I am dead, you are mistaken."

My interlocutor, dressed in the brummagem finery of a commercial traveler, was a man much browner than Victoria. His hair was black as a raven; his cheeks had the bristled look of a shaved porcupine; a large black moustache drooped around his mouth; and his eyes were hard as iron. He had two henchmen, similar in appearance to himself, with revolver barrels resting on Billy Jack's ears. "We are republicans, señor, yes. But your death—that awaits."

We hit another trestle, his revolver bumped off my nose towards the roof of the carriage, and I announced, not quite biblically, "My vengeance waiteth for no man," and drove my fist directly into his face; my other hand wrestled the revolver away from him and pressed it against his ribs. "*Touché*," I declared.

Behind us Billy Jack was still under guard. But Rachel had stood, turned, and was facing the chief villain with a derringer in her hand.

I said, "Tell your men to drop their guns on the seat beside the Indian."

He nodded to them, and Billy had those guns flipped on the miscreants faster than a dog leaps on his dinner.

Their leader pulled back from me, dabbing his nose with the back of his hand.

"You are a bastard, señor—but they told us that."

"I've heard a lot about *they*—who are *you*?

"I am Hervé Manuel Gonzalez-Gonzalez. You have heard of me?"

"No."

Victoria said, "He is an anarchist, a revolutionary! He is an enemy of my country!"

"An enemy of its Caudillo!"

"Who is this Claudio?"

"El Caudillo," said Victoria. "He is the hereditary soldier-emperor of Neustraguano; a defender of our nation and its faith."

"An exploiter of its people; defended by superstition!"

"Anarchist! Revolutionary!"

Gonzalez-Gonzalez raised his fist, grinning wolfishly; I noted the blood on his teeth, loosed there by my own strong hand. "*Viva la revolución!*"

As you know, Libbie, I have often been tempted by politics, but I have never understood politicians or their ways, and it is with no shame that I confess that I was terribly confused. I saw but one course forward. I grabbed Gonzalez-Gonzalez by his collar, dragged him past Victoria and Rachel, and shoved his face at the window. "Open it!"

He seemed flustered, and his fingers fumbled with the latch, but he finally succeeded, and with my one hand gripping his collar, and the other seizing his belt, I lifted him and heaved him off the train into the wilderness. "*Adiós!*"

I closed the window, brushed off my hands, and eyed his two compadres. They weren't such confident desperadoes now. They regarded me with shock and fear. "Billy Jack, what should we do with these two?"

"Castrate and disembowel?"

"There are ladies present."

"Hmm, I suppose they must follow their master." He said to one of them, "You open window; then I either launch you with gun or you jump."

Victoria shouted at them in Spanish—preempting Billy Jack's own translation.

Picture this, if you will: two cowardly thugs facing an Indian with two revolvers, your beloved Autie with gun drawn, Sister Rachel (who cocked the hammer of her derringer for melodramatic effect), and that Latin spitfire Victoria who, I suddenly noticed, also held a derringer. Who wouldn't lose his nerve in such circumstances? The villain nearest the window fingered the latch, and slowly, reluctantly slid the window open. He climbed into the vacancy and paused. Billy Jack stuck a revolver in the seat of the blackguard's pants, and he screamed and jumped out. His accomplice followed quickly—no doubt hoping to reunite with his co-conspirator if they survived their leap into the wilderness. Billy Jack closed the window and stuck the revolvers in his belt.

He looked pleased with himself, so I asked him, "How'd they surprise you?"

"Was mesmerized by your mystifying talk; then saw guns—dangerous fight would risk lives."

"You're getting too civilized, Sergeant."

Sister Rachel eased the hammer on her derringer and said, "And you, Marshal, are getting a little too fresh."

I did not reply, because just then Victoria clasped my arm—as a drowning woman might seize a life preserver. And I suppose in some ways I was just that, as I have often been to women in need.

On that arm to which she clung, hidden beneath my sleeve, was your tattooed image and my Cavalryman's motto "Born to Ride." Perhaps her female intuition sensed its existence, for the pools of her coffee-colored eyes swirled with passion, and she exclaimed (something Latins are prone to do), "You are the hero you said you were!"

"Yes, señorita," I conceded. "I am."

CHAPTER THREE

In Which I Acquire a Rival

The incident with Hervé Manuel Gonzalez-Gonzalez was, of course, the highlight of my journey. The remainder was spent providing comfort to Victoria, who was greatly shaken by the event. But our consoling small talk, chaperoned as it was by Billy Jack and Sister Rachel, need not detain my narrative. You already know, dearest one, how stalwart and sympathetic a gentleman I can be.

Still, by the time we reached San Francisco, I had achieved a new level of understanding with the comely young señorita. Perhaps it goes without saying that she came from a noble Spanish family, devout in religion and politically influential. She and her family were loyalists to El Caudillo, whose name, I learned, was Don Juan Naranja de la Cortez. His interests were supposedly both literary and military, and in the waspish Ambrose Bierce—or "that devil Bierce," as both friends and enemies called him—he thought he had alighted on a congenial soldier of fortune. The two had corresponded, Victoria said, and Bierce had apparently agreed to train and command an elite company of Infantry for the Caudillo. I felt obliged to make the obvious point that in the late American war I had been a Major-General and that even in the realm of journalism, in which I had merely dabbled, I was far more famous than Bierce. Victoria was suitably impressed and suggested that I return with Major

Bierce and herself to Neustraguano to volunteer for a Cavalry command. Knowing her cause to be just, I could not deny her request.

We disembarked in San Francisco (to which our train had been ferried from a wharf across the bay), loaded one coach with Victoria's rather extensive luggage and another with Sister Rachel and Billy Jack, tethered their horses to the rear of the baggage coach, and bid the drivers proceed to Victoria's hotel—the Hotel Neptune, which Bierce had recommended in his correspondence with El Caudillo. Then I saddled Marshal Ney for myself and Edward for Victoria and we rode into the city of Saint Francis, Bad Boy trotting behind.

I considered this a reconnaissance mission, and I will say that San Francisco was not, at first glance, what I expected of a saint's city, but it was bustling and handsome all the same, with wide thoroughfares (save for Chinatown, where they were narrow and menacing), sloping hills, and towering buildings—some of them mansions of the wealthy that would do New York proud. There was a nautical air about the place, with sleek and slippery black seals barking their greeting from across the harbor, longshoremen laboring on the docks, and seamen berthing themselves in saloons along the wharf. Once into the city, we saw fashionable gentlemen strolling along one street, rowdies on another, and, yes, a church spire or two. I confess, I liked it.

We drew admiring glances. It is not often done these days, of course, to ride horses into the city—where people travel in cable cars or by carriage or on foot—and we appeared, no doubt, as romantic throwbacks, a vision of chivalry, a Spanish lady accompanied by her gallant knight and faithful dog. Street urchins doffed their caps like junior peasantry; jolly sailors cheered us; men who looked like mining scamps grinned, stroked their beards, and spat appreciative squirts of tobacco juice; and gentlemen of business, top hats and oiled moustaches, cast apprising eyes on us. All in all, we were—as it seems I have always been—a center of attention.

I was enjoying myself, but Victoria recalled me to my duty.

"Señor Generalissimo, we should join the others at the hotel. We should be cautious of being seen. There may be spies."

"I fear no spies, señorita; I can deal with them."

"Assuredly, señor—but we must find the hotel and send Señor Bierce a message. We must tell him we have arrived. He works at the mint."

"At the mint—I thought he was a literary man?"

She shrugged her graceful shoulders, and my thoughts were immediately redirected by my sense of duty. Yes, I thought, we must find the hotel—and quickly. There the graceful señorita could put herself at ease, rest her dainty feet upon the cushions, restore her strength with chocolates and champagne, as I plotted strategy with Bierce.

I turned Marshal Ney towards the docks and asked a young scamp to direct me to the Hotel Neptune. I found it down a narrow alley paralleling the wharf. It was not at all what I expected. Rather than opulent, it was piratical—indeed, drowsing alcohol-soaked pirates were draped over a rail outside like so much dirty laundry; but this was surely the place, for tied at the rail were the horses belonging to Rachel and Billy Jack. I slid a couple of comatose drunks aside to make room for Marshal Ney and Edward, set Bad Boy as a guard, and escorted Victoria inside.

To our left was an enormous saloon, littered, like the rail outside, with boozy buccaneers, sprawled unconscious across tables and chairs. Only the sporadic flaring of nostrils, the occasional snore, and the twitching of extremities betrayed that they lived. To our front was the hotel clerk's counter. Behind the counter and flanking it on either side were desks, at which sat two boys wearing green visors. One had in front of him a stack of newspapers, the other a telegraph key, and both had books perched open in their hands—schoolbooks, I noticed as they put them down: Latin primers. The boys regarded me with frank curiosity. Sitting between them was a bearded man wearing a dark blue sea captain's jacket and matching peaked cap. He had a book in one hand—something by Plato—and a hunk of bread in the other. He seemed to be lost in his reading. Ever the diplomat, I coughed to indicate our presence—and he lunged at the counter like a man possessed. "State your business! What the hell do you want?"

"I remind you there is a lady present."

"And I remind you that this is my establishment, and I will speak as I like. Now what the hell do you want?"

"I believe the *lady* has a room booked in your hotel."

He looked past me, took in Victoria, and tried to moderate his tone. "*Oh, señorita, eres la amiga de Bierce?*"

I looked at him askance. "You speak Spanish?"

"I'm married to a Mexican, aren't I? Have to talk to her sometimes; can't always be at sea. And these two sons of mine—can't have them conspiring in a foreign lingo behind my back."

I regarded him blankly, but Victoria said, "Si, señor, I believe he arranged a room for me."

"Aye, so he was. A room for one, I might add."

"How dare you!" I said, and balled a fist, but Victoria's graceful hands circled my bicep and restrained me.

"I run a tight ship here, Mister High and Mighty."

"The name is *Marshal* Armstrong." I angled my chest to highlight the badge.

"Marshal? Well, then, Mister High and Mighty, you'll call me Captain, Captain Briggs." He ran his fingers along the brim of his cap. "You'll mind your manners around me." With that he belched, and a cloud of garlic arose between us.

"Do you have a room suitable for this lady?"

"Suitable, you say? Aye, it's more than suitable. I had to give her baggage a room of its own. Bierce didn't tell me about the luggage—or about you."

"Does he know we're here?"

"He knows *she's* arrived—and he's waiting for her upstairs. He's a bit surprised she didn't come with the luggage. I gave him a pint of ale to calm his disappointment."

"Room number?"

"Up the stairs, three rooms down, number 206, baggage is next door, number 208. And mind your manners: there's a nun staying here. And if you don't mind your manners: there's an Indian staying here—and I'll have him scalp you. Bierce is in 206. You should knock first; he's generally armed."

There was a stairway to the right. I led the way and knocked on the door of 206. I was greeted by a command—unmistakably that of an officer: "Come in!"

Bierce stood upon our entry. He made a most immediate impression. He is a man of unwavering icy blue eyes overhung by a prominent forehead and intimidating eyebrows. His posture is erect and martial; his manner sharp and formal; his clothing as immaculate as if ready for inspection; his moustache slightly dandified. The overall effect was of a formidable character.

He eyed me for a moment before stepping toward Victoria. "Ah, señorita," he said kissing her hand after the French manner. "You are a most welcome arrival. And you, sir," he added, "are not." His glance fell on my marshal's badge. "I do not require a lawman."

Victoria eyed me an apology and said to Bierce, "This kind gentleman saved my life."

"Really, señorita, I'm not *that* dangerous," he replied.

"No, I mean he threw an anarchist from the train—whoosh, *por la ventana*."

Bierce cocked an eyebrow, "You did, did you?"

"And he, too, wants to fight for Neustraguano."

"A United States Marshal? Do you have business there?"

"I am on leave, Mr. Bierce."

"And that entitles you to act as a soldier of fortune?"

"I could ask the same of you—are you offering El Claudio your services as a government clerk, or as a correspondent, or as a soldier?"

"In San Francisco, Marshal, the printed word is only as strong as the man behind it." With a slight movement of his hand, he exposed that beneath his coat he wore an Army Colt revolver on his hip. "My job at the mint is temporary, and could be done by anyone—and, in fact, I have anyone to take my place while I am gone. Most government departments are run by the living dead. They'll never notice my departure. So depart I will. I am recently returned from England; I can find that country on a map. Of Neustraguano I had been ignorant. I thought I should improve my education. War is God's way of teaching Americans geography—and, as anyone will tell you: I am the Lord's tool. I was reasonably well trained in killing my fellow Americans for the greater glory of God and the Union. I see no reason why I should not entrust my sword to this young lady's cause; it seems as worthy as any other."

Victoria said, "El Caudillo himself has summoned you, Señor Bierce. It is a great honor."

"Yes, nice of him, isn't it? I rather like monarchies—the fewer people involved in government, the better, don't you think?"

"We face a revolution, Señor Bierce."

"Yes, I know. I dislike revolutionaries. They wreak havoc for that great mass of stupidity, the people. They overturn injustices—and inflict viler ones of their own. I am, Marshal, lest you wonder, a conservative. I am enamored of the present evils—in fact, they are my business; I delight in exposing them. And man being what he is, I expect nothing better. From revolutionaries I expect only worse."

"The Marshal was also a General—a commander of Cavalry."

Bierce's eyes drew a bead on me. "Is that so? A General? Some political appointment?"

"Earned on the battlefield, I assure you—a *Major*-General to be precise, brevet rank. I am, it would seem, your superior officer."

"I'd like to see you prove it."

"Surely that won't be necessary."

"It is if you mean to go to Neustraguano."

"I only state the rank I earned in the Union army."

"That was a different army, a different war. El Caudillo admires my pen; he desires to employ my sword. He has sympathy for the predicament of my current employment. But no man, not even he, will command me. I oppose all men with missions; I serve no cause fully but my own. I go to Neustraguano as a paid assassin—to serve a king with literary taste and to observe man's normal inhumanity to man."

"An interesting sentiment."

"It is mine, Marshal."

"And my sentiment is that a man should do his duty."

"A very Marshal-like sentiment. But you know, Marshal, for most men, duty is an excuse for profit and desire."

"My duty, Mr. Bierce, is to Señorita Victoria. My only desire is to serve her as an officer and a gentleman. The only profit I seek is duty done. On her behalf, I will offer El Claudio my sword, and he can assign me as he wishes."

"Yes, we'll see about that. In the meantime, señorita," Bierce took Victoria's hand, "let us partake of dinner in the saloon downstairs. And you, Marshal, can stay here and guard the lady's luggage."

"I have seen her safely to San Francisco. I will not abandon her now."

He paused. His eyes had the icy stare of a duelist. Finally, he said, "Very well. I suppose every Spanish lady needs her *duenna*. Try not to get in the way."

He led us down the stairs, and as we entered the saloon, I saw that Captain Briggs had cleared a table for two and was polishing it with a rag. He glared at me. "Three is it then, eh? You, Mister High and Mighty, turn up like an unwanted cormorant." He turned and called to a small boy to bring another table setting.

"It is perfectly safe for us to talk here," said Bierce. "These gentlemen," he indicated the panorama of snoring sailors, "don't awaken until four in the afternoon. A bottle of wine, perhaps, Briggs?"

The wine bottle, glasses, and a corkscrew were delivered by a girl no more than twelve. Indeed, the saloon appeared to be operated entirely by an army of Mexican children who swept the floors, dusted around the sleeping pirates, cooked in the kitchen, waited at our table, and apparently had command of the wine cellar. I had not expected wine in an establishment like this, or for it to be delivered by pint-sized peons, but San Francisco was a city full of surprises, and I will say that Bierce became much more convivial with each glass of wine that passed his lips, though he mocked my own abstemiousness. "Really, Marshal, only a weak man accepts the temptation of denying himself a pleasure."

"I have no idea what that means, Mr. Bierce, but I deny myself no pleasure." I motioned to our snoring companions. "I take pride, on the contrary, in not dulling my senses. I stay loyal to my vow and take pleasure in preserving my wits."

"Wit? Since when have Marshals had wit? I have a friend who's a Marshal—but I value his marksmanship, not his wit."

"My wit is the wit that guides strategy and tactics."

"Ah yes, the wit of the butcher, the widow-maker—I've seen plenty of that."

"The victor."

"Pyrrhic, no doubt."

"My record speaks for itself."

"Enlighten me."

"It was a record of singular accomplishment and unparalleled success, save for one grievous massacre."

"Yours or the enemy's?"

"Señor Armstrong tells me he and his men—all dead, wiped out. I do not understand how that could be…"

"Really? Dead, are you? Lucky man. I assume, then, Marshal Armstrong, that your brevet rank has officially expired."

"Yes, I suppose it has."

"And your rank when you died?"

"Lieutenant-Colonel."

"Interesting."

"Tragic, I'd say."

"In my experience, living officers outrank dead ones."

"Perhaps in action, if not in the annals of history."

"Ah, history—an account mostly false, of events mostly unimportant, featuring rulers who are mostly knaves, and soldiers who are mostly fools. I take it, then, Marshal, that you are a fool—or a late fool."

"I'm not entirely dead."

"So I see. You interest me: I knew dead men voted for Democrats; I didn't know they served as U.S. Marshals."

"I am serving in a semi-secret capacity."

"No doubt—or semi-fraudulent as the case may be."

"I take that as an insult."

"You can take it with salt and pepper, for all I care. I've shot men before, Marshal, and I wouldn't mind shooting you—just to keep in practice."

"Señors, por favor, please, there is no need to fight—you can both be of service to El Caudillo."

I said, "As you wish, señorita. Only a blackguard would issue threats in the presence of a lady."

"Only a fool would think it's a threat and not a promise."

"Please, señors, enough. We have much to do. We must book a ship."

"That can be arranged," said Bierce. "Marshal, you can attend to that. A dead man will attract less attention. The proprietor of this establishment also happens to be the managing director of Briggs and Company, Shipping Agents. He can provide a disreputable ship and a crew of impressed cutthroats at an affordable fare. Give him my regards. And have him stable your beasts; they'll be safer that way. Some of these gentlemen might be French—and they eat horses, don't they?"

"What about Señorita Victoria?"

"Surely, Marshal, you would not confine her to a stable. She will stay with me—for her own protection."

"It is all right, Marshal Armstrong. I trust Señor Bierce."

"Bierce, I want your word as a former officer that this lady will come to no harm."

"If you pledge me as an officer and a gentleman—with these slumbering sailors and Briggs's children as witnesses—well, then, Marshal, even I have no choice. I do have one request of you, though."

"Name it."

"Tarry as long as you can."

"I am a man of action—I never tarry."

"And I, Marshal, despite my reputation, am indeed an officer and a gentleman—at least as much as you are. You will find that our friend Briggs has a shack about a hundred yards or so down the wharf. It is there that he conducts his shipping business. Take your time."

I met Bierce's basilisk glare with my own, bowed to Señorita Victoria, and left the saloon. I was surprised to see a matronly Mexican woman seated where Captain Briggs had been. The boys on either side of her ignored me; they were reading books—catechisms, by the look of them. "*Mis hijos te sirvieron bien?*"

I could guess her meaning. "Yes, you serve wonderful tortillas, thank you."

It was with relief that I stepped outside to breathe in the clean, salty sea air—and to be reunited with Bad Boy, who looked at me keenly for instructions.

"Come along," I said, and with Bad Boy trotting alongside, I led Edward and Marshal Ney by their reins down the wharf where, as Bierce had foretold, I saw a small wooden shed with an American flag flying from a lanyard and an engraved shingle announcing BRIGGS AND COMPANY, SHIPPING AGENTS.

"You again? What do you want?"

"I'm looking to book a ship. Bierce sent me."

"The hell he did. That man's too wicked to employ someone like you. You look vaguely respectable: no eye patch, no scars, Marshal's badge. Aye, but wait, those eyes—those are killer's eyes right enough."

"I am not in his employ. We are merely traveling together."

"Traveling together—and where the hell would you and Mr. Bierce be traveling if not to hell itself?"

"Really, Mr. Briggs, I must again ask you to mind your language. I myself know how to swear like a soldier, but what if a lady were to pass by?"

"If any lady passes by here, she'll have heard worse. And I am a Captain, Mister High and Mighty, and can do as I like. I have been in my own employ for lo these past twenty years—and do you know why?

Because no one will have me—and I won't have them; I am an independent Captain, with me own ship and beholden to no man. I have a seafarer's saloon, a respectable hotel, a telegraph office, and a newspaper, the *Captain's Gazette*, for the employ of my family. I am completely self-sufficient. And you, mister, have still not answered my question. Let me state it plainly: Where the hell are you and that devil Bierce going?"

"We embark for Neustraguano."

"For what? Say that again."

"Neustraguano—in South America, I believe."

"Neustraguano, you say."

"You've heard of it?"

"Of course I've heard of it. I'm an educated man, Bowdoin College, Maine. You've heard of *it*, of course."

"About our destination…"

"Yes, yes, in my youth I sailed there weekly—just for their bananas, occasionally for their rum, sometimes to discuss theology with learned Jesuits. Somewhere down south, you say. I need to get me a map so I can pinpoint just the place. But yes, somewhere south, near Mexico, I'm sure of that. An island, isn't it—in the Pacific, across the Spanish Main?"

"Indeed, Captain. Now about the ship…"

"You shall have mine—I have no other at the moment—*The Columbian Cutter*. It's just you and Bierce, then?"

"And the lady—as well as my horses and my dog."

"What is this—a zoological expedition?"

"The Indian might come as well—and maybe the nun; I hadn't thought about that; and they have horses too—back at the hotel, your hotel."

"You hadn't thought about the nun and her horse?'

"No."

"But you know the nun?"

"Of course I know her. We traveled on the train together. And, truth be told, she saved me from the Indians—twice, in fact."

"I see—truth be told; and now she's traveling with an Indian herself, as I saw with me own eyes."

"Yes, a friend of mine; served in the Cavalry. He and the nun will both want to come along, won't they?"

"It sounds to me, Marshal, as if everyone wants to come along."

"Can your ship accommodate us all?"

"Aye, as cutters go, she's big enough. I'll have to crimp me a crew—but that's not hard; plenty of sailors hereabouts; shanghai some from the saloon if needs be. We have us a concoction—whiskey dashed with opium. That softens 'em up; then I cosh 'em over the head."

"Your crew is your concern, Captain. Mine is merely to book passage. When can we leave?"

"Well, let me check my schedule book. If you can afford the price of passage—that's one hundred dollars each for you and Bierce and the woman and the nun and the Indian and the horses and the dog—let me see…it appears I have an opening at midnight or at four in the morning depending on how long it takes me to find experienced crewmen."

"A hundred dollars is a great deal of money, Captain. For that price, I expect you will also provide us with suitable fare to eat and drink—both for my companions and for my dog and horses."

"Suitable fare to eat and drink? For your dogs and horses, you say? You're lucky I take you at all—let alone at my most reasonable and inexpensive rate. It'll ruin me reputation, so it will, to carry Bierce and you and a woman and an Indian and the beasts. Ah, but there's the nun, and I'm a fair man and a kind man, though few recognize it—and a convert to the Holy Mother Church, which saved such a sinner as me. So, aye, you can have what I have. I'll increase my stocks nine-fold, and your beasts can dine with the crew—does that sound suitable?"

"That sounds most satisfactory. Can you stable my animals until tonight? Bierce said you could arrange that."

"Very presumptuous man, that Ambrose Bierce—but, aye, I can arrange that; I've got a shed next door for holding cargo. They can stay there until we embark."

"And they'll be watered and fed?"

"Of course they'll be watered and fed. What do you take me for—a villain like Bierce? That'll be an extra five dollars."

I ferried a coin from my pocket. "Will this gold coin do?"

He examined it closely. "Where the devil did you get this?"

"It's from the Delingpile treasure. You've heard of it?"

"This is San Francisco. I've heard of everything to do with gold claims, gold rushes, and even a crazy Englishman up north—Montana, I believe—who passes off gold coins with his own blasted image on them. But Delingpile—no, that wasn't it. Delingpole, wasn't it?"

"As you say—but that'll do?"

"Aye, it'll do. But you'll come back tonight and claim your animals. I'm no Noah; my craft is no ark; and I take no long-term responsibility for your beasts."

I nodded.

"And who shall I write down as booking the passage? I know Bierce. I know you're supposed to be a Marshal, but what the devil's your name?"

"I am Marshal Armstrong Armstrong."

"Marshal Armstrong Armstrong? And now that I think of it: Why should a Marshal go to Neuvoguerrero…or whatever it is? Tracking a villain? Exporting American law? Or is Bierce taking a vendetta to the edge of the earth?"

"My business in Neustraguano is my own concern. Yours is merely to get me there."

"Watch your tongue, Marshal. I know my duty as well as any man."

"In that case, Captain, I suggest you see to it."

"I'll see to it as I see fit. I am an independent merchantman, with an emphasis on the word *independent*, do ye hear? I've had no complaints, because I brook none, and I'll have none from you. And as for your fare, Marshal, am I to reserve your booking now with a cash deposit—I can't imagine you have that many coins—or do you ask me, do you entreat me, do you beg me to grant you credit? Do you mean to be in my debt?"

"I will bring the money when I bring my companions. Your payment will not be a problem. El Claudio himself of Neustraguano has requested our presence. That most delightful woman who accompanied me is his emissary and our guide."

"Oh, I see. El Claudio himself, you say; and that woman is his emissary. It's a wonder I take you at all. But I will. I have a wife and a crew of children to feed, a dozen of them, if you must know. Luckily—being Mexican—they subsist happily on beans. But I require beef and rum, and therefore must needs earn a living renting a ship to the likes of you. And you look honest enough—for a friend of Bierce, at least. Truth be told, that wicked man is a soul of honor, be it peculiar and his own. Come back here after midnight, bring your money, and I'll have a ship and crew waiting, or my name ain't Briggs—it'll be Claudio or something. Now, let's stow these animals; I don't want them befouling me quarters."

After seeing to the needs of Edward and Marshal Ney—straw, feed, and water—I set Bad Boy to guard their improvised stables. His deep brown eyes radiated with a devotion to duty that I have seen nowhere else, save in the mirror—or perhaps from you, dearest Libbie. I gave his paw a shake, bid the irascible Captain good day (he damned me to hell in reply), and returned, swift as the wind, to the Hotel Neptune. The mamasita at the front desk looked up and smiled at my return. "*Hola, señor, le gustaria cenar temprano?*"

I took that to mean, "Hello, sir, you look handsomely suntanned," and nodded my acknowledgment. I peered into the saloon and espied only sleepy pirates, a few small Mexican children lounging about for lack of conscious customers, and a couple of cats daintily making their way around the tables to pick up scraps.

I turned to the woman I presumed to be Mrs. Briggs. The two boys flanking her did not look up from their schoolbooks until I said: "*Mamasita, can los boyos, take dos horses, those two caballos,*" I said pointing out the door to Rachel's and Billy Jack's horses, "*to el Capitàn Briggs?*"

She looked at me askance but nodded; the boys nodded too.

"*Gracias*," I said. "*And dondé est la señorita and el hombre Bierce?*"

"*El hombre Bierce?*" she shook her head. "*El Hombre Diablo*," and pointed upstairs, which was surely the wrong way for the devil. Her sons looked at me wide-eyed and crossed themselves with vigor.

I casually did the same to appease their papist superstitions. I ascended the stairs, knocked at room 206, and opened the door. Bierce greeted me in his customary fashion: "Go away."

He and Victoria were seated, separated by a small oval table, she with her back to me. As I approached, I saw that her derringer was pointed at Bierce. I looked at him questioningly.

"We were discussing editorial matters," he said.

Victoria returned the derringer to her purse. "Ah, Señor Generalissimo, perhaps you can tell Señor Bierce to save his ardor for the battlefield."

"Indeed, I have booked our passage: we are bound for Neustraguano at midnight!"

CHAPTER FOUR

In Which Destiny Sets Sail

I had assumed we would have little to do until boarding our ship, but I was wrong. Bierce marched us down to the saloon, pulled four dozing sailors from a curtained padded booth, dropped them decorously on the floor, and made the booth his office, barking out the most extraordinary orders, the point of which became clear to me only later.

For the nonce, I was kept busy ferrying Bierce's scribbled notes to a gang of street urchins gathered outside. They went running off with them, returning with even more indecipherable notes of reply. Bierce guffawed and chortled as he read them and dashed off responses to be delivered by his street urchin express.

"Might I ask the purpose of all these notes?"

"The purpose, Marshal, is my entertainment, our security, and the transport of the señorita's luggage."

And sure enough, like an army of ants carrying granules of sugar, a steady stream of ragamuffin boys went up and down the stairs ferrying hatboxes, trunks, and her other impedimenta.

As I watched this caravan, I was distracted by yet another presumed son of Briggs, hawking a newspaper. "*Captain's Gazette?*" he inquired.

"Go on, Marshal," Bierce chided me, "support the literary life of San Francisco. Captain Briggs edits the *Captain's Gazette*. He's an educated man, you know."

"So I've been told." I thought it was time I paid Rachel a visit, so I bought two of the boy's newspapers, and said to Bierce, "If you'll excuse me, I have other business."

"I'll gladly excuse you, Marshal—but what other business could you have in San Francisco?"

"It is business of a religious nature—this being the city of Saint Francis. Señorita Victoria, would you care to accompany me?"

Bierce put up his hand and interjected, "Marshal, you can pray in a pew before you sally forth, but the señorita will stay right here. You have your business and I have mine. Don't worry. She'll be safe."

"It is all right, Señor Generalissimo. I have my gun."

I bowed to her, scowled meaningfully at Bierce, and then strode to the front desk of the hotel, where I inquired of Mrs. Briggs, "*Donde esta la nunna y el indio?*"

"*Qué?*"

"Me amigos—a nun" (I held my hands in prayer) "and an Indian" (I made a scalping motion).

She pointed upstairs, her eyes wide as saucers (I don't know why), and the two boys smiled their approval and crossed themselves (I don't know whether with relief that I was no longer in search of that *Diablo* Bierce or in the hope that I might be scalped). I crossed myself again in the Mexican fashion and then bounded heavenwards up the stairs.

I knocked on a door, opened it, and was gratified to see Billy Jack—though he was flush against a wall and peering cautiously out a window.

"Careful," he said and beckoned me to take a position on the opposite side of the sill. "Hotel watched. Three men. All day."

I glanced through the window. Below were three swarthy men in derby hats. They appeared to be operating a fruit stand. "Those are spies?"

"Yes—more interested in movement of woman's baggage than customers."

"That's no proof, Sergeant. Victoria's luggage is like a caravan from Kandahar. It would attract anyone's attention."

"I do not trust them."

"Where's Rachel?"

"Sister Rachel? She's in town; makes collection for the poor."

"What?"

"So she said—and I assume she speaks truth."

"That's quite an assumption. No one followed her?"

"No, those men below stay at fruit stand—not interested in nun Rachel."

"Or me, apparently. You're quite sure they're spies?"

"Yes, they watch all who enter and exit hotel; they look for something."

"Well, then, Billy Jack, no use cowering. Spies hate to be discovered—so let's discover them." And with that I stood before the window and threw open the sash.

Given that we were near the sea, I opted for a nautical greeting. "Ahoy there, fruit sellers. Are you spying on us?"

"*Qué?*"

"Are you spies?"

"*Espias?*"

"Who do you work for?"

"For ourselves, *señor*—you want to buy *la fruta?*"

"You've been watching the hotel."

"Oh, sí, we watch *el hotel*. We sell to *los huéspedes*. Also we sometimes give tours of San Francisco; very fine city. You want tour?"

"Not today, thank you."

"You new to San Francisco?"

"Yes, just in today."

"You ride in on horse?"

"Yes."

"We see you. Welcome to San Francisco." He threw me two green apples, one after another. "For you and your Indian friend beside you: free, *gratis*. You want more—or carrot for your horse—just come see us. Plenty to sell—enjoy apple now; we offer tour later. *Adiós.*"

I closed the window, bit into the juicy green apple, and said to Billy Jack. "You see, Sergeant, never take the counsel of your fears. Confront them boldly, frontally—and you might come out with a delicious apple to your credit."

We retreated from the window, sat in facing armchairs, and set about munching our apples and reading our copies of the *Captain's Gazette*, which was a peculiar grab-bag of news (particularly crime stories), poetry, and short essays. Though they were credited to various classical pseud-onyms—"Papias" and so forth—the authorship of the essays, which were composed in an emphatic style and full of nautical exclamations, was in little doubt. My eyes had just drifted to an essay titled *Orestes Brownson, His Idiosyncratic Odyssey from Damned Idiot Flibbertigibbet to Catholic Man of Letters* by "Marcus Lurius," when I fell fast asleep.

It was hours later when I awoke. Billy Jack was asleep in the chair across from me, the remnant core of an apple still in his hand, the *Captain's Gazette* sprawled across his lap. I stumbled to the window. I was not so bold this time, but like Billy Jack pressed myself to the wall and peeked down. The three swarthy derby-hatted men were still there at the fruit stall. I went to the washbasin, splashed reviving water on my face, and brushed my teeth.

I shook Billy Jack by the shoulder. He blinked his eyes repeatedly, finally got his bearings, and then leapt to his feet. "Those apples— *pommes de Blanche-Neige! apples of Snow White!*—they were drugged!"

"No, my friend, *you* were drugged; I was merely put to sleep by the *Captain's Gazette*. You stay here and recover. Bierce is downstairs with Victoria in the saloon; that's where I'll be."

"You tell them about spies?"

"No, I reckon I'll keep that knowledge to myself—for now anyway. For all I know, they're his."

I inspected myself in the mirror, deemed myself suitably immaculate, and left Billy Jack alone with the admonition not to eat any more poi-soned apples.

I trotted down the stairs and saw through the parlor windows that it was turning to dusk. In the saloon, the sleepy sailors were awakening, yawning, slapping their faces, and pounding their tables demanding grog and vittles. Mexican children came scurrying forth with both— though the pirates were obliged to pay before receipt.

Several of the pirates called out greetings to Bierce, who returned the same. To me he said, "Well, well, Marshal, where have you been— not that you've been missed. I was just regaling the señorita with tales of the literary life in London—a far more sophisticated place; have you visited?"

"No, I have not, but I have hunted on the Great Plains with the Grand Duke Alexis of Russia—and that, along with occasional trips to New York City, attending to private business and the theatre, is good enough for me. Though," I added graciously to Victoria, "I am quite keen on the attractions of Neustraguano."

Bierce laughed at that, his spirits quite merry for so saturnine a soul. He asked me to sit down and renew my role as courier to his street urchin express. With each note that he wrote and received, it appeared that some deeply laid plan was taking form—and pleasing him no end. He even acted the gracious host, putting on a splendid table (I drank endless cups of coffee, trying to rid myself of any remaining torpor) and proving a delightful supper companion.

I lost track of time until nearly midnight. Bierce then turned suddenly abrupt and said, "The señorita and I must go. We will meet you at the ship. For now, you stay here. If we go together it will look suspicious. Give us thirty minutes." He dropped a pouch; it clattered on the table. "That's our fare. You keep it; it's your security." He slid from the booth, tossed me a casual salute, and said, "Be seeing you." Then he took Señorita Victoria's hand, and they were away.

I had no intention of twiddling my thumbs. I needed to alert Billy Jack and Sister Rachel, who had been out of sight and out of mind. I grabbed the pouch and bolted from the booth, tipping my hat to Mrs. Briggs at the hotel desk.

I found Billy Jack awake and at the window. "The fruit men—they just left."

"Damnation! They're after Bierce and Victoria! Come on!"

We leapt from the room and into the corridor. I rapped on Sister Rachel's door, opened it—and, to my astonishment, she was no longer a nun but a ravishing woman in an equally ravishing black spangled dress. "My, my, Armstrong—you've left things quite late. I was hoping you were taking me to supper. I'd just about given up hope; it must be midnight. I had dresses sent up and settled on this one, you like it?"

"For goodness sakes, woman, come on—there is no time to lose!"

"You *are* an impetuous man!"

We ran down the stairs, out the hotel doors, and into a cold, clammy, choking fog that hung like an endless succession of veils. You could literally push aside one veil of fog with your hand only to see another behind it. Beyond the veils I could see little, but I could hear water lapping to my left. I moved slowly, lest I walk off the wharf and into the sea, and waved at my companions to follow my path. I have, as you know, a pretty good sense of direction, and I knew that if I could maintain a course due north, I would in short order be reunited with Bad Boy.

I stepped as boldly and rapidly as I dared, gripping Rachel's hand, Billy Jack padding behind, our footfalls echoing off the wooden walkway, my eyes straining through the fog—and then I saw it, a lantern dead ahead. To my left, towards the water, I heard creaking timbers and grunting men.

The lantern was outside Briggs's shed. The door was closed and locked. I trotted round to the makeshift stables behind. My companions Bad Boy, Marshal Ney, and Edward were there, as were the horses belonging to Billy Jack and Rachel, all apparently safe, but Bad Boy's alert brown eyes signaled danger. Still, I had no time to think, only to act. Billy Jack and I quickly saddled the horses, took their reins, and with Bad Boy at my side, we led them through the fog.

I stood by Briggs's shack and called out to the sea, "Ahoy, there! Bierce! Briggs!"

Bierce called back. "Ahoy, is that you, Marshal? I didn't expect you so soon."

"Where are you? I have our horses. Where's the boarding plank? I fear you've been followed."

"Ah, you spotted them. I've had my eyes on them for days. The boys took care of them."

"I'm relieved. We came as quickly as we could. But where are you? I don't see the boarding plank—or the ship."

"No plank. We just set sail. We're off without you, I'm afraid. But it's better this way. At least you have the money."

"I didn't come here for money!"

"Most men do."

"Bierce, bring that ship back here!"

"I'd advise you to be on your way, Marshal. I've alerted the newspapers that you're an impostor..."

"What?"

"...and that you acquired the money I gave you under false pretenses. It's from the mint—and I left the impression you took it from me; you stole it."

"What?"

"Dutiful public servant that I am, I'm pursuing the thief."

"What?"

"Yes, you've said that several times. I'd recommend you ride east. Have fun."

Two seals guffawed in the distance. You can imagine my frustration: I had lost everything—well, not quite everything. I still had Bad Boy and Edward and Marshal Ney. And then there's you, of course, dearest one, always forefront in my thoughts. But I had lost Victoria and my future as a soldier of fortune. Both had disappeared in the San Francisco fog. And Bierce, that cackling reprobate, had sullied my reputation as a Marshal.

But I had this consolation: with Marshal Ney, Edward, and Bad Boy, I had the makings of a Cavalry troop. As a bonus I had an Indian scout and two additional horses. I also had a beautiful woman in a black spangled dress who was expecting supper. Together we would make Bierce pay for this impertinence. I jumped aboard Marshal Ney. With a bare touch of my heels, I was off, due south, leading Edward by his reins, and with Bad Boy bounding behind: Custer and his Critter Company in pursuit of Ambrose Bierce.

And then I heard a voice: "I haven't had my supper yet!"

I looked down at Bad Boy. His jaws were shut. I looked behind me and there in the distance, fogging swirling around her, was Rachel, arms akimbo, high-heeled foot stamping.

ᱬᱫ

Thankfully, the Hotel Neptune kept late hours, and at the hitching rail Bad Boy had only to growl to keep the drunken sailors away from the horses. Seated in Bierce's booth with my striking companion and an Indian, I was, as ever, a focal point of attention.

"I have to say, Marshal, this is not exactly the sort of restaurant I had in mind."

I smiled wanly; my mind was consumed with strategies for rescuing Victoria.

"Still," she said, "I suppose it's the company that counts. I do wish you would talk to me, Marshal."

"Duty consumes my thought."

"Thoughts of *her*, I suppose."

"Who?"

"Your little señorita friend."

"Don't be impertinent, but yes, of course—I'd be less than a Custer," I looked nervously at Billy Jack, "I mean an Armstrong, if I didn't dedicate myself to rescuing her."

"Well, you know, *General*, I might need a little rescuing myself. Have you looked at the clientele of this place? They're certainly looking at me. Aren't I a match for that little Spanish number of yours?"

"Really, Rachel, those words hardly become a nun."

"I'm not a nun anymore, Marshal."

Thank goodness Billy Jack intervened. "Strategy simple: she go by sea; we go by land; you and I are Cavalrymen, we know how to make fast time. At the border we acquire a ship of our own. There's a port there—saw it on a map, San Diego."

"Armstrong, you're not actually chasing after that woman, are you? Who is she to you? She came here for that other man. Now she's got him. I say, let her have him, and you and I enjoy San Francisco."

"Duty bids me go, Rachel."

"Duty? If you ask me, you've got some duty closer to home. Would you leave me in San Francisco, alone?"

"Surely you wouldn't deprive me of Bad Boy?"

"No, not your stupid dog—you, you big galoot. I need *your* protection."

"Well, apparently thanks to Bierce, I'm now wanted by the law—or will be in the morning, whenever the newspapers hit the street."

"The law is not the only one that wants you, Armstrong. I've been trying to say…"

"Rachel, wait a minute—maybe there is something in that. Maybe I need *your* protection. The law, bounty hunters—they'll be looking for a crooked Marshal. They won't be looking for a married couple." I took off my badge and dropped it in my pocket. "There must be a southbound stage that leaves in the morning. We'll catch the first one."

Rarely do I ask other women to pose as my wife—but, of course, dearest Libbie, sometimes duty demands it. So, in the morning, it was not Marshal Armstrong who caught the stage to Los Angeles, it was George Autie, his wife Rachel Autie, and their adopted Indian son William Jack Crow Autie. I found an independent stage driver—in bustling San Francisco, you can find just about anything—so we had the coach to ourselves. I bought Bad Boy a seat, Billy Jack rode shotgun, and our four horses were tethered to the rear of the coach.

"They'll be fine," assured the stage driver. "I'll figger some extra rest for the horses. This here bein' a special fare journey, we can set the rules; we ain't on nobody's timeline, save your own. We'll take the old Butterfield stage route. That'll get us into Los Angeles in less than a fortnight. I know you've got business farther on. Don't mind seeing you onto Warner's Ranch, if you like. Ain't that much farther; it's a nice station; won't add but a pittance to your fare."

I clasped the driver's hand in gratitude, and Billy Jack swung up beside him. I helped Rachel into the coach, saw Bad Boy safely aboard, and climbed in after them. We were off.

"I can't tell you how honored I am to be traveling south with my dashing, young husband. George Autie—what a wonderful name—and now it's mine too."

"Rachel, you are incorrigible."

"Well, we do need to pass the time somehow. Surely you don't mind my talking—or perhaps you'd rather I talk to your dog."

"It is not your talking, Rachel; it is your making a mockery of our circumstances. Our lives are in danger."

"Your life always seems to be in danger, dearest George; and I don't see how escaping San Francisco and running off to a foreign war is going to help that."

"It is a clear matter of duty."

"Duty—*in a skirt*."

"Rachel, I served honorably in effecting your escape from the Sioux, wresting you from frontier rowdies, enrolling you in a cancan troupe, and ridding you of a criminal business partner. If anyone should have faith in me—and in my good intentions—it is you."

"I've no lack of faith, Armstrong—it's just that I know where we're heading; and it seems straight for trouble, as always."

We were well clear of saintly, nautical San Francisco, but far short, I thought, of any need to rest, when the driver roared, "Whoa!" and we stopped so suddenly that Bad Boy was thrown from his seat and into Rachel's lap. I heard the stage driver say to Billy Jack, "Lay the gun on the floorboards, sonny. I reckon I know who we're dealing with."

Outside, a voice called out. "Maybe you do, and maybe you don't. You there, hands up! You folks in the coach—come on out; slow and easy. Let me see your hands, no heroics please, no sudden movements; I hate to make mistakes."

I emerged to see something most unexpected: a man with a flour-sack over his head topped with a bowler hat. The sack had eye slits—and glittering there were eyes of cobalt blue. In his hands was a shotgun.

"Those tethered horses, belong to you?"

I nodded.

"They can stay, then, and you can have 'em when we're done. I'm only after the essentials. Driver, if you'd be so kind, I'd be obliged if you unhitched your team, turned 'em to Frisco, and just kept walking. You can fetch your coach later. I'll leave it here. If you don't bother me—if you don't try anything—you're a free man. Indian, that goes for you too."

"The Indian's with me," I said.

"And who might you be?"

"Mr. George Autie, from Michigan."

"Autie, is it? Ha! All the way from Michigan. Well then, Mr. Indian, if you'll just stand there with Mr. Autie, I'll let your driver be on his way."

"You don't mind, Mr. Autie?" said the driver. "You paid your fare."

"He may have paid his fare, but I don't see how he's in a position to mind; and he's still going to have his horses," said the sack-hooded highwayman.

"It's all right," I told the driver.

"Before you go, Mr. Driver Man," said the robber, "there's one more thing." His eyes—and the shotgun—rotated to me. "Mr. Autie, I want you to write a poem. A half dozen lines will do: a paean to San Francisco."

"What?"

"Questions aren't your friend, right now, Mr. Autie; scribbling is. I've got pencil and paper if you don't."

"Why should I write a poem?"

"It's a small request."

"Yours?"

"The poem will go to Mr. Ambrose Bierce, the literary critic."

"What?"

"For publication in the *Captain's Gazette*."

And so it was that we stood there, watching our driver lead his team of horses back down the winding road to San Francisco, bearing on his person a poem I wrote and entrusted to his care to be delivered to the *Captain's Gazette*. Even now I can remember it:

Farewell, then, oh San Francisco,
Your saintly shore I leave
With memories of your church bells ringing;
At my departure I do grieve,
For such is your natural splendor,
Such is your saintly allure,
That I am struck nearly speechless,
Except to say, bonne nuit, monsieur.

Our sack-wearing, shotgun-toting wayfarer had chuckled upon reading it and deemed it "Not bad," before handing it on to the driver.

When the driver was out of earshot, he said, "Bierce reckoned you'd hire a coach. Looks like I guessed right too. Getting that poem printed in the *Captain's Gazette* will make you out as a sort of literary bandit. Bierce reckoned that was a nice touch, a nice little story. In the meantime, I'll have that mint money, if you don't mind. It's not rightly yours and he figured I might want it. He figured right, too."

"Mrs. Autie will need to retrieve it from her bag."

"Mrs. Autie? Oh, you surely are a card. All right, then, Mrs. Autie, you go ahead and fetch it—real careful like—or I'll blast your poor innocent husband."

"Bierce knows you?" I said.

"Well, Mr. Autie, I'm not unknown. They call me Black Bart. Usual target is Wells Fargo, but you'll do for now."

Rachel handed me the sack of money. I tossed it to Black Bart. "My, my, that is a heap of coin. I'm obliged to you. Now then folks, I'll give you the same deal as your driver. You just walk the opposite direction, up that hill. Once you pass over the crest, I don't mind if you turn around and walk back and fetch your horses and belongings. I'll be long gone by then. But if you—or that dog—come after me, looking for trouble, I'll have to give it to you. As it is, all you've lost, aside from your coach and driver, is evidence of a crime you didn't commit. So, I reckon, on the scales of justice, I've done you a favor. You can repay me by doing as I tell you. So, go ahead and get walking. You won't see me again—leastways not with a sack over my head; not unless you're uncommonly unlucky."

"In that case," said Rachel, "we certainly *will* see you again—my husband and I are uncommonly unlucky."

I took my wife—or rather, my impostor wife—by the elbow and led her and Billy Jack and Bad Boy up the road. Near the top of the hill, I risked a look back—Black Bart was gone.

We had but one option: Billy Jack and I would revert to being Cavalrymen—he as a scout, I as an escort for Rachel. Billy Jack had his Indian pony; I rode Marshal Ney; Rachel took Edward; and Rachel's mount served as our packhorse.

Our new goal was the port city of San Diego, a distance of some five hundred or more miles across a landscape that could be simultaneously beautiful and harsh, with towering forested mountain ridges; barren, rugged deserts; rolling tree-lined hills; and a glittering sea to the west.

It took us about three weeks of steady riding, and for all the wonderful sights we saw, it was the meals round the campfire I remember most. Bad Boy and Rachel looking at me soulfully, Billy Jack sketching out the next day's ride in the sand, coffee aromatic in the pot over the fire, and I reflecting on what might lay in store for us in Neustraguano where there awaited a war (of what dimensions I did not know), a villain (often I dreamt of hurling Bierce from a castle keep), and a damsel in distress (Señorita Victoria). Of life's many consolations I often think the finest are dogs, horses, and my own meditations on duty.

Such meditations had their reward. In San Diego we found a pretty little town that gave us a respite from the trail—a chance to bathe and refresh ourselves at a hotel—and was our entryway to the great Neustraguano adventure. Billy Jack and I scouted the seaport village for an amenable Captain who could take us there.

I expect my Crow scout and I made a bit of a picture, riding along the wharf. We had chosen San Diego, because we expected we could pass unnoticed here. If Bierce had put further obstructions—whether spies or brigands—in our way, surely he would have put them in the much larger port city of Los Angeles, not in sleepy San Diego. The one risk we ran was that San Diego might be too sleepy to provide us with seaborne transport.

But that proved not to be the case. A young man standing in front of a fishing boat caught sight of us and approached with the rolling gait of a sailor. He was attired as a ship's Captain should be—his dark blue jacket immaculate with brass buttons glittering, his shoes polished brightly, his white trousers remarkably clean for those of a man surrounded by dirty ropes, tar, and sea water. He tilted his naval cap back, brushed a luxuriant flop of light brown hair from his forehead, and grinned. I was glad we had left Rachel at the hotel; after our long and arduous journey, a handsome young man like this might have had a bad moral effect on her.

I greeted him after the nautical fashion: "Ahoy there."

"Good day. You're new here, aren't you? Looking for a boat?"

"Why, yes, we are. My wife and I have just arrived here."

"That's not your wife, is it?"

I was flummoxed for a moment: "Oh—ha, ha—no, she's at the hotel. This is our adopted son, William Jack Crow Autie."

He nodded and said, "My name's Cameron Wakesmith."

He extended his hand and I shook it. "George Autie. We were hoping to book passage to an island down south, Neustraguano. Have you heard of it?"

"Sure have—sail by it all the time—do a little trade in its ports. It's off the coast of Mexico. Good fishing down there—but, you know, they've got a war going on."

"Could you take us?"

"It's dangerous—I wouldn't recommend it."

"I'm prepared to pay."

"It's not the money."

"Danger, Captain, doesn't frighten me."

"Why Neustraguano?"

"A newspaper assigned me to write about it."

"Oh, I see. Newspaperman, huh—you want to tell the American people about the war?"

"Yes, it's my trade—war correspondent. Fought for the Union, during the great war."

"For the Union—to set men free?"

"To defend the Union—when I give an oath, I mean it. Was a Cavalryman in that war. Been writing about wars ever since."

"Well, I was planning on a fishing expedition down there. Don't mind moving it forward a couple of days. Just you alone?"

"No, three of us: my son—and my wife has begged to come along."

"Well, at least he's an Indian; he can take care of himself, I imagine. But you want my advice: keep the wife at home. That island's dangerous. There's a lot of gunrunning in those waters. The rebels have Recruiting Sergeants on the Mexican coast. They smuggle guns and men—and they don't like people who get in the way. I sail those waters because it's my business. But I would never take a woman down there—might get caught in the crossfire."

"You don't know my wife. She's a true woman of the West. She's fazed by neither Indian war parties nor Mexican banditos—nor anything else, from wildcats to blizzards. There's no leaving her behind."

"Well," he looked thoughtful for a moment, lifted his cap, and brushed back his hair: "I suppose that's your decision—and hers. I'm only saying, if she comes, it's on your conscience, not mine. I'd keep her well out of sight. You won't reconsider?"

"No, Captain, my mind is set, my will is resolved—and I can tell you, so is hers."

"All right then, so be it."

"And the fare?"

"Don't worry about that. I'll make my profit fishing, and I'll appreciate the company. My crew are new hands; hired them just a week ago.
They take orders well enough—but they don't speak much English."

"That's awfully kind of you, Captain. Can we leave tomorrow?"

"Tomorrow? I guess I can manage that. How much luggage do you
have?"

"Hardly a thing; just what's on our horses. They need to come too—
four of them—and a dog. Do you have stalls aboard?"

"No, but we'll rig something below decks—and add a few stores. It
won't take long. You'll need a place to stay the night—you can stay
aboard the ship if you like."

"Thank you, Captain, but we have rooms in town. Shall we meet
you here at dawn?"

He lifted his cap, ran his fingers through his hair, and said, "You're
sure about your wife?"

"Yes, Captain, she is a courageous woman."

"Well, then, at dawn."

⊙⊶⊙

The first part of our seaborne passage was like something from a
dream: a limitless horizon, obscured by gauzy mist in the morning, but
bright and cerulean by day, and glowing orange and red at night; whales,
behemoths of the sea, leaping from and crashing into the foaming waves;
sea gulls and pelicans floating in the sky, then suddenly diving to snatch
fish from the roaring ocean; the salty sea air, brisk and invigorating. At
least I found it so. For Billy Jack it was a floating, rolling nightmare. He
spent most of his time at the ship's rail, looking wistfully and mournfully
at the distant Mexican coast.

At the Captain's request, and out of concern for her safety, Rachel
spent most of her time in our nicely appointed cabin, to which Bad Boy

had been assigned as well. (You can rest easy knowing that Bad Boy slept between our bunks to ensure that all Christian proprieties were observed.) In San Diego, Rachel had purchased a copy of that wonderful book *My Life on the Plains* and was understandably captivated by it. She kept a candle burning in the cabin, not only for added light, but to freshen the air, for the ship had a quite extraordinary and inextinguishable aroma. I can only call it "surf and turf" or "fishmongery and horse manure." On the deck and in the hold were barrels that, though empty, still stank of fish. Below decks, our steeds provided a challenge for crewmen obviously less experienced with transporting horses than tuna. I deputized Billy Jack to assist them. They took his assistance grudgingly. Their presence, too, encouraged Rachel to stay locked in her cabin; the crew made her uncomfortable. I was unsure of the crewmen's provenance, but I assumed they were Mexican. At first, I thought she was disquieted by their Indian-looking features, evoking unhappy memories of the Boyanama Sioux who had once held her captive. But I soon realized there was more to it than that. The crewmen were openly suspicious—if not contemptuous—of us. They seemed especially distrustful of Billy Jack—perhaps because he spoke their language. When he stumbled to the rail and gazed woefully at the green-blue swells of the ocean—or took to his berth, which was among the crew—the sailors were ominously silent or surly.

They also seemed lazy. I never once saw them fish. Most times they could be found sitting on improvised benches: stacked rectangular boxes about the size of coffins, holding, the Captain said, miscellaneous cargo he hoped to sell. The boxes were covered with canvas (like our sails) and tied down by stout ropes. There the crewmen whiled away their time whittling wooden harpoons.

Still, the Captain was a cordial host and kept us entertained in high form in his cabin, where we dined in the evening. On our first night at sea, he good-humoredly interrogated us on our backgrounds. Rachel can be a deft conversationalist, and I followed her lead, sticking closely to our lives as actually led, making only slight deviations so that our paths eventually and naturally intersected in matrimony.

She told him, truthfully, that her father had been an itinerant judge, traveling between towns, and a widower. "Unfortunately, he was murdered by Indians when I was young; and they held me captive. I know that might sound horrible, and it was, but I feel my father's legal training—and the savagery I witnessed among the Indians—has made me an excellent judge of men. In Mr. Autie, I do have the most lawless little savage, don't I?"

The Captain laughed rather too charmingly and said, "Another glass for you, Mrs. Autie?"

"Why, certainly."

Wakesmith motioned to his steward. "The lady's glass, please."

The steward looked as Mexican as his colleagues—dark and bearded, with slick black hair falling over his brow—but there was something monkeylike about him. Short and slight, his skinny arms too long for his body, he moved jerkily, as if uncertain of his footing—not a sailor, I reckoned, and not a natural steward either. He lifted her glass, put the bottle to its lip, and tremblingly filled it, returning the glass to the table as if it were a priceless Parisian vase.

Wakesmith turned to me: "And you, sir, tell me your story."

I spun a tale about how, after the war, I had migrated West, seeking new challenges, reporting on Indian wars, and how those adventures had led "to my greatest conquest of all, Mrs. Autie."

He smiled obligingly, and I asked him about his own background.

"Oh—nothing so exciting: Harvard; decided against the ministry; felt called to the sea."

"Oh, how romantic," said Rachel.

"Not really," he smiled and brushed back his hair. "Not unless you like the smell of fish."

"Oh, but I find the sea very romantic."

"I'm a New Englander; we're not romantics, but we do like salt spray. Quite a few of us in San Francisco. Not so many down here. There's the businessman Alonzo Horton and his friends. He's a Connecticut Yankee, a Republican, and a Unitarian. But otherwise, San Diego's practically the Confederacy. Could be a dangerous place for you, sir, as a former Union officer, what with all these Southerners about."

"No, Captain, we'd get along fine. I was quick friends with the Southerners at West Point—even best man to one during the war!"

"You were at West Point?"

"Er, yes, but just for a short while, you know—and then the war broke out." I thought it wise to change the subject. "More wine for Mrs. Autie?"

"Ah, excuse me for not noticing." Wakesmith gestured to the steward. "Are you sure you won't indulge, sir?"

"Quite sure," I said, eyeing the steward as he trod awkwardly to Rachel.

"*In vino veritas*, as we say at Harvard."

"Yes, I suppose you do," I replied.

"To the romance of the sea," proposed Rachel.

"To my wife's draining the bottle dry," I seconded.

It was a long night.

CHAPTER FIVE

In Which We Find Neustraguano

O ur second night at sea proved less bibulous but more eventful.
Our host was charming as ever, but I wanted information about
the war in Neustraguano, and he seemed reluctant to talk about it, especially in front of the steward.

"Ah, the rebellion, you mean." The Captain's brow furrowed. He
cast a quick glance at the steward and then back at me. "It's a fraught
subject."

I took that as a warning but plunged on. "You're familiar with the
situation?"

"Familiar enough: Neustraguano was something like a pearl down
here—not like the other Latin republics. Fair number of English speakers
for one thing—descendants of pirates, they say. The ones with treasure
bought land; those without joined the army. Some German settlers, too:
tradesmen, brewers, a few farmers. The royal family is minor Dutch
nobility from the old Spanish Netherlands. At least half the plantation
owners, most of the government, and the Church are Spanish."

"Picturesque."

"The king is the problem. His family were reformers. They talked
about abdicating, joining the Latin republics. But they didn't. When the
heir apparent was killed in a hunting accident—or murdered, as some
say—the king and queen died of grief—or poison. That brought their

younger son, El Caudillo, to the throne. He's a thoroughgoing reactionary: distrusted, disliked, and disdained—even by his own government, let alone the rebels."

"Who supports him?"

"Plantation owners—he's one of them—yeoman farmers, cattlemen, the Spanish Church, French refugees from the Mexican revolution: anyone who fears losing land, wealth, or position. I assume your newspaper backs the republicans?"

"Republicans? No, Captain, my paper supports the Democrats."

"Democrats?"

"Indeed: free trade, lower taxes, limited government, a return to the gold standard, and honest administration. Sam Tilden is our man."

Captain Wakesmith brushed his fingers through his hair—a nervous habit of his. "But, sir, in Neustraguano, I assume your paper favors the republicans—the rebels—over the monarchists, the king, El Caudillo."

"On the contrary, Captain. My newspaper supports the king. I had the honor of receiving the king's emissary; she was most convincing. And you, Captain—on which side are you?"

"I don't take sides; I avoid politics. I came out here for a reason: Emerson, Thoreau—independence, self-reliance, a peaceful, reflective life, that's me. The sea is my Walden Pond."

"I understand, Captain—well, not really, but I can pretend to. For my part, I am a slave to duty, and, having pledged my sword to his emissary, I am obliged to serve El Claudio."

"Your sword—as a war correspondent?"

Rachel glanced at me and then at Wakesmith. "My, all this talk of kings and rebels, war and peace, seas and ponds, swords and pens, it certainly raises a thirst, doesn't it?"

"Forgive me, I'm forgetting my manners." The Captain snapped his fingers and said to the steward, "*Otra botella de vino, por favor.*" To Rachel, he said, "I'm afraid I've been deprived of proper company for too long. I practically made a speech."

"Oh, I found it fascinating."

So had I. But now something else caught my interest: I noticed that the longer the steward was gone—and he was gone an exceedingly long time—the more fidgety our Captain became. He combed his fingers through his hair and offered excuses for the newness of his crew. Finally, he said, "Forgive my steward. Our wine stores are low—the Frenchmen in Neustraguano buy all I can carry."

Suddenly, the Captain's door flew open—and in leapt the steward, like a crazed, knife-wielding monkey. He smashed a huge machete into the dining table; his eyes, locked on mine, glittered with insanity. Pretty impertinent for a little man, I thought—but then behind him stormed the crew, their fists gripped around machetes of their own, their eyes, like his, reddened with hate.

The steward yelled, "Do not move—or you die!"

The Captain said, "Now hold on, Manolo. What do you think you're doing?"

The steward wrenched the machete blade from the table and, with his freakishly long arms, swung it dangerously close to my nose. "*He* cannot remain aboard ship."

"He is my guest, Manolo."

"He is a friend of El Caudillo."

"That is no concern of ours."

"Maybe not for you, Capitán, but for us."

"Be careful, Manolo. If this is a mutiny…"

"You would be dead, Capitán. *You*," he waved his machete, setting my whiskers aquiver, "outside with your woman!"

I had no choice. Two machete blades, wielded by mutineers, rested menacingly on my chest; another prodded my back. One of the blackguards grasped Rachel's shoulders.

"*No touchay la señorita! Dontay daraymos!*" I bellowed in my fiercest Spanish, and the hands withdrew. As imperious as the Indian royalty she had once been (daughter-in-law to a chief, after all), Rachel pushed back her chair, stood, and stepped bravely from the Captain's cabin and onto the deck. I followed with machetes tickling my ribs and spine. There we saw Billy Jack, trussed like a turkey and looking sicker than ever.

Behind me I heard Captain Wakesmith mutter, "If I had my pistols," which made me think of Rachel's derringer. I harrumphed to get her attention, but she kept her eyes on the rolling sea.

The steward said, "We are no mutineers, Capitán. We are only friends of Neustraguano. You keep the ship; we do not want it; we are not thieves—but we no longer sail with you. We will take the longboat, and the boxed cargo—not as thieves, but as our payment—and row to Mexico. As for *you*," and the machete came back to my nose, "Neustraguano is that way," he said pointing west. "We throw you overboard—no boat. You will never make it."

Rachel said, "So you're not a thief; you're a murderer."

"We no murderers. We leave you to fate—or to the sharks. These waters are full of man-eaters; we will whet their appetite, and then your fate will decide." He said something to his compadres, and the blades on my chest and back made swift thin cuts; my shirt seeped red. "Sharks like blood—I think your fate is death, like all who serve El Caudillo."

They shoved me to the ship's rail, Rachel beside me. The mutineers grabbed Billy Jack, his binding ropes were cut (why, I don't know; it could hardly have been a matter of mercy; perhaps they merely wanted to show off their machetes), and he was thrown over the side. Then they grabbed Rachel and me and heaved us over almost simultaneously. The water was dreadfully cold—but it revived my spirits and concentrated my mind. I had no clue how far away Neustraguano was, or how far we could swim in sodden clothes, freezing and shivering, and with the prospect of sharks tearing at our flesh. But I knew we had to try. To stay here, rolling on the waves like corks floating in a bathtub, was slow death. Life—if we were to keep it—lay to the west; and we must swim for it.

"Courage, Rachel! Fortune favors the brave!"

"Armstrong! Armstrong! I'm drowning!" Rachel gasped. Unfortunately, she had never learned the aquatic arts. With plunging strokes, I swam to her side. Suddenly, there was a dark splash in the water, and there was Bad Boy, paddling furiously so Rachel could cling to his back.

The swells rose, crested, and fell in a powerful pattern that I reckoned was aiding our westward drift. I looked back at the fishing boat. Our horses were still aboard; I was determined to retrieve them—even if I had to lead an armada and a landward invasion of Mexico to do so. For now, though, we were captives of the Pacific Ocean. An ominous darkness surrounded us, we shook and shivered and were borne upon the waves, and our skin shriveled in the frigid waters. Beneath us, unseen, could be sharks ready to feast upon the warmth of our limbs. I thought it best if we held onto each other, with Bad Boy as our center point. Alone we were vulnerable; together we could mount a defense.

Even with the cold and danger, with the wind and waves battering our faces, with the salty water seeping through our lips, flooding our ears, and swarming our nostrils, Rachel fell asleep—or perhaps she fainted from shock or exhaustion. I grasped her waist to keep her afloat. As we were married—or at least acting the part—I felt there was nothing untoward in my doing so. I have always believed in embracing every role I have been handed, and given the extremity of our circumstances, I'm sure you would agree, my dear, that it was the right thing to do. There was also the matter of sharing body heat in our vigil through the night. Billy Jack and Bad Boy acted as chaperones and swam round us as scouts.

Come dawn, I expected to see a vast, vacant horizon—and in the west, that is exactly what I saw. But from the east came salvation: a fishing boat. Waving down to us was Captain Wakesmith himself. "Ahoy, there—still in one piece?"

"Yes, and frozen solid," I replied. "What happened to your mutineers?"

"They took the longboat all right, but not very foresighted, were they, if they really wanted you to drown? I can handle this ship myself if needs must. Stand by—I'll toss you a rope. I've got a basket that might do for your dog."

And thus, my dear, we were rescued—fished from the Pacific, the Captain's catch of the day. We were reunited with our baggage, our sodden clothes set out to dry (though after being thoroughly drenched in saltwater they would never be the same), and the Captain brought us coffee.

"I knew they weren't the most efficient crew or the brightest, but I didn't reckon them for mutineers. Still, this Neustraguano business has made everyone down here crazy—you'll find that out soon enough."

"If they care about Neustraguano, why didn't they go there instead of Mexico?"

"Patrol boats. El Caudillo guards the approaches to the island. That might be why they didn't kill you—afraid a patrol boat would track them down and try them for murder."

"Well, thank heavens for that."

"We'll see Neustraguano—or one of El Caudillo's patrol boats—within a day's sailing; and then, Mr. and Mrs. Autie, it's good luck to you; and keep your heads down."

The Captain was as good as his word: the next day the island of Neustraguano rose before us. Through a grey haze a bustling seaport appeared—a long shoreline slowly filling the horizon—and green hills beyond. A small warship, cannons protruding from its gun ports, slid through the waves. Her Captain and ours shouted nautical pleasantries. The warship turned, came alongside, grappled itself to us, a rope ladder descended, and sailors came thumping aboard, along with a half dozen Marines and a naval officer who, speaking Spanish-accented English, and hardly pausing to draw a breath, issued a rapid patter of orders to the sailors to secure our boat and guide us into port while he interrogated Captain Wakesmith under the watchful eyes of the Marines.

Leaving things nautical to those who knew something about them, I borrowed Captain Wakesmith's glass and stepped to the bow and examined the looming port. Signs of the rebellion were immediately obvious. Soldiers lined the wharf, and I could see that entrenchments had been erected on the high ground above the town and along its perimeter. There were even squads of Cavalrymen, riding between posts. Looking deep in the distance, I could just make out, shrouded in clouds, what looked like a massive earthen tower with curling, wispy smoke rising above it.

Captain Wakesmith freed himself from the naval officer and said, "They've agreed to let us dock, but the Captain's a bit on edge. Apparently, the rebels struck at a town just north of here."

"Well, that could be my first big story." I handed him the spyglass. "What's that mountain way out there?"

"It's a volcano; rumbles occasionally, kicks out some smoke—that's part of this haze—but it's otherwise inert. They call it la Montaña que Eructa. For the Indians here it's sacred."

"And this town?"

"El Pueblo del Pelícano Sagrado, the chief port city of Neustraguano. If the rebels ever crack its defenses, El Caudillo could be finished. This is his lifeline to the outside world."

"Is that all he's got, this port?"

"No, he's got the eastern half of the island—and the Navy: they collect tariffs and keep a percentage, so they'll stay loyal. But be careful how you talk in the towns. You might be surprised who supports the rebels. It's not just Indians, poor mestizos, and Mexicans. A lot of Neustraguanians think El Caudillo is an embarrassment; they think monarchies are an anachronism. So, you've got revolutionaries who want to overthrow him; monarchist planters who support him; and reform-minded businessmen who just wish he'd go away. I guess you'll figure it out, all right. If you write for the *San Diego Union*, I'll read your stories."

Laborers along the dock swung ropes over the bow of the boat and helped guide her in. A Lieutenant led a detachment of soldiers trotting up portside, and the young naval officer and Captain Wakesmith took to the pier to meet him As the Marines stood guard, Billy Jack and I busied ourselves, getting our horses saddled and above decks. We had just completed that task when Captain Wakesmith returned to the boat.

"Well," said Wakesmith, "it looks like we'll be together a while longer. They're impounding my boat—temporarily, they tell me—until they know more about us. They'll be taking us to La Ciudad de Serpientes—that's the capital. No use standing here. We might as well go ashore."

Our horses' hooves clattered onto the wharf and soldiers surrounded us. Their eager young Lieutenant nodded at Captain Wakesmith, and then addressed me: "You too are an American, yes? Then
tell me, señor, your name and your business. He tells me you come to
write about the war."

"Well, brace yourself, gentlemen. That was a disguise. I am actually
Generalissimo Armstrong Armstrong, come to serve El Claudio as a
Cavalry commander. These are my companions: my Sergeant, Billy Jack;
my dog, Bad Boy; my horses, Marshal Ney and Edward; two additional
horses—and, oh yes, this is my wife, Mrs. Generalissimo."

"His Majesty expects you?"

"Perhaps—I was recruited by a woman, an agent of El Claudio. She
also recruited a man named Ambrose Bierce. I am very eager to see them
both again."

"Of Generalissimo Bierce I have heard. He forms a special regiment
at the palace. But this Capitán said nothing about you and Generalissimo
Bierce; he said you write for newspapers."

"Yes, well, one does not advertise one's Generalissimo status, does
one? My deception was a military necessity, but I am, otherwise, a man
of my word."

"You were a General in the United States?"

"Yes—and I believe that translates to Generalissimo status here in
Neustraguano. From you, Lieutenant, I require a Cavalry escort to the
palace of El Claudio."

"We have Cavalry at hand. They will escort you. But if you have lied
to me, General, they will form your firing squad."

"Oh, how delightful," said Rachel. "My husband has taken me from
a mutiny to an execution."

"Mutiny, señora?"

"Oh nothing, really—it happened to someone else, a Mr. and Mrs.
Autie. Apparently, I'm now the wife of a Generalissimo. That sounds
quite exciting, doesn't it?"

"It has been a long voyage, Lieutenant, and my wife is fatigued, having been forced to subsist on whiskey and wine. Now, about that Cavalry escort…"

It proved quite impressive—twenty riders to the front, twenty to the rear, and riding alongside me was Capitán Luis Antonio. He and his men wore kepis and were dressed in uniforms of Confederate grey with yellow and black piping and blue epaulets. The Captain was voluble, and we kept up a lively conversation, for I was most eager to be prepared for my meeting with El Claudio.

"El Caudillo is *un hombre de la tierra*. He is a king, yes, but also a plantation owner of incredible wealth and vast estates—a private kingdom. But now his realm is the entirety of Neustraguano. That has made some people very jealous. Oh yes, the government, the fashionable people, they all hate him, because he talks and governs like *un hombre de la tierra*. He is a man of our native traditions. He went to military school and respects the army. He is not diplomatic. He is not subtle. He is rude to his opponents, but also bold against our enemies. Many plot against him, but he survives; he is a hard man, and clever. You know Generalissimo Bierce? He is charged with El Caudillo's protection; he forms a praetorian guard around the palace. Generalissimo Bierce was given a position of much trust—and yet he is a foreigner; like you, an American; but El Caudillo can read a man's character."

"Maybe he should read a bit more carefully."

"Señor, what do you mean?"

Rachel interceded, "Oh, it's just my husband's jealousy. You know how Generalissimos are—always trying to prove that they're more *issimo* than the other. You should just see them, Capitán, arguing like two jealous schoolgirls smitten with the same beau."

"Smitten, señora?"

"Really, Rachel, remember your station."

"My fondest Generalissimo, you had better remember yours—and remember that you and Bierce are allies; you might need each other."

"The señora is right. Good men must stand together. Our country is horribly divided—and it is very dangerous. El Caudillo stands for Neustraguano, for our country as it has always been: the monarchy, the Church, our traditional ways. That should unify us, yes? But it does not, because the rebels want to change everything; they conspire with thieves, cutthroats, savage Indians."

Billy Jack interjected, "There is virtue in *mos maiorum*."

Capitán Luis Antonio asked me, "What did he say?"

"He's not savage enough—he speaks Latin, among other things. I believe he said, 'there is virtue in more marmalade'—an old Latin adage."

"Ah, I see."

"The way of our ancestors is best," said Billy Jack. "For civilized Indian, Catholic way is best for truth and morality; Indian way is best to ride horse and hunt buffalo."

"Generalissimo, where did you find this Indian?"

"We have quite a few like him in the United States—well, not exactly like him—but good company."

Captain Wakesmith regarded Billy Jack as if he were a talking horse. He responded in kind: "*Mos maiorum non semper optimus. Res publica semper optima.*"

Capitán Luis Antonio leaned across his saddle. "And what did he say?"

"Another old Latin adage: Marmalade is not always optimistic, but with pumpkins you can always be optimistic."

"Ah, I see—that is true, I suppose."

I looked about me. Bordering us on either side were well-organized fields: plantations of coffee, bananas, and other tropical crops. Field hands, some of them with machetes tucked in their belts, glanced up at us with mild curiosity. The road was obviously well-traveled; they had seen Cavalry many times before. Though it was late fall, the sun was bright, the temperatures mild. But I could see that looming before us was an ascent into low hills—and the jungle.

"Enjoy the sun, señor, because when we enter that jungle—the road passes through it like a tunnel. The jungle canopy blots out the sun; a mist will envelop us; it will seem like you traverse a haunted land."

"With a rebel ambush?"

"No, señor, I doubt it. Our Infantry has swept the area. Any rebels have been dealt with—but they have done their damage. I regret, we must pass through the town of San José. I wish we could avoid it, but there we meet the Minister of State. It is a scene of much horror. The rebels attacked the town—and they are without morality."

"They have a cause," said Wakesmith.

"Yes, señor, we hear often of the cause—you will see its results."

We rode on from the rich, dark, fertile soil of the plantations to a borderland of rocky soil and boulders. The land rose slowly and the rocks became gravel and were enveloped by the roots of large, scraggly trees leaning grey-green against the hills, and then came a cascade of deeper green—verdant, wilder hills covered with bushes and proud trees that reached to the sky and blossomed there. And then came the jungle, rising ever darker over us until it formed an archway of tangled green vines, filtering the sun.

The road cut east, and a chilly coastal fog rolled through the jungle, further dimming our vision, landing damp on our clothes, and loosening goose bumps on our flesh—or at least on Rachel's, I noticed. La Montaña que Eructa rumbled its earthen thunder in the distance, and our horses paused as if waiting for the ground to settle. Jungle birds squawked and trilled; ghostly seagulls (you couldn't see them) cawed far above the trees; monkeys chattered like women at a church social. Billy Jack made whippoorwill calls of his own, and was satisfied, I reckoned, that no hostile Indians responded. Brave and daring as she is, Rachel kept her horse close to mine.

Our legs bumped and she said, "Armstrong, I don't like this."

Neither did I: a roadblock in front and another behind and we would be trapped. We were no longer ascending; the road was straight and level: we had reached a plateau. Ahead of us, the grey fog became denser, sootier, until it seemed like a passage into the blackest night.

"Señora, many apologies, but we approach San José. Avert your gaze if you can. Generalissimo, mark well the enemy you will face."

The black fog was smoke. Cutting through it, like fireflies, were sparks from faltering flames. And then a scene of barbarity that I can barely describe. Lining the road, dangling from vines, swaying slightly under the fog-borne wind, were severed, blood-spattered arms and legs. They leapt suddenly to sight from the mist, then were shrouded again. Worse was to come. Pickets of soldiers waved torches, revealing adobe dwellings and horribly mutilated corpses: women and children, disemboweled, limbs severed. Sweating, grunting details of soldiers dug hasty graves; a priest wandered past, his hands moving in the sign of the cross. As we drew closer, waving torches revealed a dual purpose—not just lighting up the darkness but chasing away swarms of flies.

"Oh, Armstrong!" Rachel clutched my arm and buried her face in my shoulder.

It was a scene of gore, depravity, and evil.

Riding out of this satanic fog, illuminated only by flickering fire, came a Spanish hidalgo: dark-haired, grey-templed, proud and dignified, his eyes welling with sorrow.

He addressed Luis Antonio: "Capitán, these are the Americans?"

"Yes, your excellency."

The hidalgo nodded briefly at Captain Wakesmith, and then looked at me and Rachel and said, "I am sorry you must see this—this outrage of El Caudillo; this butchery for which he alone is responsible. But forgive me, I am Senator and Minister of State Matteo Rodríguez. I take it you are Generalissimo and Mrs. Armstrong?"

I nodded. "El Claudio did this?"

"Yes, he and he alone—though he will blame others. The man has no honor, no shame. He is a liar, a hypocrite, a brute."

"But why?"

"Vanity—he is consumed with vanity. This is the price we pay. These people had no quarrel with the rebels. They welcomed them. They hoped to work and trade together, to live side by side. But El Caudillo vowed the rebels should not have this town. And now we have it. They, the rebels, warned us. They said, 'You may take San José, but you will recover nothing.' It is worse than nothing."

Captain Wakesmith muttered under his breath, "Damn him; damn that dictator El Caudillo."

I said, "So the rebels committed these atrocities?"

"Yes, you could say so—but only under El Caudillo's provocation. That's what El Caudillo does—he provokes, he divides, he instills hate. And this is the result."

Capitán Luis Antonio caught my eye.

Billy Jack interjected, "Responsibility lies with murderers."

The Minister of State replied, "Yes—and it was El Caudillo who gave them leave to do this. You are an Indian—are you not? Your people have been provoked beyond endurance—isn't that why you fight?"

"I do not understand."

"Injustice always provokes."

"I fight Sioux, Cheyenne; I fight beside the white man when we share common cause."

"There is no common cause here. El Caudillo has divided us. He has made Neustraguano a land of despotism and war. Were it not for his vanity, we would have peace, free trade, a republic. Instead we have his dull, deadening fist. And this is the man you intend to serve, is that correct?"

"Well, yes," I said, "but I was told a different story."

"Indeed?"

"I was persuaded to come here by a young woman."

"Apparently you were misinformed."

Capitán Luis Antonio crossed himself and whispered: "*Viva Cristo Rey.*" He was looking at a religious statue smashed on the ground—it was a male figure, perhaps Jesus or Joseph, decapitated.

The Minister of State noticed and said, "Capitán, true religion does not lie in statues. It is here, in our mind, in our highest, most transcendental thoughts. Statues are but plaster; they are nothing of value."

Capitán Luis Antonio shot me a glance, but he was too good a soldier to speak.

"Well," I said, "it's not very respectful, is it—knocking down a statue, smashing it?"

"You speak of respect. That is all the rebels want: the respect of living in a progressive republic rather than a backward monarchy. But let us ride away from here. I can stand the stench of death no longer."

The Captain shouted orders, and we weaved eastward, cutting away from the town and onto a road that plunged back through the jungle and the mist.

Matteo Rodríguez rode beside me and said, "You say you were persuaded by a young woman?"

"Yes—and most convincing she was."

"That would have been Consuela Victoria Margarita Monteverde Cristóbal. I said she misinformed you. That is not entirely true. She was sent as an emissary to your country. She is indeed a lovely young woman. I am certain she was quite persuasive. She and her family share a simple, honest patriotism, but it is misguided. They fear the future; they reverence the past; they do not see El Caudillo as a blot upon Neustraguano, because they see our country as a Church and a king. They do not understand that these things, like that smashed statue, are mere appurtenances. Neustraguano, if I may speak my mind to you, should be an idea—a social compact available to all; not tied to a crown or an altar or a tradition or even a specific people. So, you see, Consuela did not mean to misinform you; she was simply mistaken. Still, her patriotism has its uses, and she is a well-meaning young lady, and I do not fault her."

Rachel said, "Well, I fault her if she misled my dearest husband. If she lured him here under false pretenses—if she told him a villain was a saint—perhaps we should get right back on that boat and set sail for San Francisco. I think this has all been a terrible mistake."

"To leave now could be a worse mistake. El Caudillo expects you. Messengers have gone ahead, announcing your arrival. And he is not a man to be disappointed." The Minister's eyes rested on mine. "You are a friend of Generalissimo Bierce?"

"I know Bierce."

"Do you come for the same reason?"

"Well, maybe not exactly the same reason, but," I glanced at Rachel, "I reckon you could say we were allies."

"Bierce is a good man—a man of deep understanding."

"Really?"

"Oh, yes. Our two countries are in many ways alike, you know. We have a constitution, laws, elected representatives, a supreme court, cabinet officials—of which I am one. All tools to restrain El Caudillo. On my advice, he made Bierce de facto Minister of War."

"Bierce?"

"You seem surprised."

"I thought he was managing some household guards. El Claudio hardly knows him."

"So much the better—for them both. El Caudillo does not keep Ministers long. He loathes government ministries; he delights in abolishing them; he eagerly agreed when I suggested eliminating the Army and Navy departments. Bierce, one man, has taken their place."

"If Bierce is his military adviser, who's his naval adviser, Captain Kidd?"

"No, it is far worse; it is another embarrassment. El Caudillo's Navy adviser is—a priest. He has two qualifications: he is El Caudillo's confidant, and he tinkers with boats. So naturally, he should advise our Navy. Absurd, is it not?"

"Not absurd," said Billy Jack; "a man who knows biggest truth, theology, can master smaller truths of science and mechanics. *Disce quasi semper victurus vive quasi cras moriturus.*"

The Minister looked curiously at Billy Jack, and then went on: "It is absurd that we have a Navy at all. We are a small island. Navy patrols are an impediment to free trade and free immigration. I have tried to abolish the Navy many times—as a waste of money."

"And the Army?"

"The Army too—but fear not, Generalissimo, you will have your soldiers. The king enjoys military parades too much; they feed his insatiable vanity; they make him feel strong."

"After that massacre, I'd say you need an Army."

"If Neustraguano had no Army, would we have such massacres? Do not armed forces bring on the very violence they are meant to prevent? I am no anarchist. I recognize that we need men to enforce the law—especially on El Caudillo. But we are an island. Our Army is only used against our own people. If we had no king, we would have no Army—and there would be no war."

After that, we rode a while in silence. To say that I was disconcerted would be an understatement. I was baffled that a Minister of State would condemn his own king before Luis Antonio, a serving Captain of the royal Cavalry, and me, a putative Generalissimo.

The Minister slowed his horse, which fell into pace with Billy Jack's behind mine, and he engaged my scout in conversation, but I didn't eavesdrop. I assumed it was the typical palaver of a politician. Then he slowed again so that he could converse with Captain Wakesmith.

Capitán Luis Antonio looked warily at the skies. He told me that sudden torrents of rain could cascade through the trees, turning the roads to mud. He was not worried about the mud's impeding our way, but he fretted about the men's uniforms becoming soggy, spattered messes: the king was a stickler for appearances. An officer whose men were not impeccably turned out could be reduced to the ranks. The Neustraguano Army, I noted, would be no place for Sam Grant.

Rachel's mind, of course, was elsewhere. "The Minister is a handsome man, isn't he?"

"I'll let you judge that."

"Well, he is then."

"I wonder, though, about his sense of duty."

"I knew you would; I wonder if he's married."

"*We're* married," I reminded her.

But that was only to keep her in line. When it comes to wives, my dearest Libbie, you are the only genuine article.

CHAPTER SIX

In Which I Meet
El Caudillo

L uck was with Capitán Luis Antonio. The rains held off.
The road descended from the jungle plateau down a rocky slope
to the plains, the sun reemerged, and cultivated fields rolled out before
us. A man sat astride an elegant trotting horse next to a road-bordering
stream. He was dressed in a ruffled white shirt, black tie, and brown vest
and coat. He lifted his sombrero in salute. The Minister acknowledged
him with a nod and called out: "You fare well, Don Gilberto?"

"Very well, indeed, Matteo Rodríguez! San José has been avenged,
and once more I sleep soundly. *Viva El Caudillo!*"

The Minister smiled wanly.

"He seems to value the Army," I said.

"It is because of men like him that we have El Caudillo."

The fields eventually gave way to a narrow strip of forest, beyond
which came a town. Its dirt roads were full of people going about their
business—wagons loaded with produce, vendors and tradesmen hawking their wares, women carrying baskets of fruit on their heads. It was
dusty and reminded me of Texas during Reconstruction, because there
was a profusion of soldiers (albeit these soldiers wore grey rather than
blue). The most notable buildings—amid a town of shacks—were the
stout adobe guard posts.

Looming behind the town were the high adobe walls of the capital: La Ciudad de Serpientes. Soldiers paced on the walkways behind parapets. Flanking the arched wooden gates into the capital were sentry boxes, each with a squad of soldiers keeping watch behind sandbag breastworks.

The Minister remarked: "Would a popular president—rather than an unpopular king—need such protection?"

Past the saluting sentries and through the gates was something far more remarkable—a vision from the Spanish Middle Ages, or at least how I imagine them to have been: a tremendous Spanish plaza paved with black and white tiles that made it appear like a checkerboard. At one end was an astonishing cathedral, its cross casting a giant shadow over the plaza, its spires rising heavenwards like stone hands in prayer, its enormous bell tower festooned with a great golden bell, its gargoyles looking like busts of Sam Grant in one of his fiercer moods. Opposite the cathedral was a squat white-washed stone castle that appeared to be crouching, intimidated by the cathedral. On its roof were soldiers, rifles at port arms, officers gazing down at our entry.

Matteo Rodríguez pointed at the castle: "El Palacio Blanco, the official residence of El Caudillo—hence the guards. These other buildings are mostly government offices. You'll notice that they—unlike the cathedral and the palace—are in the neo-classical, republican style; and no guards."

Actually, after the awe-inspiring cathedral, what I noticed most was the milling crowd on the cathedral square. It was full of people dressed in imitation, it seemed, of Black Bart, with flour bags over their heads. A strange, spiky, herky-jerky figure—a woman who looked like a stage witch, perhaps touched with fever—was haranguing them, but I could not make out what she was saying.

Matteo Rodríguez said, "Ah, you wonder at the protest? It is a protest for science—and against ignorance as represented by El Caudillo and that cathedral. Our nation's square should not be dominated by a Church or represented by a monarchy—both relics of the dark, unenlightened past. We need to join your nation as a republic, don't you agree?"

"Why the bags over their heads?"

"The speaker is Lucretia Borreros. She works with the Indians on the borderlands. They suffer from a plague. The people wear bags as protection from it."

A phalanx of Infantry marched from the Palacio Blanco. We stepped down from our horses, and the guards stepped forward to take them.

Looking back at the Black Bart crowd, I said to the trooper leading Marshal Ney to the stable, "Does the plague affect horses?"

"I do not know."

"Well, if you think it necessary, cover the horses' heads."

"With a feed bag?"

"If that's sufficient protection, yes."

Matteo Rodríguez bowed to Rachel. To me he said: "I leave you here—for your audience with El Caudillo. I must attend to other matters. But I will be apprised of your interview. We shall talk again soon, Generalissimo."

The phalanx halted before the iron gates that separated the castle from the plaza. An officer and four household guardsmen—wearing breastplates and steel helmets, like conquistadors—became our new escort and directed us into the palace. The entry hall, like a miniature edition of the plaza, was floored with checkerboard tiles. The hall was long with high stone walls; its decorations were shields, crossed weapons, and medieval suits of armor, neatly separated by alcoves with conquistador guards. We were ushered into a large sitting room full of overstuffed chairs and sofas. The walls were painted red and festooned with pastoral paintings of the island landscape. Against one wall was a line of doors that admitted to small rooms, closets really, with water basins and mirrors so that we could freshen and tidy ourselves: a reminder that appearances were important.

We were not kept waiting long. A uniformed footman entered and asked us to follow him. He led us down a corridor that ended abruptly before two massive wooden doors. He pounded on these, opened them, and announced our arrival: "The captured foreigners, Your

Excellencies of the Council and Your Majesty." We entered, and he closed the doors behind us. We were left in a circular stone room with vaulted ceilings. Halfway up the wall was a platform where guards stood by barred windows. The room's perimeter was devoted to statuary, busts, and paintings—each an artistic representation of El Claudio in some sort of heroic pose: dressed for battle, on a rearing horse, like Napoleon crossing the Alps; toga-clad, scroll in hand, like Solon, the Athenian-lawgiver; the man of the soil, a soldier-farmer like Cincinnatus behind his plow, belted with sword and scabbard. And there was the man himself, seated on his throne, elevated on a raised platform. He was an arresting sight. I had expected to see a Spanish nobleman like Matteo Rodríguez. Instead, I saw a man of almost Germanic features, clean-shaven, bronze-skinned, and blond-haired (it shined, almost like a halo around him). He was a formidable, determined-looking man, and radiated authority. Before him, on parallel lines, were two very long stout wooden tables. Seated at the table on the far side, and facing us, were the members of the king's council. Footmen directed us to the unoccupied near table. My eyes riveted onto an officer seated in a chair just in front and to the right of the throne platform. It was Ambrose Bierce—grey tunic set off by blue epaulets and a maze of gold braid. Opposite him, in another chair, just to the left and slightly in front of the throne platform, was a man in a cassock and dog collar, a Catholic priest—and, I presumed, from what Matteo Rodríguez had told me, the king's naval adviser. His hair had flecks of grey, but he looked remarkably vigorous, a bit like Colonel Nelson Miles. He seemed to be stifling a smile.

El Claudio said, "Go ahead, *americanos*, sit down. Welcome to Neustraguano. I am told you wanted to see me."

The others sat, but I stood and bowed, "Your Majesty, I am Generalissimo Armstrong Armstrong, an associate and superior officer of Generalissimo Ambrose Bierce. I wish to offer you my sword as a commander of Cavalry."

"And who are these other people?"

"Your Majesty, might I introduce my wife, Rachel..." She stood and curtsied. "My Indian Sergeant and scout, Billy Jack..." He stood and bowed. "And Captain Cameron Wakesmith, merchant seaman." He stayed seated.

"Do you have children?"

"Your Majesty?"

"Do you have *niños*, children?"

"No, Your Majesty."

"Well, you should you know; you are a handsome couple. I understand if you can't—that's very sad—but I've noticed in our cities—have you?—that increasingly it seems husbands and wives go into business together and get very busy and never have any children; and if the most attractive people in Neustraguano never have children, won't our people, over time, become uglier and uglier?"

That sounded like pure science to me, and hard to gainsay, but I noticed that—aside from Bierce who sat stone-faced and the priest who was still stifling a smile—the cabinet officers were rolling their eyes or burying their faces behind their hands.

"Of course," His Majesty continued, "it's not half as bad as the rebels—they're utterly barbaric. Their Indians—not your Indian, I see—actually stick bones through their noses. Can you imagine? Bones through their noses—how do they even do that? And they do weird things with their earlobes, sort of distending them. And they scarify themselves with tattoos. Of course, they're not Christians. They do not know that the body is the temple of the Holy Spirit. They are ignorant in that regard. But they are clever in their own way. They have a tradition of cutting off heads and shrinking them. How do they do that? It's their ancient secret. I thought we should stamp it out as barbaric, but my councilors tell me that instead we should apologize to the Indians, because if our plantations hadn't crowded them out, they wouldn't be raiding, decapitating people, and shrinking their heads; they'd just be shrinking each other's heads, and that would be all right, because that's their business—or that's what they tell me.

Personally, I want a country where we don't apologize for replacing head-hunting with farming."

"That sounds reasonable, Your Majesty."

"I'm glad you think so. The rebels we face are horrible. They make war on our churches—and on our women. And our women are much better than theirs. For one thing—ours are actually women. Theirs are some horrid third sex—like human pack animals. They load them with supplies and march them through the jungle. I ask you: Would you do that to a woman? Would you do that to your wife? Is that what a woman is supposed to be—a pack animal? I don't think so. Our men are trained in Christian chivalry. So, they don't want to shoot women. But luckily their women are so big and hairy—like overgrown pigs; they grunt under their own weight, not to mention their packs. They're really too ugly to be women—as you and I understand the term. And chivalry is harder to come by when you see a snarling hog with a pack on its back. People will tell you it's a woman, but you will find it hard to believe. 'Really, is that a woman?' you might ask. And I hate that. We have to kill the snarling hogs—so I don't mind that—but I hate what the rebels are doing to our country. I want a country where the women are smaller than the men, don't you? I want a country where beauty is celebrated and passed on to the next generation; we shouldn't hold it to ourselves, selfishly, and let it expire. I want a country full of children; I prefer them quiet and well-behaved, but I like children. I have five, you know."

"Yes," sighed one bearded old cabinet officer in a stage whisper, "by a wife and two mistresses."

"You see the respect I get—and I'm the king. But my wife loves me, and as the Minister well knows, those mistresses were matters of state, trying to seal some pointless European alliances. We have this custom in Neustraguano: if a woman is a mistress to a prince or a king, no matter for how short a time, she is entitled to a plantation and her off-spring gain a title. The custom was meant to discourage affairs, but my Ministers wanted to curry favor with European aristocrats who needed money, and they convinced me it was a matter of patriotic necessity. Isn't that true?"

The old cabinet officer nodded unhappily.

"I'm surrounded by councilors whose counsel I can't trust. Do you know what these Ministers of mine tell me? They tell me we should get the Church out of educating our young people, because the rebels don't like it. I have a Minister who wants education to be *his* responsibility, a *government* responsibility. He and his allies want to remove crucifixes from our government buildings. *'The Church is bigger than that,'* they say. *'It is a small gesture to pacify the rebels.'* But I say, and my special councilor Father Ricardo Gonçalves says, *'Why should we give ground to the rebels?'* If we remove the Holy Catholic Church from our schools, from our government buildings, something else will take its place. We will replace one set of beliefs with another, with a worse one. It will be the rebels' monstrous beliefs—beliefs that lead to ugliness, tattoos, shrunken heads, bones through noses, distended earlobes, and women who are bigger than men—and worse horrors that we can't even imagine. My councilors want to elevate barbarous paganism to an equal level with our Holy Mother Church. You've seen la Montaña que Eructa? It is a smoking, belching volcano that they warn me will someday explode and kill us all. To prevent that day, the Indians offer it sacrifice—they throw infants, babies ripped from wombs, into its steaming volcanic pit. And my Ministers tell me we should tolerate that! They don't want me to even talk about it. And the Indians—they sometimes even *eat* their own children. Can you believe that? We're supposed to ignore it, but we all know it's true, and it's wrong, but we're not supposed to say a word. And even our newspapers—we have three newspapers; all run by the government—and none of them will talk about this. Why we support these newspapers is beyond me. One is nothing more than an outlet for the rebels. Okay, fine, they can have their say, but why do *none* of the newspapers support me? I can tell you why: because these councilors, *my councilors*, use those newspapers to pursue their own political ends against the country—and me! After I was crowned, do you know what they did, some of these councilors of mine? They organized a protest in the cathedral square—the one happening right now; you saw it, no doubt—declaring their support for *science and progress*. Let me say that again: *science and progress*. A protest for science? What does that even mean? Are they performing experiments out there? Are they studying plants or naval architecture as Father Gonçalves does? I don't think so."

"Your Majesty, if I may..." said a bearded councilor.

El Claudio ignored him and asked me, "You've heard of this theory of evolution? Father Gonçalves disproved it by a simple experiment. Darwin—and I have studied him closely—believes that through a miracle, which he calls 'time,' you can turn a fish into a frog, a frog into a lizard, a lizard into an eagle, an eagle into a monkey, and a monkey into a man. I might have the sequence slightly wrong, but it's something like that; it's about adaptation over time. *But it doesn't work.* I am a farmer, Father Gonçalves is a farmer, and every farmer knows you can take breeding only so far. Breed a horse and a donkey and you get a mule, not a tiger or a rat—and I don't care how long you do it. But Father Gonçalves, being a scientist, gave Darwin's theory a try. He put pigs in trees around his farm to see if they would adapt to their environment and grow wings—and did they? No, they merely fell splat on the ground and died. We turned them into ham for the Navy. Did I get that right, Father Gonçalves?"

"Yes, Your Majesty, it was something like that."

"Yes, I thought so—you see? And as for *progress*—progress to what, I'd like to know. And they invited that horrible woman, Lucretia Borreros—who has a government job, by the way—to be the ringleader! She's the one who is supposed to convince the Indians that head-hunting, cannibalism, and child sacrifice are wrong. And you know what she does instead? She tells the Indians to avoid our bad, corrupt, *civilizing* ideas and pursue their own barbarism."

A Minister said, "Please, Your Majesty..."

But the king held up a hand for silence and asked me, "Do you like beef?"

"Why, yes, Your Majesty. I hope it's what's for supper."

"Bierce, make a note of that—make sure he gets a beef ration tonight." To me the king said, "We have a few cattle ranches here. Now, I want you to imagine a cattle ranch. If you're a rancher, you take good care of your stock. You protect them from predators, right? Now imagine yourself as a cow. You roam, you graze, you're content because your rancher provides you with lovely green fields and cool clean water. He builds rail fences so you don't accidentally trespass on the neighboring farmer. And so, you lead your life, untroubled, as happy cows do; and the happy rancher thinks about something I once read."

A counselor smirked. "*Read*, Your Majesty?"

El Claudio stared at him, "The rancher never mistakes a dozen noisy grasshoppers—even those that sit in his council—as outnumbering his hundreds of contented, quiet cows." He looked at me. "You get my point?"

"Actually, no, Your Majesty."

"Then let me explain it to you. Being king of Neustraguano is like being a rancher. I ensure that our people are free to work and support their ranches. I protect them from predators; I guard our borders; otherwise, I try to leave them alone, just as ranchers leave their cattle pretty much alone, to graze and enjoy the sun; and I ignore the grasshoppers, no matter how loud they get."

A large, well-fed Minister forced himself to his feet and said, "Your Majesty, I object to your comparing the people of Neustraguano to cattle."

The king held up his index finger and said, "I like cattle. I like them better than many of my councilors. But Lucretia Borreros—that crazy woman—is opposed to cattlemen and their cattle. She berates them at every opportunity. Her Indians steal cattle and put them in pens. You will find this hard to believe—I find it hard to believe—but it is true: she and her Indians shout at them, curse at them, their Indian medicine men shake shrunken heads at them; they chastise the cattle—the poor, dumb, uncomprehending cattle—for the error of their ways, and the cattle stand there and take it. They don't get it, of course: they rotate their ears, and swing their tails, and expect they'll be led to water and grasslands. But after Borreros thinks she's made her point, she and the Indians lead them up la Montaña que Eructa and push the cattle over the edge—the poor, lowing, mooing cattle; the poor big-eyed calves—as yet another sacrifice. She thinks we shouldn't have cattle because the Indians didn't have cattle. They were introduced by settlers. But I like beef, you like beef, what's the matter with beef? I like milk too—very much in fact. So, why not leave the cows alone with their ranchers and leave our country rich in milk and beef? The cows are happy, the people are happy, everyone but Lucretia Borreros is happy."

A Minister began, "You will forgive His Majesty…"

But I quickly interjected, "There is nothing to forgive. I appreciate His Majesty's wisdom. I too want a country where the women are smaller than the men, where beauty is perpetuated, where beef is freely available, where milk can be drunk happily, and where children are not thrown into volcanoes or eaten for dinner."

"I like this man," said El Claudio. "You're a Cavalryman, right? I could use an officer of household Cavalry, couldn't I, Bierce? Wouldn't that work well with your men?"

"So it would, Your Majesty. Generalissimo Armstrong is a man of high moral character—practically a lawman in his own right—and an extremely clever Cavalryman, capable of eluding the best set traps of his opponents."

"You're hired," said El Claudio. "Bierce will work out the details. And these other men?"

I gestured towards Billy Jack. "I assume, Your Highness, that I might keep my Sergeant and chief scout?"

"Certainly, we need more Indians on our side; and I like the fact that he doesn't have a bone through his nose. And what about the naval officer?"

Cameron Wakesmith stood and bowed and addressed the king: "I, sir, am not in the Navy; I am a merchant seaman; I ply the waters as a

fisherman and as an importer and exporter of goods. I have no interests
here—I only rescued Mr. and Mrs. Autie; I mean, the Generalissimo and
his wife, after they were cast adrift."

"I like you, Captain; you are a man of enterprise, humanity, and
good sense. I want to offer you a job."

"I am content to return to my boat, Your Majesty."

"I can make you a better offer. You may have your boat—and a
crew. Bierce will arrange your pay—and it will be generous. I commission you a Captain in the Royal Navy of Neustraguano for a period of
five years or until the end of the rebellion. We need more boats, and
yours happens to be here. You will join our coastal patrol. Anyone you
need transported to our shores—wife, sweetheart, children—tell Bierce
and he will arrange it. I know this might not be what you want, but we
will make the transition as happy as possible, and it is far better than
the alternative: which would be seizing your boat for violating our
sovereign waters and throwing you into prison until the United States
government ransoms you, if it ever did. We had another man, another
ship, a Captain Briggs, but he had too many children—we had to let
him go."

"Sir, Your Majesty, I have no interest..."

"I know you don't, but that is all, Captain—hard times mean hard
measures, and even if you did so with the best of intentions, you illegally
crossed into our territorial waters. Our naval intelligence officers tell
me you have done so many times before—on the pretext of fishing. You
have also traded extensively with Mexico—and we are forced to regard
Mexico as a hostile power, though I believe that will change under el
Presidente Porfirio Díaz; he seems a good man. So, you see, I either make
you a prisoner or a naval officer. That's a great choice, isn't it? So easy
to choose. But if you refuse my offer, I have the best lawyers in Neustraguano. They will convict you of violating our sovereignty. On the
other hand, if you accept your commission, you will have the authority
of a naval officer and the freedom of Neustraguano. All I require is your
loyalty, your service, and, of course, your boat."

"He accepts," I said, "with thanks, Your Majesty." I sensed Wakesmith was about to protest, so I thrust him forcibly into his chair. "*There*, Captain Wakesmith, you may rest your case. And I, Your Majesty, rest mine. I look forward very much to renewing my partnership with my old comrade Ambrose Bierce. I am at your service, Your Highness—eager to lead any troops I am given."

"I really do like this man," said El Claudio. "In fact, I might have a mission for you now. Would you like that?"

"I would like nothing more, Your Highness."

"You came through San José, didn't you? Well, the rebels are trying to take another town from us. It's on the western side of la Montaña que Eructa, which means enemy territory. It is surrounded. It is a small town named Santiago. My councilors say we should abandon it—but why abandon ground when you don't have to? A road, El Camino Real, directly links Santiago to the capital, which means you can put your Cavalry on that road, Generalissimo. The rebels want Santiago badly, because it has a great, big, beautiful statue of our Spanish hero El Cid. You should see it. You will see it. He is mounted on a horse and holding a lance above his head—it's a symbol of victory. And they want that statue. They want to topple it and destroy it. But you are going to save that statue. If you must evacuate the town, I will accept that, provided you return with the statue intact. We will erect El Cid in the plaza, where he will be a rallying point for our martial spirit. As he drove the Moors from Valencia, so we will drive those rebels and protestors for science from Neustraguano. Do you accept this mission?"

"Yes, with pleasure, Your Highness."

"Bierce, give Generalissimo Armstrong as many men as you and he deem necessary. I want them to be Cavalrymen with carbines. I leave the other details to you." He looked at me. "Generalissimo Armstrong, if you require political information, talk to these men." He waved at the cabinet officers. "Just don't believe anything they say. And don't believe our newspapers either—they get all their information from them. Now, if you will excuse me; I have a troop inspection to make at the barracks at Santa Maria."

He rose from his throne, the cabinet officers stood and bowed, and the king made his exit, escorted by two guards. I saw now that El Claudio was tall and powerfully built. Capitán Luis Antonio had called him a man of the soil, which made me think of a stout yeoman farmer. But given his prosperity and station and martial bearing, I thought El Claudio better resembled a Prussian *Junker* or a paladin of the South—a Bismarck or a Wade Hampton, only clean-shaven and with luxuriant golden hair.

Captain Wakesmith grabbed my forearm: "I did not need your intercession. I have no interest in serving this king or any other. I am a merchantman and a citizen of the United States."

"For now, Captain, you are a free man because I spoke on your behalf. Gratitude would, I believe, be the appropriate response. I too am a citizen of the United States. I too intend to return there. But for now, we are bound up in this thing, and our only choice is to make the most of it. Surely, it cannot be such an imposition—for you, a Harvard man— to take up the duties and obligations of an officer and a gentleman. El Claudio has called you to be not just a fisherman, but a fisher of men, casting aside those who don't belong here."

As he had grabbed my forearm, Rachel grabbed his, "Captain Wakesmith, my husband is right, and I don't say that lightly. Usually, he has an unerring nose for trouble, but in this instance, I think we have no choice but to serve El Caudillo—and serve him well. When he's victorious, we can all leave. And if I'm any judge of men, he will be victorious."

"I need hardly add," I said, "that my wife is an excellent judge of men."

And with that, I broke free from Wakesmith, left any further persuading to Rachel, and strode boldly to meet Bierce. His icy blue eyes twinkled above a smirk. "So, my fellow Generalissimo, you made it here after all."

"Yes, no thanks to you."

"You'll soon wish I stopped you."

"We'll see about that. Now about my troops…"

"We should discuss that in my office. There's a lot you don't know." He snapped his fingers and an aide stepped towards him. "Lieutenant, get the other Americans billeted. Generalissimo Armstrong and I will be in conference in my office; we are not to be disturbed." Then, to me, he said quietly, "You, Marshal, have entered a pit of vipers."

CHAPTER SEVEN

In Which I Encounter a Conspiracy

B ierce sat behind a desk, with pens and papers aligned like battalions, and a skull, a memento mori, staring at him. He was twiddling a miniature sword letter-opener. Behind him maps were tacked to the wall.

"So, Marshal Armstrong—or Generalissimo, is it?"

"That seems to be the style."

"Well, Generalissimo, you can have no conception of the mess you're in."

"I can make some guesses. I saw how heavily fortified your port city was—and this one. I saw the atrocities at San José. I rode here alongside Matteo Rodríguez."

"This city—this government—is full of people who want El Caudillo dead. They want you dead, too."

"Should I suspect anyone in particular—beyond you?"

"You should know we have no friends at court."

"I got that from Matteo Rodríguez."

"He's hardly the worst of it."

"He supports the rebels, doesn't he?"

"No one in the cabinet does, officially—but they're all copperheads. So, for the most part, is their congress. It's called the Casa de Aire Caliente. Unlike our rebels back home, who had the courtesy to secede, the rebels here still get to vote, if you can believe that—and the lower house has a rebel majority. But the upper house, their Senate, is appointed by the District governors, and most of them are plantation owners or ranchers, so it generally supports the king. The Casa de Aire Caliente appoints the king's cabinet—and they settle on compromise candidates, prosperous businessmen from the towns for the most part, men like Matteo Rodríguez, de facto copperheads who think they can buy the rebels off."

"Can they?"

"You saw San José—that's your answer."

"So, El Claudio, surrounded by enemies, needs a man he can trust—and he made the terrible mistake of hiring you."

"He didn't hire me; he'd never even heard of me. It was that charming, earnest gentleman, Matteo Rodríguez."

"Rodríguez? He's an ally?"

"He's nothing of the sort. He hired me to assassinate the king."

"What?"

"Yes, he figured I'd have every opportunity, as commander of El Caudillo's household troops."

"But why choose you?"

"Because, apparently, my fame has reached even unto the shores of Neustraguano—or at least unto him—and he assumed, from my writing, that I'd be the perfect assassin: a former soldier, interested in the macabre, who hates politicians. And anyway, I'm a foreigner—somehow that makes it better, more moral, more politically acceptable; I represent no Neustraguano faction, tribe, or party—except his."

"What do you mean by that?"

"The idiot thinks we're co-religionists."

"What?"

"You heard me."

"What religion?"

He lifted the skull from his desk and stared into its eye sockets. "I despise religion: its ignorant hypocrisy; its manipulation of hope when there is no hope…"

"Then why does he think you're co-religionists?"

"Because when I married…"

"You're married?"

"Yes, damn it," he said, replacing the skull on the desk, his blue eyes boring into me. "I'm married—and have three young children, if it's any of your business."

"But…"

"And I was married by the Reverend Horatio Stebbins of the First Unitarian Church—and Matteo Rodríguez somehow knew this. He's a Unitarian, of all things, in an island full of Catholics. He read my animadversions against religion and assumed it was Unitarian proselytizing. Don't ask me why—you'd have to ask a Unitarian."

"So, he hired you because he thinks you're a Unitarian assassin?"

"Rodríguez wants to be president of the new republic. He didn't tell me that, but it's obvious. Instead, he blathered a lot of pious twaddle about El Caudillo being unworthy of the throne, a disgrace to his country, a pompous, bumptious buffoon, a congenital liar and hypocrite, a man who revels in humiliating his enemies, a man deaf and blind to necessary reform, a man whose sole gift—if he has one—is energy, and whose sole purpose is the glorification of himself. When I said he was merely describing a politician, he said, no, no, no, El Caudillo was 'corrosive to the political life of Neustraguano.'"

"And assassination isn't?"

"Precisely."

"But you've not assassinated him."

"No, not yet."

"And you don't intend to—you're still loyal to El Claudio?"

"I told you before, Marshal, I serve no cause fully but my own. But I'm not in the habit of smiling on treachery. I came here to command troops, not to kill a king. Right now, I'm stalling for time. I'm gathering intelligence on El Caudillo's enemies and making my own assessment of him."

"Which is?"

"He's arrogant, like McClellan; bullheaded, like Grant; and vicious, like Sherman, thank goodness. He's a bloviator—a politician, even if a king—but at least he understands what the cabinet doesn't: the rebels will never be appeased. Kill him, abolish the monarchy—they will still come with fire and sword and revolution. The rebels aren't Confederates; they aren't people who just want to go their own way and be left alone; they're not mannerly Southern aristocrats; they're Jacobins. El Caudillo knows that—and he knows he can defeat them on the battlefield."

"What about San José?"

"The rebels needed a demonstration—to show they weren't beaten, weren't intimidated; and San José was easy pickings. The town wasn't garrisoned; the town burghers didn't want a garrison—they thought it would be a target. The rebels came anyway; the burghers extended the happy hand of friendship; and you saw what happened: those burghers' heads were pitched down the street like bowling balls; their families lay butchered in the gutter. That's the future—they didn't see it coming, and neither does the cabinet. They're too focused on El Caudillo's *vulgarity*; they think *that*—not the rebels—is the real problem."

"No one in the cabinet supports him?"

Bierce's eyebrows hung like clouds on his face; he picked up his sword letter-opener. "That Catholic priest sitting by the throne—he's loyal; the king's naval adviser."

"He doesn't know you're a Unitarian assassin?"

"Damn it, Armstrong, I am neither a Unitarian nor an Episcopalian nor a Baptist nor a snake-charming Hindu! He knows exactly where I stand on that—but he also knows that for now, anyway, I stand with the king, who is himself a rather profane defender of the faith, which I suppose makes it more palatable."

"How close are the rebels to the capital?"

"They can mount raids like San José. If they mounted a raid here, the copperheads would hand them the keys to the city. But I've got things pretty well-guarded; the capital is very defensible. We've got two rivers crisscrossing behind us; we could easily withstand a siege. The likeliest approach would be from the northeastern hill country. It's broken ground—easier for guerillas to hold. From there, they might sweep down and cut us off from the coast. And if they got that hill country, they'd have Father Gonçalves; that's where he lives. His family is rural nobility. He's a farmer, when he's not saving souls or advising the king; and his farm overlooks the ocean, where he experiments with boats. The rebels hate him more than anyone, except for El Caudillo himself."

"Interesting."

"Isn't it? You remember that señorita whose life you supposedly saved—the one who brought me here—she's his niece. She lives at her parents' hacienda. Her father is one of my Colonels—or I would spend more time there. That area's potentially vulnerable, so we keep Cavalry on patrol. And some of those troops, you lucky man, will soon be yours."

"And with them I ride on Santiago?"

"That assignment was going to the Colonel. Now it's yours, I guess, by royal decree."

"Tell me about the city."

"It's the westward-most town under our control. The rebels have chipped away at it, never cracked it, but now it's surrounded. You'll have to fight your way in and fight your way out."

"How many men will I have?"

"Maybe a hundred—I hate to strip our patrols, but any fewer than that, and it would be impossible."

"What's the enemy strength?"

"Easily ten times that."

"How soon can I have my troops?"

"A couple of days at most; you'll want to train them for the task—get to know your officers."

"No time for that. If I move tomorrow, I'll surprise the enemy. It's a small island, right? Santiago can't be far."

"About fifty miles—the whole island is about a hundred miles across."

"So tomorrow we could go out, as if on patrol—and then attack the following day."

"Maybe—at least half the cabinet will try to get word to the rebels that you're coming. But I doubt they'll expect you in two days."

"The road is good?"

"As far as we control it, yes—but they'll try to block it."

"When can I meet my officers?"

"I have to select them."

"If I could meet with them at four in the morning, we could be out the city gates before dawn."

There was a rap at the door. A guard announced, "The Minister of State and the Minister of Finance." The door opened to reveal the grave, handsome, distinguished Matteo Rodríguez and a thin, beetle-browed, blonde-mustached man with a receding hairline, spectacles, and the stoop of an accountant. The guard shut the door behind them.

Matteo Rodríguez said, "Gentlemen, I am sorry to intrude, but I must congratulate Generalissimo Armstrong. I understand your position is now official. I cannot tell you how gratified I am to have another American in the service of Neustraguano."

"Generalissimo Bierce and I were just discussing the details of my appointment—and my duties."

"Ah, then perhaps my entrance was well-timed, for I can tell you your duties. As Generalissimo, Bierce commands the household Infantry; you will command the household Cavalry, which I trust will be a small, elite unit: something El Caudillo can watch at parades—colorful, harmless, and taken from our existing troops. In fact, if I might introduce our Minister of Finance, Carlos Blandino—I believe he will insist on that. He will not allow you anything as elaborate as the horse guards of Queen Victoria."

"Indeed not," confirmed the Minister of Finance. "There is a difference between a monarch governed by a constitution and a tyrant, though El Caudillo blurs those lines continually. He cannot just divert funds whenever he feels like it. He cannot just snap his fingers, declare a new unit of Cavalry, and put you in command of it. That is an act of tyranny."

"My appointment is an act of tyranny?"

"You may call it that. If he spends unallocated government money on it, it certainly is. You are aware we have a legislature, and we are governed by laws. Our legislature decides how the government spends its money. That is not El Caudillo's prerogative. He must ask the legislature for funds—and he has not done that. We must have a royal submission to the treasury asking that funds be provided for a new regiment of Cavalry, and it must be approved by the legislature."

"But the legislature is full of rebels—or so I've been told. They'll try to block that, won't they?"

"Yes—and quite right they will be. We do not need another unit of Cavalry. The truth is, we do not need Cavalry at all. This is a small island. It is not your wide-open plains, your American West. The legislature understands, even if the king does not, that people will not vote for you if you insist on fighting them with mounted Cossacks. The sad fact is that we have a war only because the king and his party demand one. If he stepped aside, the war would be over."

"But if he stepped aside," I said, "if he abdicated his crown—the rebels would win."

The Minister of Finance scowled at me. "What is winning in this circumstance? There is no profit—nothing constructive—in this war. If El Caudillo were not such a cretin, he would realize that western Neustraguano is a great opportunity. That's where the rebels are. If we stopped fighting them, we could reason with them."

"Reason with them," I repeated.

"Yes. Instead, he talks about recovering statues, which is pointless—who cares about El Cid?—or defending the Church, which is divisive; not everyone accepts it."

"Or accepts the king, apparently."

"Precisely. We do not need a monarchy. We do not need statues and churches. What do they matter? As I said, we are an island. We need to trade with the world. What matters is whether we have farms and businesses and free trade that create jobs and wealth. Are you familiar with Richard Cobden?"

"A famous medieval cobbler?"

"No, not a famous medieval cobbler. Do you know what he said?"

"Was he a farrier, then?"

"No, he wasn't a farrier. He was an English statesman, a Liberal, who said that free trade was a principle that was as true as gravity and as moral as any gospel. It would draw men together regardless of race or creed or language; it would unite everyone in peaceful cooperation. Liberalism is a universal language of reason and enlightened self-interest that everyone can understand—except for El Caudillo. He would take us back to the Middle Ages of throne and altar. If he would just step aside, our country would reunite; we would be a free republic; and we could tax the rebels. We can't tax them now—it is too dangerous—but if we could end the war…"

"Do you really think the rebels want to be taxed? Do you really think you can reason with them? I saw what they did at San José."

Matteo Rodríguez said, "I told you: they were provoked—El Caudillo provoked them. And I tell you this: the king needs good advisers. Your position is an opportunity. Use it wisely; work with us. Perhaps you, like Bierce, will have special influence with the king, a position of trust and proximity. I trust you will do your duty and protect our country from its greatest enemy."

The Minister of Finance added, "The man is a menace, a moron, a disgrace."

"El Claudio?"

"Yes, El Claudio—I mean, El Caudillo. You heard him talk. The man cannot string two sentences together without saying something inane, idiotic, or untrue."

"Really? I found him eloquent, moving, even profound. I tell you frankly, his call for more attractive women and abundant children; for stamping out cannibalism and child sacrifice—that is a platform I can wholeheartedly support."

Minister Blandino scowled. "Yes, El Caudillo is full of such insights. I'm glad you appreciate his genius."

"Perhaps you forget, gentlemen, that in the United States, our president is Sam Grant. He is not nearly so eloquent—and yet he holds the highest office in the land."

Bierce said, "Generalissimo Armstrong is a Democrat."

"Ah, a democrat," Matteo Rodríguez said, "then I believe we understand each other. As commander of the household Cavalry, you serve the monarch, but you are also subject to parliamentary law. I, as a Senator and Minister of State, represent parliamentary law, democratic law—you understand that?"

"In the United States military, Senator, every high-ranking officer has the misfortune of answering to meddling politicians."

"Ah, a sardonic wit—like you, Bierce!"

The Minister of Finance, however, was not amused. "Let me say plainly, Generalissimo Armstrong, I will authorize no funds for additional Cavalry troops or for the recovery of statues. Bierce knows the penalty for violating the law. He saw the Ministers of the Army and the Navy pay the price."

"Senator Rodríguez told me they were sacked to save money."

"Senator Rodríguez is diplomatic; he said that to shield them; the Ministers were prosecuted for misappropriating funds. El Caudillo wanted a ship to patrol the inland waterways behind the capital; he wanted the army to build entrenchments in front of San José. When the legislature and my department refused those requests, the Army and Navy Ministers attempted to divert money from the Minister of State."

"Yes," Matteo Rodríguez said, "that is true. The Minister of Finance and I had allocated money for trade missions—one to Mexico and one to the outer areas of the Ottoman Empire, where we believed we could find new markets for our exports and gifted minority populations for future immigration—Albanians and Kurds, mostly. It was quite the opportunity. But the Minister of the Army and the Minister of the Navy claimed that El Caudillo's war took priority. When they tried to misappropriate those funds from us, we were obliged to prosecute them. I told El Caudillo to fire the Army and Navy Ministers for their incompetence.

I would assume those roles, and the matter would end; it would protect him legally—and save the government money."

"Those men are now in prison," said the Minister of Finance, "and that is where you will be if you overstep your bounds."

"If you call me impetuous," I said, "you'll regret it; and if you jail a prominent American citizen like me, it'll be an international incident."

"Are you so prominent?" asked Blandino. "My colleague had heard of Generalissimo Bierce; he had never heard of you."

Bierce came to my rescue. "Generalissimo Armstrong has a certain renown in American military circles—but, in any event, his duties should never put him athwart the law."

"I should hope not," Blandino huffed. Wagging his finger at me, he said, "And I warn you: if that statue of El Cid turns up in the plaza, I will authorize no funds for its protection. I see that statue as nothing more than another provocation of the rebels and their elected representatives. More than that, it would be an impediment to future Mohammedan immigration."

"Mohammedan immigration?"

"Yes, as we just said, from the Ottoman Empire. Unfortunately, our trade mission was canceled. We have lost many such opportunities because of El Caudillo."

"There are other, more immediate opportunities," said Matteo Rodríguez. "Your position gives you access to them. We ask only that you do your duty—and that justice is done."

Minister Blandino looked at me over his spectacles. "Is that quite clear?"

Bierce used his sword letter-opener to probe the eyeball socket of the skull on his desk. "We understand, Minister Blandino. We will do our duty and see that justice is done." He looked up at the Minister of Finance, smiled, and gave the eye-socket a good thrust.

The Minister's fingers fluttered about his tie. "Well, then, perhaps we should go, Senator, I have other urgent matters requiring my attention."

Matteo Rodríguez said, "I trust, gentlemen, that you will faithfully—and swiftly—execute your duties. I sometimes fear that El Caudillo might achieve his ends before we achieve ours. Good night, then, *buenas noches*."

Rodríguez reached for the door—but it slammed into his face. Rachel bustled her way into the room, shrugging off the uncertain grasp of the guard.

"I gave orders not to be disturbed," said Bierce; but then, taking in an eyeful, he added, "Nevertheless, madam, you are welcome." He waved the guard away.

"Thank you, sir—being a Generalissimo's wife should have its privileges, don't you think? And you, sir, Senator Rodríguez, I must say: you are the most statesman-looking man in the king's court. Wouldn't you say so, Armstrong? Why, you just resonate with integrity, honesty, warmth, and intelligence. And, oh my, is your nose all right?"

Rodríguez held a handkerchief to his face and said, "Yes, it just made unfortunate contact with the door."

"My, my—but it is a prominent nose, a Senator's nose, just like the noble Romans."

"I thank you, Señora Armstrong, for your consideration."

"And I thank you, Senator, for all your courtesy to us."

"I trust, señora, that I do my duty before God and man, as well as your husband does his."

"Oh—I do hope your nose is all right; your handkerchief is looking a little red—but Armstrong is the perfect slave to duty, as I'm sure he told you. And who is this other man?"

"Forgive me," Rodríguez said, tipping his head back to slow the blood dripping from his nose. "May I introduce, Carlos Blandino, Minister of Finance."

"You must both be such busy and important men, I hate to interrupt, but I just came to fetch my husband. I figure if I didn't, he might end up in some new trouble—trouble, as you know, is his business."

"Ah, so it is," said Rodríguez, moving the handkerchief up the bridge of his nose to intercept tears before they became visible, "as a soldier, an adventurer perhaps."

"Oh yes, life with Generalissimo Armstrong is quite an adventure, but I'm getting used to it."

"Good evening, madam, if you will excuse us," Rodríguez said, hastening to the door, Blandino on his heels. "I hope to see more of you in the future."

"Good night, Senator Rodríguez and Minister Blandino. It was a pleasure. And do be careful; there are other doors."

Rodríguez made his exit, and once the door was closed, Rachel looked at Bierce and me like we were naughty schoolboys.

"Let me guess, you two are devising a plan to divide the island between yourselves—or with that politician."

"Really, Rachel, we were discussing important military affairs."

"Whatever you were discussing, I'm glad to see it was civil. We Americans need to stick together. I don't mind telling you, I don't trust that Matteo Rodríguez," she said tilting her head to the door. "He's slicker than a greased spoon."

"Handsome too, I thought."

"You never mind that," she said. "And that Minister of Finance—he wasn't discussing your salary, was he?"

"We never got that far."

"Well, you, Generalissimo Bierce, can take of that. I'm taking my husband away. They've assigned us a wonderful little house across the plaza. I wanted to make sure he didn't get lost finding it. It's quite charming. Just what I dreamt of as a girl—adobe with a white picket fence outside, and two guards just to make sure we're not captured by Neustraguano Indians and fed to a volcano."

"Those guards are my men," said Bierce. "I'm responsible for the security of El Caudillo and his guests at the capital. You are quite safe here. We are far from the frontlines."

"Not far enough, from what I saw."

"If you mean San José—that won't happen here. If you mean the mob outside—they're being dispersed."

"Yes, I saw your men encouraging them—quite effectively."

"Mrs. Armstrong, may I ask you a personal question?"

"Seeing as you are an officer *and* a gentleman, I assume it won't be *too* personal."

"How long have you and your husband been married?"

"That *is* rather personal, Generalissimo Bierce."

"I am also involved in military intelligence. My sources tell me that you were once a nun."

"Well, once a nun always a nun, I suppose, but I never completed my vows, and, as you can imagine, when I came across Generalissimo Armstrong while doing missionary work among the Indians, I was simply swept off my feet. We have been together ever since—with the blessing of clergy, I might add."

What an incorrigible little liar she was, but in this game of ever-shifting alliances, I decided to play along. "Yes," I said, "with all the blessings of the clergy; and that Indian too, he's a Catholic, by the way. Dearest, did you know that Bierce is a Unitarian?"

"Damn it, Armstrong—I am not. I am a heathen and proud of it."

"Don't let him kid you," I said. "Just ask Matteo Rodríguez."

"Now, now, whatever you men are talking about—all your strategy and tactics; all your wars of religion—it can surely wait until the morning. They were fighting this war long before you got here, Armstrong—and now that you are here, victory is certain. And I'm equally certain they can manage a few hours without you. Anyway, shouldn't strolling around the plaza, looking over the city, checking out its defenses, be part of your job? I'm appealing to your sense of duty, Armstrong; come with me and let's do an inspection. Tell him, Generalissimo Bierce, give him an order that your conversation can wait."

"With pleasure—it can wait; I have work to do." Bierce thrust the sword letter-opener back into the skull's eye socket.

Rachel winced and pressed close against me. "Thank him, Armstrong."

"Very well, then, Generalissimo Bierce, I will inspect the plaza and its defenses. Summon me whenever you're ready."

Bierce said nothing, but his cold blue eyes seemed to sit in judgment as Rachel took my arm and led me away.

Bierce's office was in a building nearly adjacent to the Palacio Blanco. Between them was a very pleasant courtyard. In its center was a fountain. Three giant stone snakes sprayed water like a benediction.

"They're a little frightening, aren't they," said Rachel. "Our house has a courtyard too, with a fountain—just like this one, only much smaller; I asked about the snakes. Apparently, they're from the crest of El Caudillo."

I read the motto carved into the base of the fountain: "*Si Ellos Muerden, Nosotros Morderemos más Fuertemente.*"

"What does it mean?"

"I think it translates as 'If Ellen Murders, then Nostradamus Murders More Fiercely.'"

"Hmm."

"That's the literal translation—colloquially it's probably something like 'Don't Tread on Me.'"

"Well, I certainly wouldn't tread on El Caudillo—and it's that Senator who's the spouting snake, if you ask me."

We perambulated. The moon was full, with a hint of a moon bow, and the humid air teased impending rain. Tropical blooms released their fragrance—even in autumn. And all about us was the reassuring crunch of soldiers' boots on gravel as they patrolled the grounds.

"Oh, Armstrong, isn't it lovely here?"

"Yes, I suppose it is."

"Our house is just across the square. It's the one with the dark green shutters—and the matching sentry boxes. We're right in the center of events, Armstrong—with you and Bierce and the king. Oh, it could all be so splendid. I imagine they must have tremendous state balls and banquets and…"

"I'm sure they do. Where's Captain Wakesmith?"

"He's in that building across the street—a boarding house for visiting dignitaries, they said—but that man lacks ambition. I told him, 'Look, you're still the captain of your ship; you're still the master of your fate; why not make the best of it?'"

"Sound advice. And Bad Boy?"

"I thought you'd ask about him. They wanted to kennel him with the horses, but I knew you wouldn't approve, so he's with us—another guardian, for when you're not around."

"Well done."

"I thought I might need one. Between the rebels and that Matteo Rodríguez..."

"You're right not to trust him. In fact, until I get a better grasp on the situation here, don't trust anyone—except for Bad Boy and me."

"And your Indian?"

"Where is he?"

"The same boarding house as Wakesmith."

We had just reached the center of the checkerboard plaza, when behind us came the rumble of pounding hooves. A caped Cavalry officer, a half dozen Cavalrymen, and two riderless horses charged us, hell bent for leather. The officer whipped his saber from its scabbard. Rachel gripped me like an anaconda. A single well-placed stroke could have decapitated us both. Instead, his horse clattered to a halt and the saber swung into a salute.

"Generalissimo Armstrong?"

Rachel tightened her grip. I gasped like an asthmatic, "Yes."

"I am El Teniente Balduino Pérez. El Coronel Monteverde Cristóbal has sent me and these men. He requests the pleasure of your company. He offers you supper at his hacienda. We have two horses—one for you, one for the señora. It is not a far ride: half an hour, perhaps. You will come?"

Having just advised Rachel to trust no one, I now wondered if I could trust this young officer. I decided I had no choice. For one thing, Rachel had practically squeezed all the air out of me, and I was turning blue.

For another, if I declined, his men could simply ride us down. If I accepted, however, I had a horse beneath me—and that evened all odds. Before I could catch a breath and speak—the tropical air exploded with a *boom, boom, boom.* The plaza flagstones seemed to shift beneath us, and Rachel cinched her grip so tightly that I nearly fainted. My eyes pleaded with the Lieutenant for an explanation.

"It is merely la Montaña que Eructa," he said, "it is like a dog that has a bark worse than its bite. You do not look well, Generalissimo. Perhaps you are hungry. You will come?"

"We will come," I croaked.

"We will?" Rachel said, suddenly brightening and releasing me. "Oh, yes, indeed we will, Lieutenant—how delightful, supper at the hacienda!"

Our ride there afforded me a chance to better reconnoiter our position. I now saw in more detail how heavily fortified the city was; it was as if Bierce or El Claudio thought a siege was imminent. Nevertheless, the general mood of the city, as far as I could judge it, was calm. People strolled up and down the avenues contentedly; soldiers marched past, but the civilians barely acknowledged them, or if they did, it was with smiles on their faces that said, "There go our boys!" The people were handsome, in an Iberian way; and the buildings beyond the plaza were handsome too: stone walls painted a vibrant variety of colors, topped by red tile roofs.

We left through the eastern gate. It was much less traveled than the southern approach by which we had entered the city. The shops here were sparser—there was a blacksmith pounding his anvil, a harness-maker tending his leather, a stable-hand brushing a horse— but entrenchments were prominent. The ubiquitous guard posts were enhanced by batteries of cannon. If this was the city's vulnerable point, Bierce was taking no chances.

Sooner than I expected, we crossed a bridge over a narrow river and then into the jungle borderland that separated the city from the plantations beyond. As the jungle had blotted out the sun when we journeyed toward the city, now it blotted out the moonlight; our horses slowed their pace; and I kept a sharp lookout for tangled roots that could lame or ambushers who could kill. But the jungle tunnel was brief, and we then entered a world of moonlit fields stretching to the horizon, separated here and there by colonnades of trees.

The entrance to El Rancho del Chaparral Alto, the estate of Colonel Monteverde Cristóbal was up a long path, lined by what I was told were Italian cypress trees, imported to the island long ago. Interspersed among them were the inevitable guard posts, though these guards wore black sombreros and suits—a private security detail, I gathered. They saluted as we rode past. Ahead was a long adobe and red brick house built around a courtyard. A group of black-clad vaqueros trotted out to greet us; in their wake strode a Cavalry Colonel in full uniform. The Lieutenant saluted him and said, "Colonel Monteverde Cristóbal, I have the honor of introducing Generalissimo Armstrong."

We were assisted from our horses, and the Lieutenant led his men cantering back down the track. The Colonel shook my hand firmly. He was a burly man, whose wrinkles were hidden behind a grey goatee and mustache. He said, "Generalissimo Armstrong, I greet you for the moment, not as one of your officers, but as an honored hidalgo of Neustraguano. I will of course serve you faithfully once your appointment is official. Señora," he bowed to Rachel, "I am graced by your presence here." He returned his gaze to me. "My daughter has told me much about you. From her description, you are a remarkable man—and one to whom I owe a great debt of gratitude."

"Any man of noble sentiments, fierce devotion to duty, and marked physical prowess would surely have done the same, Colonel. It was my pleasure to serve such a poised and patriotic young lady."

Rachel whispered under her breath, "I'll say."

"Come, I have refreshments waiting inside. Neustraguano is famous for its sangria. You will have some, yes?"

I had no idea what sangria was, so I assented, thinking it the proper thing to do, but it is of course a type of wine, and as soon as I realized my error, I handed my glass to Rachel so that she had a glass in each hand. "Perhaps, my dear, you'd like another—in fact, I'm sure you would. One is never enough."

"Well," she said shrugging, "it is wonderful."

The Colonel approached me, full of concern. "You do not care for it, Generalissimo?"

"It's not that, Colonel. It's merely that I've taken a vow not to touch alcohol. But my wife has taken no such vow. I'm sure she will happily drink for the two of us."

"May I get you something else, then?"

"Alderney, if you have it."

"Alderney? What is Alderney?"

"It's a type of cow; my pet word for milk."

"Milk? Ah, that is most interesting, Generalissimo. Here in Neustraguano men drink water during the day; at night they drink tequila or beer; if they are officers, they drink wine like our sangria. But our Caudillo, he too drinks milk; he too refuses alcohol."

"I had no idea, but I'm gratified to be in such good company."

"And I am impressed, Generalissimo, very impressed by men who keep their vows—whether my brother-in-law the priest or El Caudillo or yourself."

"Oh, it's nothing, really—just a matter of high moral character."

"Just so—and we do keep stores of milk, or, er, Alderney, in case El Caudillo calls." He ordered a servant to fetch some.

Presented along with a perspiring pewter cup of well-chilled Alderney was Victoria—or Consuela Victoria Margarita Monteverde Cristóbal. Apparently, her father was unaware of her preference for being called Victoria; he called her Consuela. She was even more attractive than I had remembered—dressed as if she had just returned from a ride: black riding boots, flared grey pants, a flame-red blouse, a black vest laced tight as a corset, and, in her hand, a just-removed black, stiff, flat-topped, wide-brimmed hat. She shook her dark flowing tresses. Her face had a classical beauty about it—simultaneously noble, passionate, romantic, and welcoming—but it also seemed puzzled.

"Generalissimo, it is wonderful to see you again—and in the service of my country, but this is the sister, is it not?"

"Your sister?" said the Colonel.

"No, no, not my sister," I said.

"Oh, my dear," Rachel replied, "I'm afraid the Generalissimo and I have a little secret to share. We were married—it happened so quickly; I have yet to catch my breath. I was still a nun in training, you know, and the Church was so generous in letting me surrender those vows to take up my new vows of holy matrimony. San Francisco is such a beautiful city to be married in. This is sort of our honeymoon. The Generalissimo said to me, 'Would you like to go to an island at war off the coast of Mexico?' And so of course I had to say, yes, and here we are."

"Yes," I said, "and here we are. Perhaps, Colonel, you could pass my wife a bottle of sangria while we retire to discuss military matters."

"Ah, you jest, señor—you are just like your countryman, Bierce, in that regard. But Consuela tells me you are a much better man than he is—and it is *that* I wish to discuss with you. But first, come, supper awaits—and so does my brother-in-law, Father Ricardo Gonçalves. He is very interested to meet you both. He is presently reading his breviary in the hacienda chapel. I will have him summoned to supper. It was his idea to invite you."

"How kind."

"Yes, he suspected that the rebels might attempt to assassinate you tonight."

CHAPTER EIGHT

In Which I Take Command

We were standing around a dining table set in the courtyard when Father Ricardo Gonçalves entered and bade us sit down. The Colonel sat at the head of the table and beckoned me to sit at his right-hand side. Father Gonçalves took a seat across from me. He walked stiff-legged, but otherwise exuded a surprising air of youth; his fair hair had something to do with that, though it was greying at the sides, and his blue eyes sparkled. Like El Claudio, he must have had Dutch blood. And he still had that peculiar look—as if trying to stifle a smile.

"I am glad to see you well, Generalissimo Armstrong."

"Apparently you're glad to see me alive."

"Oh, indeed—but you are perfectly safe here. My brother-in-law takes precautions." Father Gonçalves directed my attention to an earthen bank that rose about forty yards distant and about twenty feet high, a natural parapet. Silhouetted on top were riflemen wearing sombreros.

"Yes, I appreciate that. Neustraguano seems to have plenty of guards." I turned to the Colonel and said, "I assume those men are yours—not men from the Army."

"As Father Gonçalves says, I take precautions. My vaqueros protect my ranch; my Cavalry have other duties."

"We live in dangerous times," said Father Gonçalves, "and the greatest danger is to the unsuspecting."

"You mean me."

"You are new here."

"I know there's a war—that's why I came."

"There are other treacheries."

"I'm getting a sense of that."

"Then you are wiser than many people in Neustraguano. They are willfully blind. They cannot believe our pleasant life is under attack."

"But the war..."

"Oh, they will acknowledge the war. They have eyes and ears enough for that. But they do not appreciate the nature and extent of the enemy. Not even El Caudillo himself fully comprehends the depth of the treachery around him."

"And Bierce?"

"Generalissimo Bierce? He is your countryman, yes—your friend?"

"You trust him?"

"Why should I not?"

"Matteo Rodríguez brought him here. Do you trust him?"

Victoria said, "Matteo Rodríguez told me El Caudillo himself called for Bierce. That is why I went."

"Apparently that was a lie. It is Matteo Rodríguez who wanted Bierce here—and he used you as his unwitting emissary."

"Minister Rodríguez prefers intermediaries," said Father Gonçalves. "It is his way."

"He's no ally of yours," I said.

"We have our differences, but we serve the king together."

"I rode with Rodríguez through San José. He blamed El Claudio for every rebel outrage."

"And in your country, does no one blame your President Grant when Indians have their massacres? Did no one blame your President Lincoln when Confederados defeated your armies? There are similarities and there are differences. Our rebels are not gentlemen like your Confederados. Would your Confederados—your Generals Lee and Stuart and Jackson—have done what you saw at San José?"

"They were not my Generals. I fought for the Union, as did Bierce. But I take your point; Bierce made it too. This war is different."

"The enemy is different—and what the rebels did at San José, they would do here, at this hacienda, if they could."

Boom! boom! boom! The earth shook to the sound of thunder—only it wasn't thunder.

Father Gonçalves continued smiling, "That is, if la Montaña que Eructa does not kill us all first."

⁖

I awoke the next morning with a dog licking my face. I pushed Bad Boy aside and sat up in a strange bed, in a strange room, to see a strange man, apparently a tailor, holding out for my delectation a grey uniform with blue epaulets, yellow and black piping, and plenty of gold braid. As my eyes refocused through the dog slobber, I realized the tailor was Father Gonçalves.

"I sent for your dog, and your Indian; he prays in the chapel. The Colonel's men are forming up outside. Bierce is here too. He brought you this uniform. It is that of a Generalissimo of Cavalry."

"What time is it?"

"Dawn has just broken. No doubt you seek your wife."

"My wife—she's quite far away, isn't she?"

"Not that far—she was given separate quarters, near Consuela. I knew duty would summon you early."

Duty! That was the word I needed to hear—that was the word that would clear and sharpen my mind: *duty!* I leapt up, and after tripping over entangling blankets, made my way to the washbasin, splashed water on my face, and with Father Gonçalves's assistance, slipped into the uniform, which fit like the proverbial glove. I looked in the mirror, straightened the epaulets, brushed the gold braid with my fingertips (covertly assessing whether Bierce had shortchanged me), and fitted the kepi.

"What do you think, Father?"

"*Un hijo de la estrella de la mañana.*"

"I've heard that somewhere before—and I'll take it as compliment."

"There is coffee waiting for you on the dining table. There is *leche*, or should I say, Alderney, as well."

"Well done."

Boots pounded on the tiles outside, and Bierce erupted into the room. "Come on, Marshal—we haven't got all day."

"My command is ready?"

"It's ready—and so am I. I'm coming with you."

"Why?"

"For your protection."

"I've got a troop of Cavalry—what more protection do I need?"

"Drunken assassins tried to kill you last night. They broke into your assigned quarters and wreaked holy hell on your bed—murdered it with machetes."

"Did you interrogate them?"

"Can't—they're dead. Guards heard the racket, charged in, shot 'em."

"That doesn't help us."

"Doesn't hurt us much either."

Father Gonçalves interjected, "Assassins came after Generalissimo Bierce last night as well."

"Bierce, is that true? Is that why you're here? Are you hiding in my command?"

"I don't have to hide anywhere in this country. They never got close to me—my quarters are guarded. The invaders were Indians, like your assassins—pawns in a bigger game. It was a warning, not a serious attempt."

"Serious enough for them, I reckon."

"If you're quite ready, Marshal…"

"A moment," I said, and returned to the basin, unbuttoned my tunic, removed my foldable toothbrush from the Indian medicine pouch I wear around my neck, tipped a dab of salt onto the brush, and cleaned my teeth. "All right, come on, Bierce; let's inspect my command."

Four horses stood outside, saddled and ready. One of them was Marshal Ney, a gun belt draped behind the pommel. I stepped up into the saddle, tied on the gun belt (which had a sheathed knife on its left side), adjusted the revolver in its holster (it was an American Navy Colt), and gazed at the long column of twos arrayed on the path connecting the hacienda to the main road.

"Well," said Bierce, mounting his own horse, "there they are. You give the orders to the Colonel; he'll do the rest. My recommendation—which you can take as an order—is that we follow the northern road, the mountain road, that loops around the capital. Our enemies won't expect that. It's rocky and indirect. It'll mean pushing these men hard."

"That's what we're here to do, Bierce—push these men hard: to victory."

Father Gonçalves sat a horse beside me. "I shall bless the men, Generalissimos; then I shall be at your disposal and follow your orders."

"Surely you're not riding with us, Father."

"As I said, you are a visitor in Neustraguano. There are more dangers than you know. You might need my help."

"Chaplain to the troop?"

"If nothing else—my naval studies have taught me something about war. I am less a novice than your wife was."

"Father Gonçalves," said Bierce sternly, "was that a pun?"

He turned his horse, galloped beside the column, and raised his right hand in benediction. The men bowed their heads and made the sign of the cross.

"Good discipline and good order," I said.

"Appeasing fate," replied Bierce. "Let's go."

We spurred our way to the head of the column. I had no blessing to offer the men, only the inspiration of my presence. But I was sure it was enough—it certainly was for me.

It felt wonderful to be back in command. I looked down and saw Bad Boy loping along, keeping pace, his sense of duty equal to mine.

Colonel Monteverde Cristóbal saluted us. "Generalissimos, your orders, sirs."

"The northern road," I said, "and we will move with all due dispatch. I want us at least halfway to Santiago before the day is done. Press the men as hard as necessary, Colonel."

He saluted and rode to his officers. Billy Jack galloped up and saluted. "Ready for orders, sir."

"Do any scouting last night? Checked out the northern road?"

"Have not slept—expecting action. Northern road looks good: rocks, hills, slopes, trees, but no near-jungle for ambush. I ride ahead, take dog?"

"On your way, Sergeant; you too, Bad Boy." I turned in the saddle and surveyed the long grey line behind me. "Well, Bierce, this is what we came for—a chance to lead men into battle."

"It's your command, Marshal; just do as I say."

I lowered my arm and pointed to the road's horizon. "All right, boys, forward ho!"

The mountain road was indeed a rugged climb for our horses, but we managed it—if not as rapidly as Stonewall Jackson's foot Cavalry might have done, still well enough. At an eastern turn along the path, I looked back and could see the ocean. Father Gonçalves came alongside and pointed in that direction.

"My farm is just over that hill. And at the beach: you see that brown shack, near the dock with two small boats? I experiment with naval engineering there. I knew Matthew Fontaine Maury of your Confederate States of America. I met him when he served the Emperor Maximilian, and we corresponded when he taught at the Virginia Military Institute. He was a very brilliant man. I consider myself one of his naval students."

"Let's hope you have better luck than he did."

Billy Jack's scouting was accurate. The road was steep but clear, and bordered by open rocky terrain that only gradually gave way to jungle.

The weather was pleasant. The sun shone brightly, and my spirits rose the closer we advanced to the enemy. In that first day's ride, we never left the northeastern hills. Occasionally, on the plateaus, we passed well-tilled plantations, but the area seemed sparsely populated—much like our own Western frontier. We made camp on a forested bluff, from which, Billy Jack told me, we would make a long descent in the morning. With luck we would be scouting approaches to Santiago the following night.

⟨∞⟩

"No sign of the enemy, Sergeant?"

"None, sir."

Bierce, Billy Jack, Colonel Monteverde Cristóbal, Father Gonçalves, and I were crouched around a campfire having an impromptu council of war.

Bierce said, "Last we heard, the eastern approach to Santiago was lightly held. Santiago projects like a salient from government-held territory. At the base of the salient is a river spanned by a bridge. The rebels have undoubtedly blown that bridge by now. The river's fordable, but if they reinforce the opposite bank, we're sitting ducks."

I said, "What if we surprise them? Father Gonçalves is a naval engineer. How hard can it be to build rafts big enough for ten men? Suppose tomorrow we make our descent as planned, move down El Camino Real, and pitch camp on our side of the river, close enough to entice the enemy, but not close enough to engage him. Under cover of night, we leave a small holding force in the camp, while the rest of us sneak into the jungle with rafts—we can build those now; there's plenty of suitable wood in that forest over yonder—and instead of a head-on Cavalry assault from the road, we'll hit them from the north as dismounted Infantry."

"We haven't scouted the area," said Bierce. "If we flank them—that's enemy territory; we could be badly outnumbered."

"I'll take surprise over numbers." I turned to Colonel Monteverde Cristóbal. "How are the rebels in a standup fight?"

"We can beat them, but my men are Cavalry men. They are not trained as mounted Infantry. They have carbines now, yes, but they are trained on lances and swords. They are not trained to creep through the jungle, to ford rivers, to attack on foot."

"More firepower means better morale. Officers lead the way."

Father Gonçalves said, "Give me men and I'll make rafts. How many do you want?"

"Nine, I reckon, if you can make them big enough for a squad. We'll leave ten men for the holding force." I looked at Bierce. "You think that's enough?"

"To fool rebel spies—it'll do."

I looked at Father Gonçalves. "You'll stay with the holding force, Father. You're the perfect decoy."

"I can be of more use in Santiago."

"No, my mind is set on that. We'll assign you good men—nine men and a Sergeant. If we gain El Cid but lose you, it's a bad trade—so keep your head down."

I had already marked Father Gonçalves as an officer of promise— and I was swiftly proven right. He gathered the men around him for a quick lesson in raft-building. It reminded me of God instructing Noah on the ark, down to the cubits. In short order he had the men gathering timber; whittling it into shape with knives or bayonets; lashing the timbers with vines; fashioning oars; and ensuring that the resulting rafts were long enough and stout enough to support ten men.

By dawn, Colonel Monteverde Cristóbal had the assault-force troops divided into units of ten, each assigned a raft, each raft to be carried by a four-man team. The assault force was eager, though we still had a hard march ahead. Father Gonçalves had not slept all night, but he exhibited no fatigue at all—indeed, he seemed even more energetic now that he had a small command of his own.

We descended the plateau to the main road, El Camino Real. The rocky terrain receded, and the jungle crept closer until the road was level and narrow and the jungle swarmed its sides. Bierce assured me that

Infantry patrols regularly swept the area, though we saw no troops—ours or the enemy's. We pressed the men hard and did not make camp until dark. When our fires were up, I had the officers around me and reminded them that stealth was now more important than speed.

We were lucky, in a way, in the weather. Clouds obscured the moon; droplets of rain hinted at an impending storm. Our men moved into the jungle, squads of ten, at five-minute intervals, using the picketed horses as a screen. The spattering rain intensified, cutting through the jungle canopy, noisily splashing on leaves and mud, and finally turning into a downpour, the cloudbursts covering the grumbling of troopers and the hissing of Sergeants as they trudged through the mire and around soggy vines.

We made it to the river without serious incident. Bierce, the Colonel, Billy Jack, and I crept to the water's edge, the men staying about ten yards behind. The current did not look overly swift. On the opposite bank, we saw a large tent illuminated by an interior fire that highlighted the shadows of four men. Two disgruntled rebels huddled outside, neglectful sentries, griping, one could guess, about the rain that dripped off their sombreros onto their dark ponchos and soaked their white shirts and pants. We saw no entrenchments and no sign of supporting troops.

"Billy Jack and I will go across," I said. "I'll enter the water about thirty yards to the left. Billy Jack, you go as far right as necessary to avoid detection. Move cautiously, but with all due haste—if we can coordinate our movements, so much the better. We'll take the sentries—alive if we can—and the ones in the tent too. Have the men ready to support us. Once the Sergeant and I have the enemy subdued, bring the men across on the rafts."

We inched our way back into jungle cover. The jungle was thick enough, the rain heavy enough, the underbrush high enough, and the rebel sentries lethargic enough, that I felt confident I could move without being seen. Still, I was careful, hiding behind tree trunks and swift-walking rather than running—I didn't want to trip—into position.

I found a muddy rivulet and used it as a path to slither down to the river. The water was cold, but as I ducked beneath the surface, I was invigorated and swam with strong strokes. Reaching the opposite shore, I scrambled into the undergrowth.

I stayed reasonably close to the shoreline to remain in view of our men and keep a line of sight on Billy Jack. I crept forward. The rebel sentries had their heads bent against the rain. I stepped lightly. I could hear them talking in Spanish. The nearest one was now only two jumps away. I saw Billy Jack crouched behind a fern on the opposite side. I unsheathed my knife. Billy Jack took that as a signal, and together we sprang. We clasped hands over the mouths of the sentries—and prodded cooperation with blades pressed against spines.

In a hoarse whisper I said, "No sound; no moveoremos. Savvy?"

We bore our captives away from the tent, tied their hands, and gagged them with vines. We directed their attention to our men across the river. They got the point. With these two secure and effectively guarded, we moved on to the tent. My revolver was wet, of course, but I drew it from its holster, shook out the barrel, and reckoned it would do well enough. With knife in one hand and revolver in the other, I stepped through the unsecured tent flap. The unsuspecting rebels were stunned, their eyes darted nervously at the entry of Billy Jack, and their hands shot up in surrender. They were a sorry-looking lot. For men besieging a town, they seemed remarkably bedraggled and demoralized. We marched them down to the river in triumph, and our rafts started across. First one, then another—the men initially tentative, afraid of tipping over, but then using their oars with confidence and bounding from the rafts onto the shoreline with undisguised glee. It was a glorious if soggy moment.

Bierce was in the lead raft. He ambled over to me, examined our captives, and said, "If I didn't know better, Marshal—I'd say you were a Marshal. Best job of rounding up rebels I've ever seen. Not too spirited, are they?"

"No, they're wet—and alone."

In the distance, to the southeast, there was an unmistakable eruption of gunfire.

Bierce said, "That sounds like our holding force."

Another raft had landed, and I heard a voice say: "We have achieved tactical surprise. But we must hurry." It was Father Gonçalves.

"Damnation, Father, can't you take an order?" said Bierce.

"Damnation is not your business, Generalissimo—and I have followed orders: I created a diversion. I am aiding and abetting your advance. The rebels have attacked an abandoned position. We withdrew the horses to the main body of government troops—down El Camino Real about five miles. We left behind our tents and a dummy Father Gonçalves who is probably hacked to pieces by now." He turned his attention to me and said, "You see, Generalissimo, there is something you should know about me." He removed the plain dark blue overcoat he was wearing and there was a glitter of brass buttons and gold braid reflecting the moonlight. "It is the uniform of a Commodore in the Royal Navy. And I too have read about strategy. The rebels took the bait. They have attacked a phantom position—and they have done so in force. That means the way to Santiago is clear. Let us make haste."

"You don't give the orders here," said Bierce.

"No time to argue," I said. "Let's get these men moving inland, in columns of five, advancing in echelon—and noisily. We don't want Santiago's garrison firing on us; we want them to know we're coming. Father, tell the men to sing your national anthem, as loud as they can—and in English; the rebels wouldn't do that, would they?"

"They most certainly would not!"

I ordered Colonel Monteverde Cristóbal and Bierce to get the men into formation. The lines formed, we advanced into the jungle, and the men belted out this tune:

> Glory to Neustraguano,
> Fair island of our king,
> Glory to Neustraguano,

Of its noble men I sing,
Strong to win their battles,
Swift to sheathe their swords,
Our men, they are not cattle,
Our men, they love the Lord!
Glory to Neustraguano,
Fair island of our king,
Glory to Neustraguano,
Of its fair maids I sing,
Their love is our salvation,
Their beauty transforms all,
Their love, it is redemption,
When we answer duty's call!
Glory to Neustraguano,
For Holy Mary's prayers,
Glory to Neustraguano,
The Holy Family's heirs.

Their voices competed with the pounding rain, and the low rumbling of la Montaña que Eructa provided an eerie accompaniment. Our boots squished through the undergrowth, and our eyes were wary in the dark. I hastened to join the lead echelon. Bierce was there too. The jungle thinned, our boots accelerated as they met less resistance, and I trotted ahead until I was first out of the jungle and into a moonlit clearing and in sight of Santiago, its sandbagged walls shining white in the near distance.

I expected a sentry to have a bead on me, so I shouted, "Don't fire! I am Generalissimo Armstrong of the Neustraguano Cavalry. We have come to rescue Santiago!"

A voice shouted back, "Generalissimo Armstrong? We have heard of no such Generalissimo."

Bierce came up beside me. "This is Generalissimo Bierce. I expect you've heard of me. Open your damn gates!"

Colonel Monteverde Cristóbal reiterated our bona fides in Spanish—and a cheer came from the garrison.

"Come, sirs, come—we are saved!"

We strode in like the conquering heroes we were, with the garrison soldiers swarming around us, cheering, and waving their rifles. An officer snapped to attention. "I am Capitán Aurelio López, commander of the garrison of Santiago. Thank goodness you have come, sir. There seems to be fighting on the other side of the river."

"Yes—and with any luck, we've drawn the rebels into a trap. Did they blow the bridge?"

"No. They used it tonight."

"Did you hear that, Bierce?"

"I did—another example of man's innate stupidity."

"Good fortune for us—they'll be coming back, and we can make them pay. Bierce, get our men arrayed to cover the bridge. Captain, I want half your men assigned to our support. If the enemy tries to cross that bridge, we will destroy him—and if we do, the siege is lifted, at least for a while. Have the remainder of your men reinforce the town's perimeter, in case the enemy brings up more troops."

Bierce, Colonel Cristóbal, Captain López, and I surveyed the ground behind the bridge. You could not have asked for a better defensive position. From the base of the bridge the enemy would have to ascend a slope of about fifty yards. At the crest of the hill was a wonderful stone wall. We would use that wall as the Confederates had used the stone wall at Marye's Heights at Fredericksburg. Another fifty yards behind the stone wall was the city of Santiago, its entryways blocked by sandbags. The rebels would never get that far. By my reckoning, they'd never get past the stone wall.

The enemy had the advantage of numbers, but we had the high ground and good cover. Granted, the rebels might not cross the bridge. They might ford the river as we had done. But if we still had the element of surprise, they'd start with the bridge.

Capitán López patted the stone wall and said, "The rebels have maintained their siege from this wall. They withdrew tonight; then came gunfire; we feared a trap."

"It's a trap all right—for them. Keep the men behind the wall. No one is to fire until I give the order. If the rebel commanders have any brains, they'll send scouts or a skirmish line. We cannot let them see us."

We organized the men into rifle squads and positioned them behind the wall.

We heard the rebels before we saw them. Billy Jack said, "Skirmish line, southeast of the bridge."

I saw them. Another line came from the northeast, their white shirts and pants easily visible in the night. They came incautiously—apparently confident that Capitán Aurelio López's men were still behind the barricades of Santiago. The rebels established a slack firing line by the bridge. Chasing a phantom enemy is frustrating. It's worse in the dark and pouring rain. Now they had to sit and wait.

The main force, however, was not far behind. They were not organized into platoons or any regular formations. It was a mass of grumbling stragglers who crammed themselves onto the bridge until they formed a giant grub worm pressing onto the span and inching itself across. The head of the worm had just pressed onto the grass when I stood and shouted: "Fire!"

Midway down the line, Bierce popped up, took aim with his revolver, and said, "Fire! And get those skirmishers first!"

At the other end of our line, the Colonel and the Captain leapt up and shouted, "Fuego! Fuego! Fuego!"

The rattling of our rifles was like a tonic to my soul. I roamed our line, encouraging the men—who didn't need much encouragement. For the soldiers of Santiago, it was vengeance. For our men, it was vindication of them as mounted Infantry. "Pick your targets and fire! Make every bullet count! Don't stop until I give the order!"

The rebel skirmish line fell under a torrent of lead. The rebels on the bridge tried to surge forward and then tried to fall back, but they were trapped. Some leapt into the river, with our bullets pattering after them. Rebel officers, identifiable by colored sashes, scrambled to lead a retreat to the southwest on the far shore. We peppered them, but we couldn't stop them. The bridge was clogged with dead—and that was the best we could do. I passed the word to cease fire, and silence replaced the crash and thunder of battle. We strained to see enemy movement across the river, but there was none: no furious shaking of tree branches, no jungle fronds jarred by wild-eyed flight; the rebels were gone. I looked down the line at our men and raised my revolver skyward.

"Soldiers of Neustraguano—you have won!"

They leapt to their feet, waved their rifles, and shouted their joy.

Bierce sat on the wall, revolver in his hand.

I said, "I'd call that victory."

"Yes. I forgot what victory looks like—up close."

"No regrets?"

"None—not even if El Caudillo gives you a medal."

"I'll put in a good word for you. Now let's get a look at that statue."

The main square of Santiago was larger than I expected. It was dominated by a church, of course, much smaller than the cathedral in the capital, but still quite ornate and attractive in its own right. It, however, did not command my attention. Right dab in the center of the square was the statue of El Cid, or as they called it, El Cid Campeador. The statue must have been at least twenty feet high. Imagine, if you can, a formidable bearded, bareheaded knight aboard a prancing horse; on one arm a shield; the other arm raised overhead, its mailed fist holding a pennoned lance. I can only hope that someday my own devotion to duty might inspire an artist somewhere in our United States to capture me in such a manner on horseback and in bronze. Perhaps, my dear, you could start a collection to that end. Possibly Bad Boy could be part of the sculpture as well.

I spent a great deal of time communing with the statue. Indeed, long after Bierce and the Colonel and the Captain had retired to a cantina to meet the mayor and celebrate our victory, Bad Boy and I remained in the plaza admiring it, pacing around it, captivated by its detail and struck

by the way the rising dawn illuminated it. Hours passed before Billy Jack
appeared and interrupted our reverie.

"Have been scouting perimeter; was worried that garrison was distracted by celebration—but no sign of enemy."

"Well done, Sergeant. My own sense of duty has kept me here pon-
dering this statue—what an extraordinary tribute it is to duty, duty such
as we pursue here: For was not El Cid both a patriot and a soldier of
fortune, as we are?"

"The inscription says he was a caballero católico."

"Ah, and a cat lover, too."

"It is a fine statue."

"Indeed it is, Sergeant. I wonder: If a statue were ever done of me,
should it be erected here, do you think, or at Gettysburg where I beat
Jeb Stuart, or perhaps in Monroe, Michigan, where I met my wife?"

"Which wife?"

"What do you mean, which wife?"

"I mean which wife?"

"Sergeant, I am a Christian gentleman. I have but one wife."

"You told me in Bloody Gulch you had a wife. It was not Sister
Rachel. Now it is."

"You know quite well that *Sister* Rachel, as you call her, is no more
a religious sister than she is my wife."

"You tell people she is."

"Rachel and I are acting incognito. I don't need to tell you, of all
people, what that means."

"I am not acting incognito."

"You don't need to."

"And you do?"

"Of course I do."

"Why?"

"Because my actual identity is a matter of the utmost secrecy—
and right now I am obliged to play the role of Generalissimo Armstrong Armstrong."

"Not so different from Marshal Armstrong—only a different wife."

"Sergeant, perhaps you should return to scouting."

"Have scouted all night; the sun is rising. Other eyes can watch now."

"Where's Father Gonçalves?"

"At the church—there is a hospital attached. He is there treating Indians—local tribe, old people who live in land just west of here, look skeletal. They suffer from some disease."

"He's not a doctor too, is he?"

"I do not know, but it is Christian duty."

"To every man his duty, but I'm surprised his includes doctoring."

"With your permission, I rest from scouting: go to church, pray, morning Mass, then sleep in pew."

"You go to church, Sergeant. You've done your duty. I'll know where to find you."

I knew where to find Bierce, too. He had spent half the night at the cantina with the mayor and the Captain of the garrison. I wanted information on the government forces across the river. I pushed open the cantina doors and found Bierce in his element, his chair leaning against the wall, a cigar in one hand, a glass of wine in the other, attentive señoritas and an audience of junior officers, the Colonel, the Captain, and a man I presumed to be the mayor because of his wide girth and voter-catcher's grin.

Bierce guffawed at my entrance. "Ah, here he is: the conquering hero; the architect of the hecatomb at the bridge; the ditch-diggers' friend. Have a drink, Marshal. You're a bit late to the party. I've used up my best stories, but I've got plenty of others."

I said to the fat man, "You, sir—you are the mayorissimo?"

"I am the mayor, yes."

"I am Generalissimo Armstrong, commander of the Cavalry who have broken the siege of Santiago. Generalissimo Bierce has been temporarily assigned to my command. He normally commands parade ground troops at the capital."

Bierce waved his cigar and said, "I remind you that I have El Caudillo's ear."

"That may be—but I have his prize."

"I told you men: Generalissimo Armstrong is quite the soldier—and quite the devotee of duty."

To the Captain I said, "Where are the government troops across the river?"

"Not far—five miles perhaps down El Camino Real. The rebels kept them frightened and away—but you have delivered us; a toast to you, sir."

"We need to get them here. We need to fortify this position. My men can't stay indefinitely. We have other work to do."

The Captain stood slowly, his head bowed and full of wine. "They were recently reinforced; they should have plenty of men."

"Excellent. Get them word that Generalissimos Bierce and Armstrong demand their advance—and our horses; in fact, make the latter a priority. Have your messenger return with my horses Marshal Ney and Edward."

"Yes, Generalissimo."

"I was told that Santiago was a salient into enemy territory. That you are bounded by a river, almost like an island."

"That is correct, sir."

"Well, your eastern front has been relieved; we've reestablished your supply line to El Camino Real; it is time to advance. I want your reinforcements to form a new front line west of the city gates, overlooking the river."

"Oh, Generalissimo, you should not do that, " said the mayor. "You should not leave Santiago. It is not safe in the countryside beyond."

"Nonsense. I will find that new front line myself, with the help of my Sergeant—and you Bierce. We will scout it together."

Bierce was gazing at his glass; his eyes shifted to me. "As you say, Marshal; you know your business. It's still a butcher's business, but I don't mind if the enemy gets butchered."

"That reminds me—we need a burial detail."

The Captain said, "I can arrange that."

"Excellent. I've been contemplating El Cid's statue. Let his devotion to duty be our own."

Bierce harrumphed. "Didn't I tell you boys? Duty, always duty—even in a statue."

The mayor stood and looked at me eagerly. "You like the statue?"

"Yes, of course. It is a masterpiece of martial art."

"You want it?"

"What?"

"To take away."

"To take away—you mean, as a spoil of war?"

"Yes, take it to la Ciudad de Serpientes, present it to El Caudillo. I think you should take it."

"But why—it belongs to your town."

"I want to replace it."

"With what?"

"Anything—maybe we have a contest: maybe a piñata; maybe a statue from the church; maybe a statue of me, I have often thought of it. But Generalissimo, that statue is yours—a gift from the people of Santiago."

"You don't want it?"

"I do not care for it so much—it attracts rebels. So, please, take the statue, Generalissimo; you are a man worthy to defend it."

Well, there was enormous truth in that. Still, I was surprised. Perhaps, though, I shouldn't have been. People express their gratitude in different ways—and why, after all, should the mayor not express his gratitude by presenting me with a giant bronze statue that had been in his town's square for decades. "The plinth too?"

"Everything—take whatever you need. We can even supply reinforced carts and mule teams. You take it—and all in Santiago will remember you as the man who rid us of the rebels."

"Very well then—El Cid is mine!"

CHAPTER NINE

In Which I Journey with El Cid

While waiting for the reinforcements to arrive, Bierce, Billy Jack, Father Gonçalves, Capitán Aurelio López, and I scouted forward positions for the new troops. We found a perfect line of high ground—a stone outcropping that afforded some cover, with scraggly trees and scattered boulders, and that had enough dirt to dig shallow trenches. It overlooked the jungle where the river, coming from the west, divided north and south to encircle Santiago. Rising dramatically from the tangled forest behind the river was the volcano, smoke curling from its apex.

We crept to the cliff's edge, hid behind some naturally formed cairns, and looked down on the river. It was wider and obviously deeper than where we had crossed because it was dammed on the rebel side; the northern and southern branches that encircled Santiago were merely overflow streams. Adjacent to the dam was a dock, perfect for bringing up men and supplies. If the rebels were to rally, it would be here.

"Captain," I said, "this is ideal ground. Why didn't you entrench it before?"

"We had orders not to—this is Indian land."

There was thunder again. The ground shook and black smoke shot from the volcano.

Billy Jack pointed at the dam. "Look—the enemy."

His Indian eyes were sharper than mine, but then I saw them—white-shirted figures barely visible behind bushes near the river. He directed my vision to something else: a line of rebels ascending the lower slope of the volcano. Trees obscured our vision, but it appeared their destination was a crevice in the volcano's side.

I said, "That's a camp—or an ammunition dump. I wonder if we could raid it."

Captain López shook his head. "Even with reinforcements, it would be very difficult—the terrain is hard; their men…we do not know how many."

"What do you think, Sergeant?"

"Better to watch from here—provide warning for town, if necessary."

"Odd to build a camp beneath a rumbling crater." I shifted to get a better look at the volcano but had an eerie sense we were being watched.

My foreboding was confirmed when Father Gonçalves grabbed my shoulder. "I fear the enemy has found us."

I turned, instinctively pulled my revolver, and was confronted by a line of hostile-looking Indians: bowmen on the flanks, their arrows drawn, spearmen in the center, spears aloft. They stood on a ridgeline about thirty yards above and behind us. Their war paint—red, yellow, and black—was in the pattern of a poisonous snake; their hair was greased and their bodies bore serpentine tattoos; their noses and ear-lobes were threaded with bones—from their victims perhaps, for they looked as gaunt, savage, and primitive as the hungry cannibals they undoubtedly were. They regarded us silently, malevolently. And then a tall haggard woman, with wild eyes and tangled long curly brown hair stepped amongst them, mumbling to herself. Her skin, even if badly wrinkled and sunburned and smeared with dirt, was unmistakably white. Unshined boots extended from splotched pants and petticoats. Her blouse was mottled and mud-caked. She was slovenly in appearance; her manner was pure disdain—and her language far more profane than I care to record.

The Captain groaned, "It is Lucretia Borreros, the government agent to the Indians, a very difficult woman."

"What the hell are you doing here?" she shouted. Her eyes rolled like an insane minstrel's. "You have no right to be here. You bring contagion, disease, and death. We kill all trespassers."

"Listen, you damned bureaucrat, I am Generalissimo Ambrose Bierce. I ended your little party in the capital the other day—and I'll end this one too. Get out of our way."

"Try to intimidate me because I'm a woman, would you?" She waved her skirts and petticoats. A dress that had been worn in a coalmine and then left out in a sandstorm wouldn't have shed more dirt. "You see my Indians? They are cannibals. They work for me. They're my muscle. And they'll castrate you—castrate you, I say! And then they will eat you—if I give the word. I am Lucretia Borreros, Appointed Administrator to the Indians. I am in direct correspondence with the Minister of State. Only he can supervise my work."

"Well, that's fine," I said, trying to act the peacemaker, "we're doing government work too."

"No you're not; not here; not with him." She pointed at Father Gonçalves. "He has no authority over these people."

"He's here as a Commodore of the Royal Navy."

"He's a priest, isn't he?"

"Well, yes, but…"

"The government has specifically said the Church has no authority over the Indians. They are not to be converted to his lies. Damn him! Do you hear me? Damn him! And damn his Church!"

Father Gonçalves said, "Miss Borreros, we are not here to discuss my religion."

"Don't talk to me! I want no instruction from you! My Indians worship nature—and that's their right. It is how they explain birth and death."

"With cannibalism and child sacrifice?"

Bierce said, "We're wasting time. Clear off, woman, and take your diseased Indians with you."

"You violated our quarantine! You trespassed our property! You are now subject to Indian law—and the punishment is death."

Bierce cocked his revolver. "We'll see about that."

Father Gonçalves said, "Wait a moment. Lucretia Borreros, all we ask is our safe return to Santiago."

"Santiago is a pig sty—with a pig for a mayor. Its pestilence infected my Indians."

"I cannot help that, but the Church does run a hospital."

Lucretia Borreros convulsed, as if possessed by demons: her legs stamped the ground, her arms whirled, her grotesque mad eyes rotated in their sockets, her fingers made bizarre gesticulations, she grunted like an animal and then suddenly blurted, "We do not need you, your Church, or your hospital! We do not need your oppression or your superstition."

"Not superstition, Miss Borreros. That hospital is no superstition. And my Church is no superstition; it rests on the historical fact that Jesus Christ stands in history just like Plato or Julius Caesar—but with a much greater message."

"Shut up, priest. I don't need your false morality."

"Try this morality," Bierce said, stepping forward. "Have that Indian throw his spear at me. Have him kill me—if he can."

Lucretia Borreros screeched at the Indian nearest her. He hurled his spear, and it clattered harmlessly a foot in front of Bierce. Bierce then raised his revolver and as casually as you would swat a fly shot the Indian dead; his red corpse came tumbling down the rocks like a log, his skinny limbs cracking like dry tree branches against the stones. The other Indians glowered, but remained silent and still.

I said to the Captain, "They're like the living dead."

"They are. They smoke a narcotic plant; the government reserves it for Lucretia Borreros and the Indians; they use it as medicine."

"Or stupefaction," I said.

"The next bullet is yours," shouted Bierce.

"You wouldn't dare! I am a woman protected by the Minister of State."

"I don't care if you're protected by the Grenadier Guards. If you get in our way, I'll kill you—you and all your cannibals."

"You're a murderer, then!"

"Just another sacrifice in your book, isn't it? And it's science. I just demonstrated the science of ballistics. I hope your subjects took note. Get out of the way! We're coming up."

"The government will hear of this."

"I am the government—and yes, it surely will. You'll be hanged for this. You let the rebels attack Santiago."

"I let them attack the church!"

"They attacked the city."

"You are an abusive bastard!" (That was the least of her epithets.) "How was I supposed to stop them? Why should I want to stop them?"

"If you want to save your life—get out of here."

"Oh, I'll get out of here all right—but don't you try to follow. My Indians might be in quarantine, but these guards, *my* guards, will kill you bastards—you damn superstitious, pestilential bastards—if you try to follow us!"

She swung away, screaming profanities. She moved with a weird herky-jerky gait into the forest, her Indians slow-marching behind her, until they were lost to sight and the cries of the jungle birds finally subsumed her noxious ranting.

Father Gonçalves, Billy Jack, and the Captain covered the Indian corpse with stones.

I ascended the hill with Bierce, glancing sidelong to make sure there were no ambushers in the brush. "Well, that was interesting," I said, "science, theology, and Indian-fighting all at once."

"Bunkum and balderdash combined with murder."

"Well, you said it, I didn't."

"Just don't try to arrest me, Marshal; your writ doesn't run here. Anyway, you saw it: he threw first."

"So, he did. I wonder what Father Gonçalves thinks?"

"I don't care what he thinks: his god got bushwhacked by his own creation."

"Bierce, you'd make a hell of a preacher: all fire and brimstone—and no redemption."

"You won't live to see it."

Bierce took my horse Edward and rode to la Ciudad de Serpientes to deliver news of our victory. I worked to get El Cid ready for the journey to the capital. The mayor provided us with two transport wagons, hitched together—one for the plinth, one for the statue—and a team of ten mules to pull them. Loading the plinth and the statue into the wagons was a challenge involving hoists and pulleys and the muscle power of more than a dozen men, including my own. It was not just a matter of lifting the weight, but of taking due care to ensure that neither plinth nor statue was damaged. In the end, a corps of West Point–trained engineers couldn't have done it better.

The mayor sat at a table just outside the cantina and watched us with amused detachment. He was enjoying an early morning brandy while the rest of us sweated.

"Generalissimo, next time you want to kill someone, make it Lucretia Borreros; you would do us all a favor." He gave his comrades a jowly laugh.

Captain López was beside me, making sure El Cid was secure. He said, "She is from here, you know. Her appointment was a sort of exile. No one could stand her."

"Who appointed her?"

"The Minister of State, Matteo Rodríguez—and it was good to be rid of her, but she is no ally: the rebels travel Indian lands—and we are kept out. Of course, she tries to keep the Indians away from Santiago—she fears the Church will convert them."

"I noticed that."

"You know, Generalissimo, it is ironic. The Minister of State ordered us to abandon Santiago, to retreat across the river; our position, he said, was untenable. But before we could retreat, the rebels cut us off."

"Now they wish they hadn't. And this is the prize they wanted," I said patting the fetlock of El Cid's horse. I stepped back to admire the statue in the wagon. "What a noble bronze animal it is, Captain; and what a noble bronze knight: strong, dutiful, and proud. It would look wonderful anywhere, don't you think—in Monroe, Michigan; in New York; in your capital; even in a jungle hideout."

He shrugged. "There are some who like it."

"But not the mayor."

"No, not the mayor."

"Yes, I can see why," I said casting my eyes from the noble bronze statue to the fat, cowardly, conniving drunk at the cantina.

Colonel Monteverde Cristóbal strolled over and slapped me on the shoulder. "It is excellent work, Generalissimo—and a true prize, in good hands."

"I wish you could come with us, Colonel."

"Ah, we have our separate duties. I don't know what delays the reinforcements, but I will wait with my troops until they arrive. Father Gonçalves will drive the wagon?"

"Yes, with my Sergeant; I've detailed eight troopers to come with us."

"Not much of an escort."

"It'll do." I mounted my horse. "I'll see you in the capital."

"*Vaya con Dios, Generalissimo.* Don't take *all* the credit for our victory. Save some for an old soldier."

"Colonel, if we each do our duty, there will be glory enough for all."

And so, my darling Libbie, we set off. Needless to say, taking credit for the relief of Santiago was hardly my primary interest. My reward for this gallant act, whatever it might afford me personally—a medal, the offer of a plantation estate, or perhaps the hand of Victoria in marriage (which of course, dearest Libbie, I would decline)—would be as nothing to the reward of seeing El Cid, in all his chivalric glory, centered on the capital square, smack between the grand cathedral, with its magnificent giant cross and glorious golden bell, and the palace-fortress of El Claudio.

Lest there be any mistaking our direction, I rode to the head of our column. The city gates were open, the barricades had been removed, and the people had turned out with cheers and flowers to strew before us. I waved my kepi at the appreciative throng. Pointing the way with my hat I bellowed the order, "Forward, ho!" and away we went, through the gates, and down a path to the stone wall, where we halted briefly and surveyed the former scene of battle. The corpses had been cleared away and buried in a mass grave. The lines of the burial trench were still visible, but the burial detail had worked hard to restore the lawn of green. Bierce himself, I was told, had stamped the ground back into place; he probably saw it as stamping his enemies to hell.

Our column meandered around the stone wall, our horses stepping carefully down the slope and to the bridge. I thought it wise to inspect the span before we crossed. It was still spattered with blood and detritus but looked structurally undamaged; I reckoned it could bear the weight of El Cid and the plinth.

I rode to our muleskinners and said to Father Gonçalves, "You're an engineer; any qualms about the bridge?"

"If we don't stop in the middle, those girders—and our prayers—will see us through."

"We stop for nothing! Pray away, Father!"

I led our Cavalry escort across the bridge. Then I called to Billy Jack: "Make a running start for it."

The slope of the hill made that practically impossible, but Billy Jack slapped the reins, the mules took a slightly hastier step, gained speed as their hooves hit the bridge, and bounded safely across, with the statue and the plinth tottering barely at all.

We traveled the main road to the capital, El Camino Real; it was clear and straight, and more than once I rode off to the side to watch, in wonder, the progress of El Cid in his wagon. There he was: lance aloft, encouraging us forward. Bad Boy was in the wagon and frequently struck a similarly heroic pose. It was, I'm sure, an inspiring sight to the pickets of government troops we passed occasionally. Indeed, I thought of our procession as a triumphal march, such as might have graced the streets of ancient Rome. In our case, it was a march of two days before we reached the outskirts of the capital city—and a surprise.

I had the men polish their buttons, shine their boots, and brush their uniforms; I wanted our dramatic entry to coincide with the noon ringing of the golden bell in the cathedral tower. We would, in turnout and appearance, be everything that El Claudio would want us to be. We did not neglect our animals either, currycombing each horse to an immaculate sheen. In the late morning, teeth agleam from a fresh cleaning, I paused to imagine our reception. In my mind's eye, I could envision the crowds swarming us. I could hear the cheers and the chants of "El Cid! El Cid! El Cid!" I could see myself waving my kepi at the crowd and saying to Father Gonçalves. "Well, Father, we survived the siege—but will we survive the celebration?"

But then reality intruded. Coming towards us was a contrary procession: two massive columns of Infantry with mounted troopers on the flanks. At first, I thought it must be our (surprisingly large) escort into the city. But then I saw they had their own wagons: enclosed wagons with barred windows, wagons for prisoners apparently, and an oversized, reinforced wagon like our own—bearing the golden bell from the cathedral.

My Cavalrymen and I withdrew to the side of the road and watched as the column advanced—an unstoppable force. I felt an odd sense of dread: there was no cheering; no huzzahs of victory for El Cid; instead, the troops looked sullen and suspicious. They halted just before our mule team, and a young Captain rode up to me.

He did not salute, but said, "Mr. Armstrong?"

"Yes, I am Generalissimo Armstrong. What is the meaning of this? Why is that golden bell being moved?"

"That is not your concern. I have my orders."

"Don't be impertinent, Captain. Where is it going?"

"To Mesa Santiago, to Lucretia Borreros, Administrator to the Indians."

"By whose order?"

"Minister of State Matteo Rodríguez."

"Does El Claudio know about this?"

"I do not advise the king, Mr. Armstrong. I am a Captain, not a Minister of State."

"And I am a Generalissimo, Captain. Father Gonçalves is right there. He runs the cathedral—not Matteo Rodríguez."

"The priest returns to Santiago. He is under arrest."

"What?"

"House arrest—at the rectory."

"Are you mad?"

"That Indian—he is yours?"

"He's my lead scout."

"The Indian Administrator, Lucretia Borreros, will take him into custody."

"She has no authority over him—he is a Crow Indian, from the United States."

"I have my orders."

"Forget your orders. I'll take the responsibility. I am a Generalissimo and I countermand them."

"You are not a Generalissimo, Mr. Armstrong; you have been stripped of your rank and have no authority."

"Stripped of my rank? That's impossible. I serve at the pleasure of the king."

"Generalissimo Bierce has ordered your arrest."

"Bierce?"

"You are charged with treason. If you resist arrest, I am authorized to use lethal force. I hope that won't be necessary."

Half a dozen of the Captain's Cavalrymen surrounded me.

"What about my men? What about the statue?"

"Your men will join the column; the statue returns to Santiago."

"But you can't. They don't want it."

"Those are my orders. You are my priority. You men," he said to his troopers, "take his gun and his knife—and let us move along now, Mr. Armstrong."

His Cavalrymen crowded around me and relieved me of my weapons. Then my horse and I were effectively bundled onto the road. I saw my troops reformed under their new commanders. Infantrymen boarded our wagons and grabbed the harnesses. The mule team was turned about. From the column's two barred wagons, Spanish voices hurled catcalls and abuse.

I looked at the Captain for an explanation.

"Criminals," he said, "released from the prison at la Ciudad de Serpientes. We don't want them; the rebels can have them. They helped us with the church bell; in return, they won their freedom. La Ciudad de Serpientes is under martial law. The prisons have been emptied—to make room for conspirators like you."

"Conspirators? You do realize I just freed Santiago; I broke the rebels' siege."

"That is not my concern. I have my orders; I am charged with preventing a coup, led by you and other foreign mercenaries."

"A coup? What is your name, Captain?"

"I am Captain Royce—and you are now my prisoner. I would advise you to say no more."

So there it was: one moment the conquering hero, the liberator of Santiago, the deliverer of El Cid; and now—for reasons I could not fathom, and that Captain Royce would not explain—I had been adjudged a traitor. And by Ambrose Bierce! The man was incorrigible, but he would not outmaneuver me.

There were no raucous crowds at la Ciudad de Serpientes, no cheers, no accolades, no waving flags, no bands playing, only guards and more guards and an eerie silence punctured by the occasional bellow of a Sergeant marching troops.

Captain Royce turned me over to conquistador-uniformed guards who bustled me to the office of Ambrose Bierce.

Bierce's smile was devilish; he toyed with his sword letter opener. "Ah, excellent; a messenger told me to expect you. Senator Rodríguez should be on his way." To the Captain of the Guard, he said, "You may leave us. I have no fear of this traitor. Just wait outside. If you hear a scream, it'll be his." After the door closed, Bierce said, "I'm afraid you've lost your commission."

"Of all the dirty tricks you've played, Bierce, this is the worst."

"It's not a dirty trick at all. It is an act of high statesmanship. Charging you with treason keeps me in Matteo Rodríguez's confidence."

"How can you possibly charge me with treason?"

"You trespassed on Indian land, violated their quarantine, killed one of them, contradicted orders from the Minister of State, and one of your confederates recently landed in jail—shall I go on?"

"What?"

"That's your favorite word, isn't it? In Spanish it's *qué?*"

"That's a lie!"

"No it's not. I have an English–Spanish dictionary on my desk. I can prove it."

"You know what I mean, Bierce. If we trespassed, we did it together. If I violated Rodríguez's orders, so did you. And you killed that Indian. I have witnesses."

"They're not here, are they? And anyway, that's not really the issue— murder never is in Neustraguano. The issue is your *motives*. Rodríguez doubts them. He thinks you're here to fight for El Caudillo."

"Well, yes, aren't you?"

"I'm the one asking the questions, Marshal; you're the one guilty of treason."

"I serve the king—how is that treason?"

"That's how Matteo Rodríguez sees it."

"What about you?"

"I work for the Minister of State. He recruited me; he didn't recruit you. Your motivations were different. They were sincere."

"And that's treason?"

"Of course."

"So what happens to me now?"

"That's up to Matteo Rodríguez. He'll be here soon. He wanted to question you himself. I expect a firing squad."

"And you'll accept that?"

"Why should I make a scene?"

"So that's it, then? You led me all the way to Neustraguano just to kill me?"

"Marshal, I tried to stop you—every step of the way. Your mad infatuation with that girl..."

"I am not infatuated with Victoria Cristóbal; I am a married man."

"You think that makes a difference?" He looked at the skull on his desk and tapped it with the sword letter opener. "There's something else you should know. When I said they jailed a confederate of yours—that wasn't a figure of speech. They've arrested a Southerner; a former Confederate officer; a man named Beauregard Gillette—says he's a friend of yours. You know him?"

"Major Gillette? Yes, but what is he doing here?"

"I thought you'd know. I don't. Anyway, Rodríguez suspects you're hiring mercenaries to overthrow the government."

"You know that's not true."

"I could be convinced."

"What does that mean?"

"Nothing, but I am curious about the Minister's methods of interrogation—aren't you? Inhumanity arouses my curiosity. That's why I came here, remember? And so far, Neustraguano hasn't disappointed."

There was a knock at the door, it swung open, and the guard announced: "The Minister of State." The grave and stately Senator Matteo Rodríguez entered. He turned, nodded to the guard, and the door was closed behind him. He looked at Bierce and then at me.

"Mr. Armstrong, I regret your arrest; I regret even more what happens now."

"Torture?"

"I fear that is inevitable. Mr. Armstrong, you need to understand your situation. You are charged with treason. Anglo-Saxon legal principles do not apply in Neustraguano. You are not presumed innocent. You are not guaranteed counsel. You are not guaranteed a trial. It is my sole responsibility to find you guilty or innocent—and I must say the evidence is overwhelming."

"What evidence? You have none."

"We have enough—and torture will provide more."

"Does El Claudio know about this?"

"He cannot help you—and he wouldn't want to. I told him the plain truth: that you are conspiring against this government."

"In what way—by winning battles you won't fight?"

"I understand the larger diplomatic picture. The United States wants improved relations with Mexico—and Mexico wants to annex Neustraguano. What better way to curry favor than with a soldier-spy? You send information to Washington; it is relayed to Mexico City; and when Mexico City gives the word, you lead an armed revolt against the government."

"That's fantastic—you know I'm not a spy."

"On the contrary, I know very well you are."

"You can't prove that."

"I need only prove it to myself. What else explains your occupation of Señorita Cristóbal's private train compartment? Why else insist on a commission in El Caudillo's army?"

"That's not how it happened."

"You call her a liar?"

"No."

"You call Generalissimo Bierce a liar?"

"Yes, as a matter of fact, I do."

"Generalissimo Bierce came at my request. His actions justify my trust in him."

"His actions are self-serving lies. I can prove it."

"We have our own methods for deciphering truth. Normally I disapprove of torture, but in this case it would be unconscionable not to use it. There is too much at stake. We must know your plans. We must know the depth of your treachery. And then, we must execute you. It would be unjust to put my own feelings of mercy against the punishment you deserve for your crimes against the state."

"What crimes?"

"We will torture you for the details, but the general picture is plain enough: You came here as Napoleon came to France from Corsica. You intended to depose the government and become military dictator, acting in the interest of Mexico. This I have pieced together—and so informed El Caudillo."

"Those are lies—and you know it."

"Your perfidy has been exposed. You brought this upon yourself."

"You have no evidence."

"We have the best evidence: a co-conspirator. Your fellow mercenary, Señor Gillette, has been captured. His appearance confirms everything I have just said."

"Major Gillette said nothing of the kind—he couldn't have."

"Who cares what he said? His being here is enough. He will share your torture—and your execution. You will not die alone. Take comfort in that."

Bierce said, "Will you conduct the interrogation yourself, Senator?"

"No—these things are messy; the prison guards know what to do."

"With your permission, sir, I think I should attend. The prisoner's testimony might need interpretation."

"Yes, I suppose that makes sense. Well, then, Bierce, see to it. I will take my leave."

"Wait a moment," I said, "what happens to my wife?" (By which, of course, dearest Libbie, I meant the woman impersonating my wife; you, I was comforted to know, were safe at home.)

"Your wife? She should fear nothing. You alone are guilty, Mr. Armstrong; you led her astray. In fact, Bierce, that's another charge against him—enlisting that innocent angel into his conspiracy. The more I think about you, Mr. Armstrong, the more anger I feel. I am a righteous man, and you fill me with a righteous anger. Generalissimo Bierce: inform me when justice is done; I will convey the news to El Caudillo."

"Excuse me, Senator," said Bierce, "will you witness the execution?"

"No, Bierce, I will leave those gruesome details to you. It is a military matter: a firing squad will suffice. I have important business, so you will excuse me. I hope your execution, Mr. Armstrong, will serve as an example to dissuade others from a life of treason."

"So I'm guilty of treason and the rebels aren't?"

Matteo Rodríguez had opened the door. He paused, looked me up and down, as if measuring me for a coffin, and said, "That is all, Mr. Armstrong. You are guilty. Every word you utter confirms your guilt.

But I warn you: others could share your fate. In my mercy, I would rather spare them. You should say nothing more. Good day." He closed the door, and Bierce and I were alone again.

Bierce said, "Any last words?"

"I thought torture came first."

"We can do it that way. Guards!" The door flung open. "You will take Mr. Armstrong to the prison. You will place him in the same cell as Mr. Beauregard Gillette. You can knock him about as necessary, but he is not to be seriously harmed—or tortured—until I arrive to supervise the interrogation. Is that clear? Now bind him and take him away."

The guards pinioned my arms behind me and threw me to the floor. My wrists were locked together with rope and I was heaved to my feet.

Bierce smiled. "Hogtied and delivered for the slaughter," he said.

The guards frog-marched me out of his office, through the military headquarters where I caught glimpses of officers studying maps and jotting notes on papers, and then down a narrow stone hall. At its end, a wooden door was thrown open. Waiting there was an enclosed wagon, like the prison wagons I had seen on the road. Its rear door hung on rusty hinges. I was lifted and hurled bodily onto its straw-strewn floorboards. Three guards were seated on plank benches on either side of me. There were small barred windows for ventilation, but they were high on the door and walls; and the guards took no chances; their boots pressed me into the straw. We rattled along for ten or fifteen minutes, it seemed, and then I was dragged out again and led down a stone corridor of empty prison cells. At the end of the passage stood a guard by an open metal door. They thrust me before the cell, and there sitting on the edge of a cot was Beauregard Gillette. He stood at my appearance. I imagine he looked exactly as when you saw him: tall, well-built, dark of hair, courteous in manner, and wearing an eyepatch embroidered with the rebel battle flag. Did they know, I wondered, that he was also a federal agent for President Grant?

The guards hurled me inside, slammed the metal door shut, and locked it. Beauregard worked to untie the rope that bound my hands.

"Well, Yankee General, sir, I do declare, I did not imagine we would meet under these circumstances—in jail, in a foreign country. Mighty fancy uniform you got there; they don't seem to respect it, though."

I rubbed my freed wrists and said, "All right, let's start from the beginning, Major. How the heck did you get here?"

"Well, sir, I delivered your letter, as ordered. Your wife is a delightful woman—and quite solicitous about your health. She sent me to find you. I've been tracking you ever since. I must say, sir, you do lead an interesting life."

"You make it more so, Major. They've imprisoned me because they think I'm recruiting American filibusters like you to take over Neustraguano—that's this country, by the way."

"Oh, I confess, sir, I knew nothing of this country before, but I made a quick study on my way here—and I can say with confidence that our government has no interest in this country and President Grant no knowledge of it."

"Of that, I'm certain, Major."

"But that could change, sir. I reckon we have the makings of a diplomatic incident. The United States government might overlook the disappearance of Miss Rachel, who I gather is with us, somewhere on this island; it might overlook the disappearance of your Indian scout; it might even overlook the disappearance of a man named Ambrose Bierce. But my disappearance, as a federal agent, could raise some eyebrows, especially if your wife were to make enquiries. And you, sir—you are in a very delicate situation, given your own desire for anonymity."

"Yes, Major, that's true."

There was thunder and the ground shook.

"Begging your pardon, sir, but what was that? The ground has been shaking since I arrived."

"It's a volcano; they say it's harmless."

"Well, sir, I'm no expert on volcanoes—but that one sounds like a drunken artillery officer; mighty dangerous, I reckon. We should expedite our departure."

"Yes, Major, but we need a plan."

"I've an inkling of one, sir. Our cell, you might have noticed, is last in this row. The door, as you can see, is made of steel; it is set into a rock wall. The corridor is made of rock. But have you noticed, sir, that the walls are adobe? I reckon we could dig right through this wall. Don't know what's on the other side—could be guards or could be freedom."

"By George, Major, you're right." I went to the wall and pressed my fingers against it. It felt stout, but there was no doubting we could chip away at it—and if we dug low, the hole could be hidden by one of the two bunks. If the guards didn't inspect the room, and we burrowed swiftly enough, it just might work.

I asked, "Have you a knife?"

"Never without one, sir. As a gambling man, it pays to keep one handy—and where your opponents won't find it." He pulled a six-inch blade from his boot and pointed at the grill in the metal door. "If you keep watch, Yankee General, sir, I'll whittle that wall something fierce."

I needed no further invitation but took my place; Major Gillette took his; and operation breakout was underway. His facility with the knife was remarkable, and his progress astonishing—so much so that I found myself worrying less about guards in the corridor than about the possibility of guards outside watching the rapid-fire deterioration of the prison wall.

The volcano continued rumbling—more constant and pronounced than before—and perhaps that gave us some cover, perhaps it distracted attention. Before you could recite Grant's first inaugural speech, Major Gillette had driven his fist through the wall.

"Well, I do declare, sir; their previous prisoners weren't very enterprising, were they? If we're not spotted in the next twenty minutes, we'll have a hole big enough to run through."

I abandoned my post at the door and joined Major Gillette at the wall. While he filleted with his knife, I used fingers to expand the existing hole. I still had my Cavalry gauntlets, so I allowed myself the occasional punch to loosen the crumbling adobe. And sure enough, we started knocking out handfuls of the stuff at a time. The hole got big enough that we actually took turns sticking our heads through, looking for trouble. If anyone had seen us, they might have thought we were being pilloried, so tight was the hole initially. But all we could see was jungle. The prison was apparently on the perimeter of the city. Once we were through the wall—and if no patrol came by—we'd be away to the forest.

The hole grew, and we attacked it with ever greater enthusiasm, kicking out its final contours with our boots. Then we crouched down and stepped through it. Freedom's grass was beneath our boots. We saw no guards—and heard nothing, save for the low rumbling of the volcano and the jungle birds beckoning us into the welcoming forest. We plunged into the maze of vines and trees until we were surrounded by wilderness, and then paused just a moment to try to catch our bearings. We did not stop again until we had put a goodly distance—easily more than a mile—between us and the prison. We were dripping sweat by the time we sat on a log to catch our breath and have a council of war. I picked up a twig and drew a circle in the dirt.

"That's the capital, Major. We cannot take it by ourselves—and our hopes for gaining an audience with the king are slight. Our first duty then, as I see it, is to go here." I drew a second circle. "That is Santiago— about two days' march to the west."

"What's there, sir?"

"Allies—albeit in the hands of the enemy."

"That rather complicates things, doesn't it?"

I drew a line connecting the two circles, and said, "That is El Camino Real, the main road connecting Santiago to the capital. On that road is an army—and among that army's prisoners are our allies, including Sergeant Billy Jack Crow—you remember him; my Indian scout."

"Yes, good man."

"And a naval Commodore named Father Gonçalves."

"Father?"

"He's a priest as well."

"Ah, to be sure—Chaplain and Commodore; quite efficient, sir."

"And El Cid's statue."

"El Cid, sir?"

"Spanish hero."

"Undoubtedly."

"With that statue—we can rally the island's patriots."

"Those would be our people, sir?"

"Yes, of course they're our people. And that column also has the cathedral's golden bell."

"I see."

"The statue of El Cid will rally every patriot; the golden bell will rally every Christian."

"So, our chief allies, sir, are a church bell and a statue?"

"Yes, Major—but the bell is golden, and the statue is a hero on horseback. You will be impressed."

"I am already, sir."

"Of course, we have to rescue them first."

"Rescue the statue?"

"Yes—but also Billy Jack and Father Gonçalves."

"I reckoned there'd be a complication—from whom, sir?"

"If that column reaches Santiago, Father Gonçalves will be held at the rectory, under house arrest. I'm not sure what that means—but if he is guarded by elderly bishops, priests, and nuns, surely we can spring him. Nuns can't stop us."

"I would think not, sir."

"Billy Jack is in a worse situation. If the column reaches Santiago, he'll be given over to a crazy woman with an army of cannibalistic Indians who practice human sacrifice."

"Yes, I thought it might be something like that."

"She has one desperate fear—that her Indians might be converted to Christianity. So Father Gonçalves is essential to freeing Billy Jack."

"So, we rescue him first."

"No, Major: second. First we rescue Bad Boy."

"Bad Boy."

"Yes, my dog—remember?"

"Oh, yes, sir, your dog."

"He is a fine Lieutenant—a valorous, dog-faced pony soldier. I imagine he is already working diligently behind enemy lines. He was with the statue, you see. And he has teeth."

"Yes, I assume he does, sir."

"Large ones—and right now, Major, we have only a knife between us."

"Not much in the way of armament."

"But that is no excuse for inaction. We must move quickly and rescue Billy Jack."

"The two of us, sir?"

"Four of us, once we have Bad Boy and Father Gonçalves."

"Do we have an estimate of enemy strength, sir?"

"Not precise numbers, but between the hostile Indians, the rebels, and the recalcitrant government troops, it will be hundreds at first, then thousands, and then possibly tens of thousands."

"And there will be four of us, sir?"

"Five, once we have Billy Jack, six if you count El Cid, seven with the golden bell, and once I recover my horse..."

"I see, sir, a simple matter of addition."

"Exactly—each victory makes us stronger."

"Shouldn't be much of a problem then, should it?"

"My thoughts precisely, Major."

"I reckoned they were."

"But, Major, all this assumes the enemy column beats us to Santiago. What if we get there first?"

"Yes, sir, what then?"

"I left Colonel Monteverde Cristóbal and his Cavalry at Santiago."

"He's an ally?"

"Yes—but I don't know if he's still in Santiago."

"Could be riding around like Jeb Stuart."

"Yes—or perhaps even aligned with the enemy. Bierce or Matteo Rodríguez might have sent him orders. We need to operate, Major, as if every hand is against it."

"That seems a fair reckoning."

"Just so. In which case," I made an X over the circle representing Santiago, "our best stratagem is to reach Santiago before the enemy column does."

"That'll take some swift marching, I reckon."

"Swifter than you know. We must beat not only the column, but the enemy's communications. If a dispatch rider reaches Santiago before we do—well, that's a complication. But if we get there first, perhaps we'll confuse the enemy about who is on which side."

"That would be a good start, sir."

"Well, then, Major. I believe due west is that way. Let's get marching."

"Yes, sir, I reckon there's nothing else to do."

CHAPTER TEN

In Which I Fight Innumerable Foes

The way west—without road, path, or trail—was fraught with difficulty. It meant pushing through tangled vines and undergrowth. High thickets of green blotted out the sun, and thus our ability to get our bearings, and even small detours around a densely packed copse, a barricade of boulders, or a trickling stream could throw us off course.

But I have always been blessed with a good sense of due north, and I was determined to beat the government column to Santiago. Major Gillette was a worthy companion, a man inured to soldierly deprivation, uncomplaining, and eager to execute his duty. Hour after hour we slogged on—and in the end, we had our victory.

It astounds me still—even as I write this—and fills me with pride that we reached the river encircling Santiago before the government column did. Granted, that column was encumbered by the golden bell, the glorious statue, and the recalcitrant prisoners. But they also had Cavalry and a clear road in front of them. Our success, if I say so myself, was a tribute to our stamina, natural speed, and native woodcraft.

We paused at the river. It was an hour, I reckoned, before dawn. We strained our eyes to discern pickets, guards, or scouts from Santiago. There was a faint aroma of smoke in the air—perhaps from hearth fires in the town, I thought—but we saw nothing, heard nothing: no fire silhouetting a camp, no squelching of boots in the mud, no cough from a sentry. We were happy with that result, but curious just the same. Why did Santiago's defenders think it unnecessary to post guards at the bridge or pickets along the river? We assumed there were guards at the city gates, but we saw none; and, strangely, we heard no noise, not even the barking of a dog or a murmur of voices from the cantina.

"Fortune favors the bold," I said. "Shall we cross at the bridge?"

Major Gillette's eyes scanned the darkness. "Yankee General, sir, if the entire garrison is asleep, if they have no sentries posted—why, it beggars my military imagination."

"Major, I left Santiago a hero. If dispatch riders have not arrived from the column, they may still regard me as one. Even if they see us cross the bridge—we might be welcomed."

"Or lynched. But I reckon it's worth the risk. No sense soaking in a river when you can saunter over a bridge."

And that's what we did—without subterfuge or fear, neither creeping nor sneaking, but with shoulders back, chests out, we made our way to the bridge.

"Major, do you have a harmonica?"

"Sir?"

"I thought you Southern boys always kept one around."

"Why, I surely do—I just didn't reckon on needing it now."

"Whistle me out a tune, Major. It does not matter, which one. I do not remember their national anthem precisely, but I will do my best to sing it, to announce our presence." And so I began:

> Oh men of Neustraguano,
> You should not be sleeping,
> Oh men of Neustraguano,
> Your watch you should be keeping,
> For Generalissimo Armstrong,
> That man he has arrived,
> May all the saints preserve him
> And keep him at our side!

"Yankee General, sir, are you sure those are the words?"

"The song has many verses, Major—that surely must be one of them."

Finally, a voice from the city gate called out: "Who goes there?"

"It is I, Generalissimo Armstrong, your city's savior."

"Why you come back?"

"Well, that's hardly the way to greet a conquering hero."

"Santiago is under quarantine."

"Quarantine?"

"By order of the new mayor: no one may enter or leave. The Indians have a foul disease and sought refuge in the church—putting us all at risk. If you value your lives, go away."

"You have a new mayor—who is it?"

"Lucretia Borreros."

"What? You can't be serious—you surely didn't elect her. What happened?"

"She bore an order from the Minister of State. We imprisoned the old mayor in the church. We set it on fire—the hospital too—burned them down. Perhaps now the disease goes away."

"Burned them down? You burned down the church, the hospital—with people in them?"

"Yes, it was necessary. The new mayor ordered it. Now you must go."

"When did all this happen?"

"Over the last two days. We burned the church this morning."

"Have soldiers arrived from the capital—advance riders from a column?"

"No one dares approach Santiago. You should go away."

"What about Colonel Monteverde Cristóbal? What about his Cavalrymen?"

"Lucretia Borreros had orders for him from the Minister of State. He was to go to the northern coast and prevent an invasion."

"An invasion?"

"Yes, from the sea; from Mexico."

"Mexico?"

"Yes—now you must go! There is great danger here. Be gone—*vaya con Dios!*"

The ensuing silence was broken by Major Gillette: "Yankee General, sir, let us cross over the river and rest under the shade of the trees."

"Shade, Major? The sun hasn't risen."

"Only a bit of prosing, sir—I reckon we need another council of war."

It seemed a prudent suggestion. We retraced our steps across the bridge, set our backs against two large tree trunks at the forest edge, and sat for a moment in silence.

"Major, the column can't be far away."

"No, sir, but I do detect an opportunity to switch things to our advantage. I doubt our opponents know about the quarantine."

"Yes, I've been wondering about that: the rebels surely know—they're just across the river. But the column, maybe not."

"And this new mayor, sir?"

"Lucretia Borreros? Major, that woman is insane, utterly insane; I had to deal with her earlier. Quarantine's likely her idea; she probably never informed Rodríguez. But we don't need speculation; we need scouting. We need to know the location of the column."

"I don't suppose it can wait 'til morning, sir? Maybe get some coffee and hardtack from Santiago. Boiled water can't be that dangerous, can it? And hardtack…"

"Major, we move immediately, under cover of darkness, while we have it. The column is coming up that road. If they suspect no danger, we will shock them."

"Shock them, sir? By ourselves?"

"Yes, we'll follow the road along the jungle verge—and when we meet them, we will shock them."

"I see, sir. What do you have in mind?"

"I don't know, but our footsteps will accelerate my thinking—and when we find the enemy, he will be ours, and we will shock him."

"Yes, sir, shock him."

And with that, I stood up, brushed insects and dirt from my uniform, and led Major Gillette on another jungle march, this time alongside El Camino Real. As we marched, my mind raced through the possibilities before us, and an idea formed.

"Major, there is—or was—a line of government troops about five miles away from Santiago. They might still respect my uniform, my rank as Generalissimo."

"I reckon that's a strong possibility, sir."

"It could be, Major, that through simple command presence, we could make that force our own. We could then confront the column with our own body of troops."

"Well, sir, having an army would be a great benefit."

We kept relatively close to the road, where the jungle was thinner, moving speedily through the brush until we saw a lounging picket line. Behind it were rows of military tents. I approached the pickets boldly—and was encouraged to see the men snap to attention. A Sergeant trotted up and saluted. It seemed appropriate to start issuing orders.

"Your name, Sergeant?"

"Sergeant Esteban, sir."

"Sergeant Esteban, I have just been to Santiago. The city has been quarantined. Did you know that?"

"No, sir; we have orders to hold this position and advance no far-ther—not even with scouts—lest we provoke the enemy."

I raised an eyebrow at that. "Sergeant, I'm giving you new orders. With Santiago quarantined, the rebels might take advantage. Take these pickets and do some scouting. Keep an eye on the city but be careful: spies might lie behind those walls. Keep me informed."

"Yes, sir."

"And Sergeant, get me your commanding officer."

"Yes, sir."

That proved to be Captain Manuel Obregón—a man who looked as neat and capable as his Van Dyke beard. "Generalissimo, I had no idea you were here; I thought you were in la Ciudad de Serpientes."

"Captain, you and I have a mission of the utmost importance. There has been a mutiny within the army. A mutinous column is coming this way. They have the statue of El Cid—and they have other hostages, including my dog. They must be stopped. How many men do you have?"

"Minus the pickets: about four score. But a mutiny, sir—I'm stunned."

"As was I, Captain, but we have no time to wool-gather. Instead, I want these tents down and the men in trenches."

"Trenches, sir?"

"These roadside ditches will do. Put your men in enfilading positions—both sides of the road. I will command this side; you take the other side."

"Yes, sir."

"And Captain: at our command, the men must fire without hesitation, even if the enemy wears our same uniform. Do you understand?"

"Yes, Generalissimo."

"Make sure they do—and we must move quickly, Captain. Take Major Gillette with you and make the appropriate introductions."

I decided to scout our position. I stepped into our trench line, the road-bordering ditch, and followed it down El Camino Real for a few hundred yards. I reached one of the few bends, and saw movement on the far horizon, a jostling of tiny dots: cantering distant Cavalry, slow-marching ant lines of Infantry, wobbling rectangular carts led by minuscule mule teams. I reckoned they were still an hour away—but we needed to be ready.

I raced down the trench line, dodging soldiers as they filed in, speeding them along with words of encouragement.

To my amazement, the tents I had ordered taken down were still upright. Standing next to them, with a handful of lollygagging men, was Major Gillette, a cup of coffee in one hand and a biscuit in the other. He appeared to be spinning yarns about his service in the great war.

"Major, this is no time to chew the molasses. See to your duty. The enemy is within sight. We must move quickly. These tents must come down."

"Well, beggin' the Yankee General's pardon, but I was wondering, sir, if you'd reconsider. As I was just telling these young soldiers here, there's more than one way to skin a hungry, mangy panther that's coming your way."

"What the devil are you talking about? Take that biscuit out of your mouth. The enemy marches upon us. We have no time to reconsider. We must act now."

"On the contrary, sir, if you'll forgive me, but I reckon you haven't had time to fully appreciate our situation."

"I appreciate, Major, that the enemy is nearly here, and that you are ignoring the legitimate order of a superior officer."

"Not ignoring you, sir, but if you'll hear me out…"

"I appear to have no choice, Major—but make it quick."

"Well, then, sir, bear with me: I reckon you're looking to surprise the enemy."

"Yes, that's the general idea."

"Well, we have two ways of going about that: we could collapse these tents and hide the men in the jungle and the trench here."

"Yes, that's precisely it."

"But think about those men in the advancing column. They've probably been on the road a long spell to arrive here at dawn. They're likely hungry and thirsty and tired. Don't you reckon they might drop their rifles a little lower, that their discipline might be a little slacker, if they see tents ahead? They might expect beans and coffee—maybe a bunk down. Those tents might be an effective decoy, attracting enemy fire."

"A decoy?"

"Yes, Yankee General, sir, drawing fire to where we ain't."

"Did Bedford Forrest say that?"

"Not that I'm aware, sir."

"In any event, Major, I see your point."

"I figured you would, sir."

"I just needed more time to appreciate the situation."

"I figured that's what it was, sir."

"Indeed, Major, there are times when you know my thoughts before I do: tents stay up; men in the trenches."

We made good progress now. I had stakes driven along the road. Each stake marked the target area of a squad on alternating sides of El Camino Real. By this tactic, we increased our effective firepower and minimized the risk of crossfire killing our men.

Gallopers advanced—the enemy's vanguard. Behind them came the creaking wheels of the wagons: the golden bell gleaming in the sunlight; El Cid magnificent, with his lance raised high; the Infantrymen looking a little bedraggled; and then, charging up the line to join the gallopers—Bierce!

The shock of seeing him inspired me to dramatic action. I climbed from the trench, stood athwart the road, and let dawn's shimmering sun reflect my gold braid. Bierce halted the column, rode ahead of his gallopers, and sat his horse about ten yards away. He locked his eyes on mine and stepped down from the saddle. He stood by his mount—a shield against rifles in the trench opposite.

He said: "It's an ambush, isn't it?"

"No worse than anything you've sprung on me."

"Well, brace yourself, Generalissimo: we're allies again."

"You expect me to believe that?"

"I command this column. These men will follow your orders, and mine. I've restored your rank."

"Why?"

"I never intended to keep you in jail. That was temporary. But you escaped before I could spring you. Now the fat's really in the fire. Matteo Rodríguez has made his fatal move—and he put me in charge of it."

"And what's that?"

"In the name of saving the country, he's going to abscond with the state treasury, steal that golden bell, and blow the island to hell by packing that volcano with explosives. You remember that sea captain friend of yours, Wakesmith?"

"I'd forgotten all about him."

"Turns out he's a confederate of Rodríguez—and a fellow Unitarian."

"Another Unitarian assassin?"

"Not an assassin, a thief—and before that a rebel gun-runner. He's bringing his boat to that landing behind Santiago. They'll load the golden bell and make their getaway. Rodríguez is nothing if not greedy—he's also got a wagonload of Treasury gold. Carlos Blandino authorized him to take it as an emergency measure—to keep El Caudillo from spending it unconstitutionally."

"But it's constitutional to steal it?"

"The whole island will soon go to Hades anyway. Lucretia Borreros and the rebels are packing that volcano full of explosives to make sure it does."

"How does that benefit Rodríguez?"

"He expects to live as a millionaire exile—in Albania or someplace."

"You consented to all this?"

"Only in theory—not in fact; for one thing, Rodríguez kidnapped Consuela. I can't consent to that as an officer and a gentleman—in fact, I wish I'd thought of it myself."

"Kidnapped her?"

"Yes, he's also captured your wife. I'm not sure whether Unitarians believe in polygamy, but maybe Albanians do. Anyway, I've been talking with Father Gonçalves."

"About polygamy?"

"About explosives: he says they won't erupt a volcano."

"Well, that's something."

"Not really; he says it's going to explode anyway—and soon, based on the strength and frequency of the tremors. This island is exploding one way or another."

A low rumble of assent came from la Montaña que Eructa.

I said, "We must rescue Victoria and Rachel."

"I thought you'd say that—and in that order too."

Behind me I heard a commotion. An Infantryman—one of our pickets—came running from the direction of Santiago.

"Good Godfrey, man," I said, "did you come from the city?"

"I didn't get that far, sir. We had a skirmish with Indians. They had a rebel officer—and we captured him."

"Yes? And?"

"Generalissimo Armstrong—Santiago, the entire city, it is aflame!"

"What!"

"Administrator Borreros ordered it burned."

"But the people?"

"Many are dead, killed by the rebels; the others she marches to la Montaña que Eructa to be sacrificed as a burnt offering. She hopes to turn away the plague that afflicts the Indians."

"Good gracious, man, are you serious?"

"I was sent to bring the news. The detachment dispersed the Indians and is advancing to the river. Sergeant Esteban awaits your orders."

"You run back and tell Sergeant Esteban that I will be there, in force, with all due speed. If the rebels approach the bridge, harass them. If he must retreat, he should do it stubbornly along El Camino Real."

"Yes, sir!"

Bierce eyed me a warning. "Rodríguez is a day's ride behind me. You've got rebels in one direction and Matteo Rodríguez in another. We either make an alliance right now, Marshal, or I might play my hand with Rodríguez."

"You might do that anyway. What if I don't trust you?"

"Then I'm prepared to shoot you—just like I did that Indian. You're not wearing a gun, Marshal. That's a big oversight."

"You're covered by nearly a hundred rifles."

"Those rifles will soon be mine. When one Generalissimo shoots another, someone's a traitor. I'll tell them it's you. I've got a reputation— General of the King's Armies. You're just an adventurer who went bad. So, what's it going to be? I kept my distance for a reason. I'm a dead shot at ten yards."

"I will not be bullied, Bierce."

"How about bribed? I'm offering you command of an army, Marshal—and a chance to rescue Consuela…and your wife, of course."

"You appeal to my sense of duty?"

"If that's the way you want it."

"Very well, then, Bierce, if I regain my rank as Generalissimo, we can make common purpose."

"Shake on it—in front of your men?"

I nodded, he stepped ahead of his horse, and we shook hands—both still wearing our Cavalry gauntlets. The volcano rumbled: in commendation or in fear I do not know.

I asked Bierce, "Is Bad Boy with you?"

"Bad Boy?"

"My dog."

"Oh, yes, he's back there somewhere; so is Father Gonçalves and your Indian—and I know you're a sentimentalist about horse flesh: I brought your horses."

I nodded my approval and said, "Bring them up—and then we'll make a proclamation to the men."

Bierce spurred away, and I went to brief Major Gillette. "It would appear, Major, that we're adding to our army. Have Captain Obregón bring the men from the trenches."

When Bierce returned, it was with Billy Jack leading my two horses, Bad Boy running after them.

Bierce said, "If you're quite ready, Generalissimo. I believe your stage is set."

I selected my horse Edward for this duty, as he was bigger than Marshal Ney and better suited to make an impression. I stepped into the saddle and rode side by side with Bierce, who waved his column forward until our troops met at midpoint. Bierce sat his horse facing the column. I circled my horse, addressing the men gathered round. "Men of Neustraguano, we have today forged the most consequential accord in Neustraguanian history. Scholars will remember this day as the Alliance of the Two Generalissimos. They will write about this day in books, but you will live it as participants, as witnesses, as actors on the stage, as soldiers on the field of battle.

"Battle is coming. We will be ready. And you can be certain of victory.

"For think upon your leaders: there, gentlemen, sits Generalissimo Ambrose Bierce—as fierce a cutthroat as any can imagine. And he is your commander.

"And here am I: a celebrated veteran of America's greatest war, undaunted in my courage, unwavering in my devotion to duty, undefeated in battle—for the most part—and a man who has pledged himself to your king's cause.

"Could you ask for greater Generalissimos than these?"

The men huzzahed. I nodded my acknowledgement and continued. "And with us are some of the greatest symbols of Neustraguano.

"With us is the statue of El Cid.

"El Cid, the man, never saw Neustraguano. He never had that honor. But El Cid, the statue, was forged several centuries later, on a different continent, indeed on this island—I presume—and who can deny that he has served your country nobly? He will go into battle with us and serve as a rallying point, a standard for our cause.

"And then there is the golden bell of your great cathedral. Ask not for whom that bell tolls, men of Neustraguano; know that it tolls for thee—and thine and thou.

"The enemy lies behind us. They are led by Matteo Rodríguez—a traitor. And any man who serves him is a traitor—no matter the cut, color, and general appearance of his uniform.

"The enemy also lies in front of us. The Indians of that madwoman Lucretia Borreros are on the warpath. They have burned down Santiago. Nothing now lies between the rebels and la Ciudad de Serpientes but a thin picket line—and us.

"Men of Neustraguano, we are the ones who—today, tomorrow, perhaps over the next several days, depending on the behavior of that volcano—will make history.

"Now, let each man do his duty. And let us set our faces to the task by taking this oath:

"*Viva El Claudio!*"

"*Viva! Viva!*"

"*Viva la Churcha Catholica!*"

"*Viva! Viva!*"

"*And Viva El Generalissimos—olé, olé, olé!*"

"*Viva! Viva! Olé! Olé! Olé!*"

And thus was forged the grand alliance. The men cheered wildly, but beneath the cheers came a torrent of Spanish curses from the prison wagons. I had forgotten about them.

I scanned Bierce's column and asked the obvious question: "How many men has Matteo Rodríguez?"

"Don't know. He has no reason to expect trouble, but he likely stripped the capital's garrison—just to leave El Caudillo defenseless."

"If Rodríguez has the garrison, and the rebels cross the river in force…"

"Then we're stuck in the middle, aren't we, Marshal? You should like that. Fighting back to back, I can't betray you."

"Our duty is clear, Bierce: rescue Victoria and Rachel."

"There's that interesting order of affection again."

"Bierce, turn your column and march on Rodríguez. He has no reason to suspect you. Capture him without a fight, if you can; fight him, if you must—but remember, our goal is to free the women. Meanwhile, I'll take my force to the river. If the rebels attack, we'll repel them until you can reinforce us."

"Right; what about the prisoners, the statue, the bell? They'll just slow me down."

"I'll take them: the statue is mine anyway."

"Yes, I seem to recall that. I'll keep Father Gonçalves though."

"You need a chaplain?"

"I told you Wakesmith is waiting with his boat. What if Father Gonçalves sank it? He's been working on a sort of secret weapon. You're familiar with the CSS *Hunley*? The Confederates built it: a ship that can go underwater. He's built one too; it's an ironclad, but also an underwater boat—at least that was the idea: a cross between the *Monitor* and the *Hunley*. He could flank Wakesmith and give him a hell of a surprise."

"Can it transport men?"

"Some—I don't know how many. Not enough to make a landing, if that's what you're thinking. But enough to drill a hole in Wakesmith's hull or maybe bombard him. I don't know—I only know the padre's been testing an underwater warship. And I reckon a navy might come in handy."

"So it might."

"That's settled, then—we'll hit them by land and sea. You trust me?"

"Of course not; but you're an officer, if not a gentleman."

"I think you'll find me both." Bierce saluted, a devilish grin on his face. "Good day, Generalissimo, and good luck to you."

He charged off. I watched him for a moment, wondering what mischief he would get up to next. Then I turned my gaze to El Cid. I had fewer doubts about him. Major Gillette came alongside. The volcano rumbled again.

"Yankee General, sir, that volcano's beginning to worry me."

"Major, never take counsel of your fears."

"Didn't Stonewall Jackson say that, sir—or Old Hickory?"

"Perhaps, Major: great commanders of the past have often copied my thoughts. Tell Captain Obregón that you and I will ride to the picket line immediately. He is to follow as rapidly as possible with the men and Bierce's impedimenta: the golden bell, El Cid, and the prisoners."

"Yes, sir." Major Gillette's place was taken by Billy Jack, who arrived in a cloud of dust, Bad Boy at his horse's heels. I looked down affectionately at my loyal Lieutenant and said, "We're in our element, old friend: a saddle beneath me, the prospect of action, damsels in distress, and you by my side."

The volcano belched and Bad Boy barked in reply.

Billy Jack said, "Volcano sound menacing. I think the enemy stokes its fire."

"That's not far wrong, Sergeant. We have enemies all around us, and a natural enemy to boot. Let's be off—to the picket line!"

The three of us charged up the road—Billy Jack, Bad Boy, and I. I waved my Generalissimo's kepi at the men: "To victory lads—to victory!"

I could see it in their eyes and read their thoughts: "How lucky we are to have such a Generalissimo! With him we will conquer all!"

The volcano sounded again, and the words came unbidden to my mind: "…until that volcano blows us to smithereens."

CHAPTER ELEVEN

In Which Battle Is Joined

Smoke rolled down the hill from the burning city of Santiago and from the billowing volcano. A sooty haze hung over the jungle; snowflakes of ash fell along the road.

Major Gillette said, "Without that moat around the city, we'd be eating fire."

The picket line was barely visible just ahead. The sound of crackling flames in the city was suddenly joined by the smacking of rifle shots. Arrows flew between our horses.

"Enemy on north side of road," said Billy Jack.

We spurred our horses ahead, crouching low in our saddles, hoping to avoid the zing of bullets or whiffling of arrows. At the picket line we jumped off our mounts; troopers took our horses and hurried them into cover. Sergeant Esteban crouched towards us in the roadside trench.

"Apologies, Generalissimo, the Indians watch the road. They saw you before I did—a small war party."

"And in the city?"

"Flames you can see. Gunfire has kept us pinned down."

"Indians or rebels?"

"Rebels, I assume. They sometimes use Indians as scouts."

Billy Jack looked at me. He said nothing, but I knew what he meant.

"I'll go with you," I said.

Major Gillette interrupted: "Now hold on there, Yankee General, sir; you can't flank Indian scouts, even if you knew where they were."

"Don't worry, Major, we'll find them—and there can't be many, or they'd attack this position, not harass it. I need a weapon, though."

Sergeant Esteban held out his rifle, thought better of it, then undid his holstered revolver and ammunition belt and handed it to me: "For fighting at close-quarters."

I cinched it on. Billy Jack slithered away towards the river, and I followed. Bad Boy crept warily after us. The jungle undergrowth was good cover, rolling clouds of smoke provided more, and the rumbling of the volcano and the crackling of fire-eaten timber helped muffle the sound of our movements. We paused at a gnarled knot of tree roots. The river flowed beside us, and across it were snipers. From our position, we needed to slink along a muddy ledge that extended beneath the bridge and slide into the ditch on the opposite side of El Camino Real. The Indians, we assumed, were farther up, watching for the approaching column. But the sharpshooters would be looking to get a bead on any of Esteban's men (or us) poking his head up. Still, we reckoned they'd be watching the road, not under the bridge.

Our best hope, I thought, was to time our movements to coincide with a wave of smoke. Bad Boy was beside me. I patted him on the shoulder and whispered softly in his native German: "*Leutnant Bad Boy, you musten creepinzie acrossen das ledgen und vaiten vor das Generalissimo Armstrong and Feldwebel Wilhelm der Indian, ja? Vaitin vor ein shielden ov smoken—then schnell, schnell.*" He bobbed his head in acknowledgement, pressed himself close to the ground, crawled into the next wave of sooty fog, and began his wary crossing. Like a cat stalking a bird, he moved deliberately, softly, quietly, his body low, his legs coiled springs. Had the Indians seen him, they might have mistaken him for a panther and fled in terror, but between his black coat, the muddy path beneath the bridge, and the tumbling black smoke, he crept into the opposite ditch unpursued by bullet or arrow.

I decided to go next. Immersed in a wave of smoke, I pulled myself across the dirt and mud as slowly as my beating heart would allow. Any hunter knows that it's movement that catches the eye—so I tried to coordinate every extension of an arm or shifting of a leg with a drift of smoke. When I rolled into the opposite ditch, I was breathing as heavy as if I had sprinted a mile.

I wasn't so worried about sharpshooters now as about an Indian ambush, but Bad Boy could take care of that. I pointed my revolver at Santiago's walls, ready to return fire if a sniper did spot Billy Jack. But he was over the muddy ledge faster than a ferret chasing a snake and plopped down beside me. He motioned us into the jungle, and we dragged ourselves through ferns and vines, crawling around trees and bushes, until he raised his hand and halted us. He directed my eyes to a pocket of long grass to our left in which appeared the bare tattooed backs of five Indians who looked sturdier and fiercer than Lucretia Borreros's tribe. They had arrows strung, bows pointed down, and were scanning the road for targets. If they were alone, our surprise would be total.

Billy pointed to his knife and slid a finger across his throat. I shook my head and cocked my revolver. The Indians heard it, turned instantly, and an arrow shot past me; six inches closer, and I'd have lost half my teeth. Billy Jack barrel-rolled behind a log—and I followed his good example. He fired a shot—and when I fired mine, he scrambled away out of sight. I rolled again, this time behind a bush. I popped to my knees and had an Indian directly in my sights. He saw me—but too late. I planted a perfect shot that knocked him on his back. Another Indian gave a war whoop, running at me with his bow raised. We fired almost simultaneously. He flew backwards to the ground in an awkward sprawl, and his arrow, partially deflected by the bush, bounced over my shoulder. More war whoops. Gunshots on my right. I rolled in that direction, hoping to find Billy Jack. I rested my revolver on a downed log and stuck my head up. A wounded Indian was tripping towards me, an arrow strung in his bow. He raised it to let fly; Bad Boy exploded from the bushes; and the arrow thudded into the log in front of me. Bad Boy had the Indian pinned, his teeth anchored in the enemy's throat; he snarled as he ripped him to pieces; he has a taste for enemy blood.

Billy Jack ran up and knelt beside me. "You wounded?"

"No, I'm fine."

"I see no others—but we should not stay. Back to picket."

He whistled Bad Boy to join us. We didn't crawl this time, we ran across the road, and, as we did, I shouted, "Sergeant, we're coming through!" Minié balls from the sharpshooters chased us, we threw ourselves into the trench, and scrambled away from the river toward the picket line. Waiting were Major Gillette and Sergeant Esteban. I returned Sergeant Esteban's gun belt.

Major Gillette said, "You certainly don't rest on your rank, Yankee General, sir."

"A Generalissimo must always lead by example, Major."

I heard a jangling noise from the road—the column!

I ran down the ditch and saw El Cid's wagon in the vanguard, then the golden bell, followed by the Infantry, the two convict wagons at the rear.

The rebels must have heard them too because there was a storm of lead into the jungle near the bridge. I hurried to the sound of the guns and joined Sergeant Esteban at the foremost part of our trench facing the river. We looked up at the flaming city: white peasant smocks fanned out from the city's northern wall. The smocks wore bandanas around their faces; they looked like an army of train robbers. There was a single rifle shot and then a voice shouted: "Caudilloistas! Do you hear me? Caudilloistas! Look at Santiago! Or do you fear what it portends? This is the hell we bring you—fire and death!" Another rifle shot. "You hear me Caudilloistas? Your hours are numbered. We are coming after you— all of us, thousands of us; the people's army is here!"

With the smell of cordite still in my nostrils, I wasn't about to take this blather. I retrieved my horse Edward, stepped into the saddle, and leapt him over the ditch. I trotted him up to the bridge. Another rifle shot—a warning, I reckoned—but I didn't care; I had a message of my own to deliver.

"Greetings, banditos!" I said. "I'm afraid I couldn't hear you before. I was too busy killing your Indians. Are you offering to surrender?"

"Surrender? *You* ask for surrender? *You* will surrender your life. The country is ours."

"Not yet. You need this road—and we're here."

"Your dogs in uniform cannot stop us; the county is in rebellion."

"We stand ready to do our duty."

"Duty to what: to the people—or to that pig on the throne?"

"I am Generalissimo Armstrong Armstrong, servant of El Claudio, defender of the loyalist people, rescuer of the oppressed, guardian of women, master of dogs and horses, and scourge of every rebel who needs scourging."

A clattering of ill-aimed minié balls hit the bridge and scattered round me.

My horse and I stood our ground. "Sergeant Esteban, let 'em have a volley!" Our rifles rattled a response—not the thunder of massed fire one would like, but enough. "All right, you rebels, you've got thirty minutes. Either I see a white flag of surrender, or I'm coming after you."

Another hail of minié balls came at us, but I had already pulled Edward back and was riding down El Camino Real to tell Captain Obregón to halt his column. I had a plan.

Back in our makeshift trench, I called another council of war: Captain Obregón, Major Gillette, Billy Jack, and Bad Boy were in attendance.

"Gentlemen, the enemy is right in front of us; he intends a frontal assault; he thinks that by sheer numbers he can overwhelm us. But I doubt this. His men are a mob, not an army. What disperses a mob? Determined, disciplined action. If we pin their ears back, they'll scatter—at least until they're reinforced. I reckon we're in a good position here."

Captain Obregón said, "But, Generalissimo, I have scarcely a hundred men. They could have thousands."

"They don't have them yet," I said, "or they wouldn't be waiting. And that's our opportunity: if we act swiftly, we can disperse them before they charge. As the Good Book says, 'Saul hath slain his thousands, and David his ten thousands.' First, we act as Saul; then, if necessary, as David."

Captain Obregón appeared dismayed. Major Gillette reassured him: "Ours is not to reason why, Captain."

"Precisely. Now then, Major and Billy Jack, you are going to perform a reconnaissance in force. Major, you will be the force; Billy Jack, you will be the reconnaissance."

Major Gillette said, "Just the two of us, sir?"

"Of course not, Bad Boy will go with you, as will the convicts. You are going to impersonate a detachment of Cavalry. The men's chains will be the jingle of spurs and sabres. In all this smoke, I reckon you can fool them."

"That would seem a certainty, sir."

"Billy Jack will show you where to cross the river. Horses can manage it. You'll leave the wagons behind. String a rope so the convicts can make it."

"Sounds easy."

"You're a gambler, Major; I need you to bluff them. You are to convince them that you are Colonel Monteverde Cristóbal's Cavalry returning from the north, hell-bent for leather."

"I see."

"With you distracting them, Billy Jack will reconnoiter behind the enemy. He'll tell me if we're facing a company, a regiment, a brigade, a division, or a corps."

"I must say, sir, that's a mighty big bluff—and a mighty big risk for your scout."

"Don't worry about him—and I'll support you, Major. When you're in position, send Bad Boy back to me—that'll be your signal. Captain Obregón, you will have Sergeant Esteban's detachment ready to pin down the rebels with covering fire. Then we'll charge the bridge."

"Charge?" said Captain Obregón. "But I heard how you defended Santiago. That bridge is narrow, you killed many men upon it. And now *they* have your position."

"But they do not have me—or El Cid. We'll roll him up behind us. In the smoke and confusion, they might mistake him for reinforcements. And I want those muleskinners with the golden bell ready to ring it." A black cloud rolled down from the flames of Santiago. "Let's get moving."

The drivers of the convict wagons acted as guards and unloaded the prisoners whose chains—leg irons and wrist irons—clanked reassuringly. Between that and their Spanish grumbling, I thought they'd do a splendid job of sounding like Cavalry on the march. El Cid—loaded on his wagon, a veritable chariot for horse and rider—rolled to the fore.

Major Gillette took a loan of my horse Edward, and he and Billy Jack began their dangerous mission. I do not need to tell you, my dear, that I waited impatiently for Bad Boy's return. The time passed so slowly that I had Sergeant Esteban send two men to retrieve the dead Indians' bows and arrows while I got a fire going. When they returned, I wrapped the arrows with strips torn from the men's bandanas, set the arrows alight, and lobbed a few balls of fire across the river—more smoke to cover us.

Bad Boy finally came hurtling back. The enemy had withheld their fire, which convinced me they were uncertain of our deployments; they awaited our next move. I decided to make it. I had a trooper bring me Marshal Ney. I patted the horse's neck. "Once more into the breach, old friend."

He leapt the trench, and I took him high-stepping to the edge of the bridge. I shouted out to the city walls. "I return to ask for your surrender."

The rebel leader yelled, "You want we should kill that beautiful horse."

"Both he and I approach you unarmed—except with news that spells your imminent defeat. Marching up this road, not more than ten minutes behind me, is the largest army you ever saw, with batteries of artillery to smash your bones to pieces, Cavalry to scatter the remnants, and Infantry to hunt down any survivors. I told you, I am Generalissimo Armstrong Armstrong. I have given the king a new strategy—one we used with tremendous success in the great war in America. We will take the war into your sanctuaries. We will give you no rest. We will leave you no sustenance. We will crush all resistance."

"You have not crushed us."

"Not yet—but Matteo Rodríguez, your traitorous ally, is in irons by now, or soon will be, and the full force of the Neustraguano army is directed right at this point. Now, I can ride across this bridge and you can surrender to me, or you can wait and join your rebel dead in hell. Look around you—you're halfway there already."

"You bluff."

"The remainder of my force is coming up with Generalissimo Bierce. He is not as merciful as I am. I think you know that. Still, he'd rather use his artillery on Lucretia Borreros than on you—he bears her a bigger grudge. Now, I'm coming across that bridge. If you open fire, Bierce's army will be upon you faster than a tornado."

"And you will be dead."

"I doubt it. I'll just duck under this smoke; the earth will shake with the pounding of hooves; our Cavalrymen's sabres will glisten with your blood. Colonel Monteverde Cristóbal's Cavalry is about to ride down upon you."

I heard, in the distance, Major Gillette shout the inspiring order: "Cavalry, prepare to charge!"

A handful of rebels nervously discharged their muskets, and Sergeant Esteban shouted: "Fire!" Our rifles fired one volley, then another, and another, and another.

I turned and shouted, "Get ready boys! Bring 'em on up," and Captain Obregón's Infantry fell in behind me. Just behind them the creaking wheels of El Cid's wagon announced his approach; his pennoned lance pieced through the smoke.

I gazed at the city. The white line of peasant smocks looked like a wheel block of Swiss cheese infested by rodents—it was suddenly full of holes. The rebels were in flight.

"After them, men!"

Captain Obregón's men charged across the bridge and up the hill, and Marshal Ney and I were soon at their head. A desultory discharge of opposing muskets sent a harmless, unaimed sprinkling of minié balls down the slope.

"Come on men! Bring up those cannons!" We had none, of course, but the threat accelerated the white smocks' departure. The golden bell sounded, and I hoped in their confusion they might mistake it for the sound of cannon: a Quaker gun, to be sure, but one with a big boom.

The rebels were now in full flight—few daring to look back—and then there was an enormous explosion behind the city walls, a refueling of the flames, and a towering new cloud of black smoke. They had fired the powder stores and armory; la Montaña que Eructa grunted its own knell of doom; and it seemed as though the ground shook.

I sat Marshal Ney at the northern crest of the hill. Billy Jack rode fast towards me from the western horizon.

He pulled up, saluted, and said, "Cavalry of one."

"Good enough for now, Sergeant."

"These men were only skirmish line. Main force still other side of the river."

"I think they're on the defensive now—they'll want to hold that dock until Wakesmith arrives with his boat."

"He is there now. I saw it. I had perfect view. In French *vue parfaite*. In Italian *vista perfetta*. In Latin *visum perfectum*."

"No need to go through all that. Let's find Captain Obregón."

That wasn't hard. He and his men came running towards us. "Generalissimo, do we take the city?"

"There's nothing to take," I said. "No need to pursue the enemy either. We know where they're going—across the river. Captain, your job is to keep them there. Deploy your men behind the city. There's a rocky ledge overlooking the river. Billy Jack will show you. Hold that position at all costs."

"Yes, sir."

"I'm detaching Sergeant Esteban's platoon and the muleskinners. They'll watch over El Cid and the Golden Bell—just in case."

"Yes, Generalissimo. And the prisoners?"

"They can fend for themselves. They won't get far in those chains—and the enemy is welcome to them."

"And you, Generalissimo, where will I find you? With the detachment guarding El Cid?"

"No, Captain, I have an appointment with Generalissimo Bierce."

Billy Jack led Captain Obregón and the Infantry away, and Major Gillette appeared, trotting Edward to my side. "Well, Yankee General, sir—you sure smoked 'em. Last time I saw troops run that fast was at First Manassas."

"Major, you'll kindly keep your Confederate comments to yourself. Let's ride down to El Cid."

We ambled our horses down the slope. Sergeant Esteban and his men were cheering, hoping to join their comrades on the chase.

"No Sergeant, I need you here—guarding El Cid."

"A statue, sir? But the enemy—he runs."

"And why do they run, Sergeant? Because they fear El Cid and what he represents."

"But, sir, my men want to be in on the kill."

The men were all eager smiles, shaking their rifles. I raised my hand in acknowledgement of the cheers and rode my horse among them. "Troopers of Neustraguano, today we had a great victory—but it is only the first of our many victories. Let us remember, though, that our victories will be as nothing unless we remember what we are fighting for. Why do you fight, men of Neustraguano? I will tell you why. You fight in defense of your family. You fight in defense of your Church—or you should if you are church-going men. You fight for your land, especially if you are small farmers. You fight for your history—for all those heroes of your past, the men who live in your collective memory, who tell you what it means to be a brave Neustraguanian. And who better to represent that than a medieval Spanish knight who fought against the Moors, and then fought for them, and then fought against them again. That, my lads, is the essence of Neustraguano, a kaleidoscope of loyalties that always comes back to victory. Preserve that knight, preserve that statue, and our

Reconquista of Neustraguano, our recovery of your undivided home-land, is certain. But should the enemy steal a step on you; should the enemy raid your position and abscond with El Cid and the golden bell; then, my lads, all will be at hazard. The rebels hate El Cid because he is bronze, and they are not; because he has strength and nobility and a wonderfully large horse, and they do not. The rebels know that a people without pride in their nation's past, without a reverence for their nation's heroes, without a passion for their nation's Church, will be a people deprived of any spirit of resistance to the tyranny that the rebels hope to impose upon you. For into that void of pride in your past, for into that void of loyalty, they will come, like the thieves they are, who have robbed you of these things, and they will fill that void with the belief that you should be slaves—slaves to that crazy woman Lucretia Borreros, slaves to her perverted version of science, slaves to the opium that she stuffs into the Indians, slaves to her hatred of religion. That is why we fight; that is why we support El Claudio—so that the people may have their king and so that the barbarism of Lucretia Borreros might meet its doom. Cry God for El Claudio, Neustraguano, and El Cid!"

If I say so myself, even John Wilkes Booth—in his acting days—never delivered a better soliloquy. The men let up a succession of huzzahs. Sergeant Esteban stood at rigid attention and saluted so hard that it would have bifurcated any passing butterfly. If you had been there, Libbie, I'm sure you would have thrown an enthusiastic garter onto El Cid's lance as a symbol of the great Spaniard's chivalry.

Major Gillette paid me a compliment: "Well, Yankee General, sir, that was a humdinger. Never heard a speech like that from ole Jeff Davis."

"No, I expect you didn't. But in this case, the man and hour are met."

Major Gillette, Bad Boy, and I made our way down to the noble knight and lowered our heads in prayerful respect.

Bad Boy ended our prayer with a bark. A Cavalryman raced up El Camino Real. His horse was flecked with sweat, and I recognized him instantly—the officer, that is, not the horse.

I raised an eyebrow and said, "Captain Royce, isn't it?"

"Yes, sir; apologies, sir."

"Apologies, Captain?"

"Yes, sir, for placing you under arrest—I had orders."

"And what orders bring you back?"

"From Generalissimo Bierce—he wants a report on events at Santiago."

"I will make that report to Generalissimo Bierce myself, Captain. But for your benefit: 'I came, I saw, I conquered.' Do you know who said that?"

"You did, sir."

"Quite right. I await the return of my scout, Sergeant William Jack Crow—also arrested by you, I believe. We will ride together and join Generalissimo Bierce. I intend to keep his guns pointed in the right direction."

In due course, Billy Jack arrived, and it will not surprise you, dearest one, that such fine horsemen as my scout, Major Gillette, and I sped down El Camino Real like a train on a railroad. Bad Boy's perdurable stamina was much in evidence, and Captain Royce did his best to keep up. Still, it was dusk by the time we found Bierce's column. They were digging entrenchments perpendicular to the bordering ditches of El Camino Real. Bierce sat outside the flaps of his command tent, a tin cup of coffee in one hand and a flask in the other. He said, "Care for a nip, Generalissimo?"

"Bierce, there's work to be done."

"It's being done, Marshal—and what about you? Back so soon: Have you already won the Battle of Second Santiago?"

"As a matter of fact, I have. Captain Royce can confirm that."

Bierce chuckled. "I thought you'd be eager to see him again."

"I'm astonished, Bierce, that you're not advancing on the enemy."

"The enemy, Marshal, is advancing here. We'll be ready for him. He should arrive around dawn, if not sooner. Scouts are keeping watch. I'll ambush him as you intended to ambush me."

"What about the women?"

"What about them? He'll keep them as safe as the treasury money—it's all booty to him."

"Where's Father Gonçalves?"

"Full of questions, aren't we, Marshal? I sent him on the northern road. No need to risk him—or delay him—in combat. He'll bring the Navy on our side, launch his underwater ship—and who knows, maybe even bring us some Marines."

"Well, then," said Major Gillette, "with that all taken care of, I reckon we can bed down for a spell, have a bite to eat…"

I interrupted, "Did your scouts tell you whether Rodríguez comes in force?"

"Yes—he's got the entire garrison of la Ciudad de Serpientes, save for the palace guards. He's leaving the dirty work of regicide to the rebels—though, of course, he's helping as much as he can."

"Bierce, I hate waiting."

"We've got scouts."

"The only scouts I trust are Indians."

"And during the war?"

"I was a scout myself—even as a General. I trust no one's eyes fully but my own—or Billy Jack's. We'll join your scouts."

"Very well, Marshal. But you'd better take Captain Royce. He'll keep you from getting lost—or mistaken for the enemy."

And so, we were off again. We cut a meandering trail through the jungle. We had a path just wide enough for horses, but too narrow and tangled for swift progress. They had to step carefully, and I wondered if my thirst for action had got the worst of me, because here I was in the midst of a forbidding jungle—who knew how far from the enemy—when I could have developed a plan with Bierce in a council of war.

But we rode on, my eyes sharpened, my ears whetted for sound. The eerie jungle canopy added its own dark shadows to the dusk, and our horses followed each other, nose to tail, Captain Royce to the front, I next, with Major Gillette behind me, and Billy Jack covering our rear.

The clicking, croaking, and squawking of jungle insects, frogs, and birds was a mere murmur compared to the incessant rumbling of the volcano, throwing up spews of fire that even at our far remove, and beneath the bower of trees, periodically lit the sky like red lightning.

The path took a turning north and ascended—so steeply that I found myself leaning forward in the saddle about forty-five degrees. I wondered where the devil we were, but voices carry in the dark, and my trail discipline, on a scouting mission like this, was too strong to let me speak. Suddenly there was a hiss from above: "*Quién es?*"

Our horses stopped. "It is Captain Royce. I come from the column with Generalissimo Armstrong and his aides."

There was a quick intake of breath, and a hurried thumping of boots coming to attention, rifles snapped into place.

We nudged our horses forward and emerged onto a small tree-fringed plateau. There were three soldiers before us: a Lieutenant, a Sergeant, and a Private. The Sergeant and Private took our horses to the rear, while the Lieutenant led us to a bluff overlooking the road. In the distance to the east, we saw a glimmer of campfires. Rodríguez's men were halted.

The Lieutenant said, "It is a formidable force. I have never seen so many men on the march."

"Lieutenant," I said, "it's because they're coming for me. They can't afford risks. But we can."

"Yankee, General, sir," said Major Gillette, "I get a mite anxious when you talk like that."

"Major, I see the enemy's vulnerability."

"And that vulnerability, sir—would it be the massive size of his army?"

"Precisely."

"I was afraid of that."

"Have no fear, Major."

"Of course not, sir. By my count, we have seven men—not counting your dog."

"Bad Boy will stay behind; he'll guard my clothes."

"Your clothes, sir?"

"Yes—and these scouts, they'll stay behind too."

"I see. Well then, we have four men—if we keep Captain Royce."

"Yes, I think that is advisable. Four men is exactly the right number."

"I don't mean to be obtuse, sir, but to do what?"

"To rescue Rachel and Victoria. It is a mere matter of maneuver, after that."

"Yes, of course."

"We will go in disguise, Major—as Indians."

"Not again, sir. Your last Indian adventure still haunts me."

"Nonsense. Granted, we had costume-makers last time, but that is a mere bagatelle. You're wearing long underwear?"

"Well, yes, Yankee General, sir, but…"

"Snip off the legs with a bayonet and you have a loin cloth."

"That's our disguise?"

"Only part of it, Major. The Indians often wear bags over their heads."

"Ugly, are they—or is there another reason?"

"You'd have to ask Lucretia Borreros about that—it has something to do with science. We'll just cut eye-slits in our undershirts and wear them over our heads. That'll get us into the camp."

"Very clever, sir."

"Captain Royce will impersonate a Captain because he is one. We will be his Indian scouts—you, me, and Billy Jack; and Billy Jack won't need a disguise because, you know, he's an Indian."

"And you think we'll fool them with undershirts over our heads and underdrawers with the legs cut off."

"I am certain of it, Major. Just leave it to me. Or did you forget that I am a blood-brother of the Boyanama Sioux?"

"Nothing would surprise me, sir."

"Then let's get to work."

Our disguises were quickly fabricated, and Captain Royce led us trudging through the jungle. Our plan was to move diagonally, cutting a path to El Camino Real and into Matteo Rodríguez's camp. But between the pitch dark, the entangling vines, and having undershirts over our faces, Major Gillette and I struggled to keep pace with young Captain Royce and the intrepid Billy Jack. Where they were sure-footed, we slipped; while they trotted around boulders, we felt our way like blind men. When we finally fell into El Camino Real's roadside ditch, the Major and I were dripping sweat, slimed with mud, and breathing hard. But none of that worried me; it added to our disguise.

There were pickets on the road. Infantrymen stepped forward to block us, but when they saw Captain Royce, they stood down. He said we were Indian scouts under his command; they did not challenge him.

We walked amongst the enemy, but with little trepidation. Just days before, these troops had been ours; and I still had my command presence, even as a pretend Indian scout with an undershirt over my head. Yes, we could have been unmasked. Yes, we could have been executed as spies. But what mattered those odds, Libbie, when I had a señorita and a wife to save? Granted, that wife was not you, but just imagine my ardor if it had been!

With the shirt over my head, my vision was narrowed, but I caught no hint of suspicion among the soldiers who surrounded us. It was night, they had duties to perform, and they took no interest in Indian scouts.

I nudged Captain Royce. "Rodríguez will be in that big tent—the hostages must be nearby."

As sure as whiskey is stronger than water, they were. Adjacent to the large, well-guarded tent of Matteo Rodríguez was a smaller tent. It too was posted with guards, but standing at its flap, gazing wistfully in my direction, was my impostor wife Rachel. I saw her put her hand to her mouth. Even with a shirt over my head, she recognized me—and then I realized why: not only did she know your tattoo on my arm; she had seen me as an Indian before. She knew salvation must be at hand. I took the foldable toothbrush and a pinch of salt from my Indian medicine pouch and cleaned my teeth.

"What about the guards?" said Captain Royce.

I lifted my undershirt slightly so I could spit. "Tell them Generalissimo Bierce sent you to interrogate the two women—to confirm frontline intelligence."

The guards saluted and raised no alarm. Rachel stood away from the tent flap and affixed it behind us. Victoria sat at on a cot and looked at me wide-eyed. I pulled the undershirt from my head; Major Gillette pulled his off as well.

"Oh, Armstrong," said Rachel, "I knew you'd come back."

Major Gillette said, "Yes, ma'am we're back—but, begging your pardon, the hard part will be sneaking out."

"We shall not sneak," I said. "We shall have a military escort." I turned to Billy Jack. "Return to the plateau, get my clothes, and hightail it to Bierce with this message. Tell him we're in the camp, have the women, and he needs to get here *muy pronto*, on his own—except for you, Sergeant—to meet with Matteo Rodríguez. Once he's here, we can spring our trap."

Billy Jack leapt from the tent faster than a jack rabbit chased by a coyote; he told the gaping guards as he sprinted past, "Must return to Generalissimo Bierce."

Captain Royce kept watch from the tent flap.

Major Gillette uttered a thought that had not occurred to me. "Begging your ladies' pardon, but might you lend us blankets? I reckon the Yankee General and I should cover ourselves a bit."

"Oh, I suppose we should," I said, and accepted a blanket from Victoria.

Captain Royce whispered: "The Minister of State is talking to the guards—now he's coming this way!"

I tightened the blanket around me. "Are the guards with him?"

"One is."

"Then our trap is already sprung. Quick, Major," I said, "under the cots!" I dove beneath Victoria's cot—and collided with a bag of luggage. She pushed the bag aside with her foot, sat down on the cot, and I was pinned. She draped a sheet, blocking my view.

The guard announced, "The Minister of State." I heard Captain Royce fumble with the tent flaps. I heard only one pair of boots enter.

Matteo Rodríguez said, "What are you doing here, Captain?"

"Generalissimo Bierce sent me, your excellency. He wanted me to confirm intelligence we received on the road to Santiago."

"What intelligence would that be—and why was I not informed?"

My impostor wife, Rachel, bless her heart, was ready with an answer: "Senator, I believe the Captain is trying to be discreet; it involves my husband."

"That traitor Armstrong?"

"You call him a traitor, Senator. I call him, Autie."

"Autie?"

"He oughta do this for me; he oughta do that for me."

"Come now, woman, what is the meaning of this?"

"Well," she said stifling a sob, "it's like this, Senator: they found a man—or I should say a body, a corpse—by the road. It was horribly mangled, half eaten, even. Do you have mountain lions here?"

"Mountain lions—do you mean big cats, like panthers? Yes, we have them."

"Well, it appears...one of their victims—oh, it is too horrible to contemplate—but I must face facts: it might be my husband."

"Eaten by a panther?"

"They were attempting to identify the corpse. Generalissimo Bierce suspected it was my husband but was looking for some proof—a locket or a distinguishing scar."

"And, well, was there?"

"We were still discussing it. I confess, Senator, it is hard for me to talk about; it is, as you can imagine, a very private matter, and I am so upset."

Rodríguez addressed Captain Royce: "They told me you had Indians with you—three of them."

"I sent them away," said Rachel. "I didn't want to discuss my husband in front of anyone but the Captain. He has been so very understanding."

"Very well, then. Captain, you will report to me immediately after you have confirmation from Mrs. Armstrong."

"That," I said pushing aside Victoria's legs, "will not be necessary: for I am here." And I squeezed out from under the cot and rolled out of my blanket as surely as Cleopatra did before Julius Caesar.

"What the devil?"

"No, Bierce is still with the column. It is I, Generalissimo Armstrong Armstrong." To Captain Royce, I said, "Keep your gun on that man."

"Yes, I know who you are, but what is the meaning of this?" Rodríguez's head twisted indignantly, looking one moment at Captain Royce's revolver; the other at the half-naked muscular blond Indian rising before him; and then at Major Gillette clambering from beneath Rachel's cot.

"The meaning," I said, "is that the true traitor has now been revealed—and it is you, Matteo Rodríguez." In the distance, la Montaña que Eructa belched its affirmation.

"How dare you!"

"It is daring, isn't it—to have penetrated your camp, right beneath your nose."

"The effrontery, the audacity!"

"Go ahead—say it: the impetuousness."

"All I need to do is cry out and those guards will be here—and you will be dead."

"*You* will be," I said. "All we need to do is show them the Treasury money you're stealing."

"That is a matter of state."

"It won't be too hard, I reckon, to convince your men it's a matter of larceny—especially once Bierce arrives. You've lost your man, you know."

"Bierce would not betray me. I don't believe that—you're a liar, a proven liar."

"We'll see soon enough. He's on his way."

"You do realize that while you sit here, spinning your fantasies, that volcano is endangering us all. Let me make this clear: I will not submit to blackmail, but I am a businessman, and I am willing to cut you a businesslike deal. Join my men on our march, and I will see you safely off this island."

"You will see us safely nowhere. Our safety, Senator, lies in our undershirts! Major Gillette, undershirt on your head!"

"Yankee General, sir, that is an order I never expected to hear."

"Nor I to give," I said, adjusting my own, "but we live in strange times. Now, Captain, you keep that gun on Señor Rodríguez and shout to the guards: 'We're coming through; we've been exposed to the plague.'"

Well, I must say, that announcement set the proverbial cat among the chickens. The Captain opened the tent flap to see the guards backing away to the sides.

"Tell them," I said, "to clear a way for us to avoid infecting the army; tell them that Senator Rodríguez spat blood and has a burning fever; he is delirious; we need to evacuate him to Santiago; he doesn't want to leave his men, but there is no alternative, so you are obliged to take him by force—hence, your gun, if we're challenged."

It was a tall tale but, given our bizarre circumstances, not entirely incredible. In any event, no one in the camp seemed to want to challenge us, and even Matteo Rodríguez kept silent—perhaps hoping that Bierce was in fact still on his side. We were lucky in that it was still night and most of the army slept; we had to bamboozle relatively few. Still, I give full marks to Captain Royce for seeing the captured Minister of State, two fake Indians with undershirts over their heads, the noble daughter of a Cavalry officer, and my impostor wife safely through the camp of a potentially hostile army.

With my vision partially obscured, I stumbled out of the camp and down El Camino Real.

"Captain, don't look back, but can the pickets still see us?"

"I doubt it, Generalissimo; it is dark, and we gave them no reason for suspicion."

"Excellent—then let's move into the ditch. We'll still make good time—but I'd rather be somewhat hidden if they come looking for us."

He directed us down. I confess I slipped and slid—it was a messy passage—and Rachel did not appreciate my tactics for evading the enemy. "Really, Armstrong, why must we trudge through all this ridiculous dirt and mud when there's a perfectly good road?"

I tore the undershirt from my head and hissed: "Keep quiet and keep moving."

"Such subterfuge will not save you," said Matteo Rodríguez. "You are but a handful of Americans. I have the people of this island behind me. Your sole ally is that idiotic, bullying court jester on the throne—and soon you won't have him. Captain," he said to Royce, "treason remains a capital offense. You are endangering your career—and your life—by serving these foreigners. They don't care about you or about Neustraguano. They don't care about healing our island's divisions. They are mercenaries; they are guns for hire; they work for the United States and Mexico, not for us; they seek to divide us for their own profit."

"We're not the ones robbing the treasury," I said.

"Think about it, Captain," Rodríguez continued. "Why would any foreigner serve that clown El Caudillo—unless it was for personal profit?"

"Who speaks treason now?" said Victoria, and even in the dark I sensed her eyes spitting peppered flame into Rodríguez. "*You* call the king—our nation's protector—a clown!"

"Consuela you do not understand how he abuses your loyalty and patriotism."

"He did not kidnap me. He did not betray my father—and all that he fights for. El Caudillo defends our traditions and our Church—that is his right and his duty. But you—you are practically a rebel; all of you in government, aren't you? You're all on the side of the rebels!"

"We are on the side of peace and progress."

"You are a revolutionary, just like the rest of them!"

The volcano fired an enormous cannonball of smoke into the sky.

"It may be too late anyway," said Matteo Rodríguez. "For all of us—too late."

I said, "We won't be late if we keep moving."

I set us a sprightly pace—so sprightly that it left Rodríguez and the women too winded to talk, and that meant I heard, just at the first glimmerings of dawn, the crunch of boots, lots of boots, marching up and down again. They were ahead of us—two horsemen at the forefront: Bierce and Billy Jack, Bad Boy trotting behind them.

We clambered up from the ditch, and I went forward.

I said to Bierce: "I thought I told you to come alone."

He looked me over, smiled, and said, "Trifle chilly this morning, isn't it, Marshal, to be dressed like that?"

Billy Jack tossed me my uniform. He held Major Gillette's clothes as well.

"That, Bierce, will soon be remedied," I said. "On the other hand, your direct disobedience to my order..."

"Oh, we're back to that are we? Who has seniority? I reckon I do Marshal. And I have an army. I hate to travel without one. I see you have our friend Matteo Rodríguez. What do you intend to do with him?"

"I expect he'll come in useful some way or another—but the chief challenge before us, Bierce, is getting off this island, isn't it?"

"There is only one way to do that," said Matteo Rodríguez, stepping forward. "Before I left la Ciudad de Serpientes I ordered the Navy to port; every sailor, every Marine is in barracks. There is only one boat that can carry us away—the one commanded by Captain Wakesmith—and it awaits behind Santiago."

"It awaits to be sunk," said Bierce.

"You can't do that; it's our only hope."

"Well then, Senator, there is no hope—as I always suspected—and all *your* hopes are going to a muddy and watery grave."

I pulled on my Generalissimo pants, and with them my martial ardor soared. "All right, Bierce, we march back to Santiago. Do you want the garrison column? It'll slow us up a mite."

"You get dressed, Marshal, and you can take my column. I'll ride ahead and take command of the garrison troops. We'll attack the enemy with our full force." The volcano rumbled. "And we better be damn quick about it."

CHAPTER TWELVE

In Which All Hell
Busts Loose

Rarely in military history, I would wager, has a military column been led by a Generalissimo walking in full regalia, along with a Major in civilian dress, a Captain holding a Minister of State at gunpoint, two highly attractive women, a large black dog, and a mounted Indian. Andrew Jackson at New Orleans may have done something similar, but I doubt it.

Sergeant Esteban's platoon cheered at our approach. I shouted, "Eyes front!" But, of course, Rachel and Victoria had no idea what that meant, so they waved at the cheering soldiers. Nevertheless, I kept our column in good form, saluted El Cid as we marched past, and led our force over the bridge, around the stone wall, and to a meadow outside the smoldering embers of Santiago. Here I halted the men. Lest they be discouraged by the sight of Santiago's ruins, I turned to them and declared, "It is from here, men, that we have driven the enemy. He now hides over that summit, lurking behind the river, with a volcano to his rear. He thinks that volcano is an ally—that it will scare us away—but it is really *his* enemy. He has no place to run. We will engage the enemy and destroy him."

The men huzzahed, and I raised my kepi in acknowledgment, then stepped aside to confer with my officers on our plan of action. Rachel and Victoria joined our councils, because—well, where else were they to go? I treated as them as honorary *"filles du régiment."* (Do you remember that delightful operetta, dearest one?)

More important, I spotted Marshal Ney and Edward grazing contentedly in a picket line of horses. I sent Billy Jack to fetch them. I also saw a clump of disgruntled men in arm and leg irons wielding shovels. Apparently, Obregón had found a use for the prisoners: as a burial detail.

When Billy Jack returned with the horses, I outlined my plan.

"Gentlemen, Captain Obregón is on the reverse slope of that summit, keeping an eye on the enemy. The rebels have the river to their front, the volcano to their back, and I presume armies coming from the west. I reckon our foe outnumbers us greatly, but he's also penned in. We need to disrupt him before he strikes."

"Begging your pardon, Yankee General, sir, but I seem to recollect that you had some trouble with Indians in a similar situation."

"Major, we will discuss that later—except to state that you have been misinformed and that I have better commanders this time; you among them." I handed him Edward's reins and said, "I'm giving you temporary command of the column. Take it over the summit, reinforce Captain Obregón, assess the enemy's position and strength, and get back here as fast as you can. You are my eyes and ears. Your report will determine our next move."

"Yes, sir!" Gillette saluted and I heard him give the order: "Come on boys, follow me up the hill, quick step!" I could trust that man.

To Billy Jack, I said, "Sergeant, I want you to find the jungle trail that leads from the summit to the enemy. There must be a land bridge. Is it guarded? Can we take it? Can we attack from it?"

He gave his horse a moccasin kick and shot past Major Gillette.

To Royce I said, "Captain, I'll retain you as an aide. Your first task: find the former Minister of State a shovel. He can join those gravediggers."

"This is an outrage," said Matteo Rodríguez.

"Consider it an opportunity," I said. "You might find your buried integrity and conscience."

Rachel took my arm. "That's telling him, Armstrong!"

Matteo Rodríguez shook his grey-templed head. "You are a meddling fool. You have no idea of the character of the man you serve. He is a nasty, blustering, belligerent idiot. His ignorance and arrogance have torn this country apart. Don't you see that?"

Emboldened by Rachel's grasp, I said, "What I see, Señor Rodríguez, is a man who has betrayed his king; who conspires with the enemy; and who is a pharisee rather than a patriot. You, Señor Rodríguez, are so consumed by your own conceit, your own precious false virtue, that you would sell your country to those who would destroy it."

Victoria grabbed my other arm and snarled at Rodríguez like an impassioned chihuahua, *"Eres un cerdo y un cobarde!"*

"Whatever she said, I second that! My duty is to El Claudio. He hired me to smite his foes, to punish traitors, and to defend this country—and that's just what I'll do. Captain Royce, take this traitor away and get him a shovel. If the graves are already dug, have him shovel horse dung. He's a politician, after all."

Royce jabbed his revolver into Rodríguez's back. "Move on, traitor."

Victoria squeezed my arm and said, "El Caudillo was wise to choose you. You have vindicated his trust. You are a true hero of Neustraguano. You are as brave as you are strong; as wise as you are daring; a patriot for our country."

"Yes, Victoria, that is undoubtedly true—and I am nothing if not loyal."

"I'd like you to remember that," said Rachel tugging on my other arm.

I found a shady tree for us to sit beneath: Rachel, Victoria, and I. Bad Boy stood guard and I draped Marshal Ney's reins over a branch.

"Well," said Rachel, "this really is the most perfect place for a picnic—a wonderful view of a burnt-out city, gravediggers, oh, and of course, a volcano providing lovely ashy skies. What could be more delightful?"

"We are here for a council of war, Rachel."

"Oh—every girl's dream, to attend a council of war."

"When Bierce gets here, I'll have a plan."

"I'll bet he has one already—and if I were you, Armstrong, I wouldn't trust him."

There was a rattle of musketry in the distance. Bad Boy howled.

Victoria said, "It is a battle—behind us."

I stood and looked at the ridge. The firing was sporadic, probably inconsequential, but I had to see for myself. I couldn't sit beneath a bower when there was fighting to be done. I looked at Bad Boy. His barking showed that he too yearned for the fray—but duty demanded something else.

I spoke to him in his native German: "*Leutnant Bad Boy, I musten goenzie to investigaten. You musten stayenzie und guarden die fraulein. Savvy?*"

He barked a canine equivalent of "Yes, sir!" and sat his haunches.

I took Marshal Ney's reins and stepped into the saddle.

Rachel said, "Armstrong, surely you're not leaving us here?"

"Bad Boy will protect you. I'm riding to the guns."

"But Armstrong…"

I sent Marshal Ney bounding up the slope. Destiny awaited: battle, and perhaps the outcome of this war. Major Gillette raced to me aboard Edward.

"Those guns…" I said.

"Skirmish fire. Obregón's men trading pepper with the enemy— they're massed across the river, stirring like angry ants. You can figure it: they expected to waltz down El Camino Real and guillotine the king. Now they're facing an army, a reinforced army. It's got them all a-twitter. They counted their headless chickens before they hatched."

"Headless chickens, Major?"

"Well, sir, you get my drift. They expected the king's head on a pike. Now they're in a battle. They're millin' around; not organized into platoons or companies; no effective leadership." La Montaña que

Eructa burped smoke. "And with *that* behind them, they've got to be a little unnerved."

Billy Jack galloped towards us. "Found jungle path—the land bridge. Not suitable for Cavalry—but Infantry can make it, double-file. No enemy guards, but massed enemy at the base. There is a small clearing on the trail; juts out over the river; looks down on the enemy; could be used by two ranks of riflemen."

"Sergeant, are you thinking what I'm thinking?"

"That depends on what you think."

I paused to consider that, and then said, "Well, gentlemen, what I'm thinking is that we either wait for Bierce or strike now."

Major Gillette said, "Yankee, General, sir, when you talk like that, I know what it means: unsheathe your sabre and get ready to ride."

"Well, Major, since you agree, let's go into action."

We rode to a hilltop arbor, tied our horses there, and hiked past straggly trees and bushes down a rock-strewn path to the stone outcropping overlooking the river and facing la Montaña que Eructa. We joined Captain Obregón.

"Generalissimo, thank you for your reinforcements, but as you can see, the enemy host is mighty—at least in numbers, if not in valor. And look at my men, scattered dots behind these boulders. We can fire potshots. But at this range, most often we miss. And the enemy ignores us for now. He cannot cross the river and attack this slope. The angle is too steep. But if he flanks us, I am in no position to stop him."

From our perch we saw long trails of white peasant smocks emerging from the western jungle; from the side of the volcano came a flight of running Indians. La Montaña que Eructa spewed fire and smoke. Already lava tipped over its brim and descended like a demonic red-black caterpillar inching its way down to consume everything in its path; it would soon prod the rebels into action.

But something else did first: a giant explosion ripped a gash into the near slope of la Montaña que Eructa, sending down an avalanche of rock, dirt, and blown-apart Indians and scattering the rebels at the volcano's base; then the crater threw up another torrent of ash and lava—and the white smocks swirled in frenzy. Gunfire sparked at the dock. Panicked factions of terrified rebels were battling each other.

I turned to Obregón, "Captain, we're going to attack. Move your men down the rock face; pour as much lead as you can into the enemy. I'll take fifty men to an enfilading position—somewhere over there. There's a trail, a land bridge. Between us, we should do some damage." The volcano belched; the earth rocked; and a spume of lava poured out like the dregs of a coffee pot. "That's our rear flanking force," I said.

Major Gillette gathered our platoons, and with Billy Jack on point, I led the way down the jungle path. It was easily passable; obscured from view by hanging leafy branches and vines; and studded with rocks, boulders, and clumpy tree roots. We reached the partially cleared area that jutted over the river—a former guard post, I reckoned.

Obregón's men traded rifle fire with the enemy: firing, then trotting or sliding down the rockface, kicking up scree, getting to closer range, shielding behind boulders. I set my own men into two reinforcing crescent-shaped firing lines overlooking the river and the enemy. We knelt behind a modicum of cover. Our first volley, at least, would hit the rebels with total surprise.

"Front rank: prepare to fire. Fire!"

Our rifles clattered. Rebels fell; some returned fire; others fled. But our harassment of the enemy was picayune compared to the roaring volcano and its menacing, ever-waxing flow of lava. And then, cutting through everything else: a fearsome rapid-fire crackling; a gatling gun mowing down rebels in front of Captain Wakesmith's boat.

The enemy was now a trapped animal. With the volcano behind him, the unexpected battle before him, dissension within his ranks, Wakesmith repelling boarders, and onrushing rebels colliding with deserters, the enemy had but one outlet: he would rush the trail. The enemy was coiled like a snake. He would strike at us.

Here we stood like the Spartans at Thermopylae (though the Spartans were three hundred, and we were but fifty). Against us: thousands of Neustraguanian rebels, who, if they got past us, would, in their savage bloodlust, sack and pillage their way to the capital. And in their path would be my impostor wife (no match for you, dearest one) and the noble Victoria Consuela Cristóbal, class enemy of the island's vicious *sans-culottes*.

The trail approaching us was narrow, of course—a small space to defend—but they could overwhelm us by sheer numbers. As per Zeno's Paradox of Murderous Motion, no matter the casualties, an enemy that progresses by yards will eventually reach some point or another. If they did that, we'd be cut off on this platform of jutting rock—and massacred. Having been massacred once before, I didn't want it to happen again. I needed a plan, and I needed one quick. Luckily, inspiration struck.

"Major, the enemy will be coming up this trail—fast and hard and shooting for all he's worth."

Major Gillette shifted uneasily. "If you're thinking of withdrawal, Yankee General, sir, I don't know that it'll help us much. If we retreated to the summit, they'd just overrun us and flank Obregón."

"Precisely; we're not withdrawing; we're reinforcing."

"With Bierce?"

"Can't count on him. Don't know where he is."

"Then who will do the reinforcing?"

"If we get El Cid and the cathedral's golden bell up on that summit, Captain Wakesmith might see it and think we're Matteo Rodríguez and his army. In all this confusion—with the enemy turning on himself—he might think we're trying to fight our way through; it might intimidate the rebellious rebels and embolden Wakesmith."

"Back to trickery, is it, sir?"

"That—and courage—is all we have, Major. But if Wakesmith can send out a party of Marines, assuming he has some, or if he has more guns, and can turn them on the enemy, it might even the odds."

I turned to Billy Jack. "Sergeant, I want the golden bell and El Cid perched on that summit as fast as blazes. And if you see Bierce—we need him here now."

Billy Jack was on the move instantly—and so was the enemy. A wave of them came rolling up the trail, a hailstorm of bullets preparing their way. I detached a dozen men to block the trail. They formed six rows two-abreast—one rank standing, one rank kneeling, the rest reloading—and pivoted the remaining men on the rocky platform. They would provide enfilading fire and fill the gaps as we took casualties.

The enemy surged before us.

"All right boys, pick your targets and let 'em have it!"

For every rebel that fell, more appeared, screaming hatred, swearing at their wounds, and shooting wildly.

Neither Major Gillette nor I was armed, but we planted ourselves among the men, directing fire, hoping to make each shot count. Once our ammunition was exhausted, it would be down to the bayonet. Our first few volleys had the enemy recoiling, but then they came on—pushing their stacked dead forward as a shield. Our men clawed frantically in their ammunition pouches to keep up a rapid fire. Panic was pressing the enemy onward: lava cascaded down the sides of la Montaña que Eructa; the Gatling gun hammered rebels at the dock, and the scene to the west reminded me of the poet's words, "Those behind cried 'Forward!' And those before cried 'Back!'" as the rebels were torn between fighting and fleeing.

Finally, Major Gillette came to me and announced the inevitable: "Yankee General, sir, in the race between our ammunition and their progress, things are about to get messy."

"A fighting retreat, Major?"

"I reckon that's the ticket now, sir."

A fighting retreat is one of the most difficult military maneuvers, and, inevitably, once they recognized our intention, the enemy was emboldened, lunged at us, and there was some very hot fighting indeed. The narrowness of the path was now both blessing and curse: it limited the enemy's advance, but it also limited our retreat. I reckoned we couldn't fire a volley by rank, withdraw, fire, and withdraw in seriatim because the men would continually bump into each other. So instead I sent our forward ranks running up the hill with Major Gillette while our enfilading force fired covering volleys; then I sent the rest of us out the same way, five or six men at a time. I led the last six men running up the hill.

The rebels pushed their shield of dead off the path, over the precipice, and now it was a footrace, in which, thankfully, we had the lead. There is nothing like the bloodthirsty cries of enraged Neustraguanian rebels to add sparks to one's stride, and I believe I may never have run faster in my life. I actually regretted, dearest one, that you and Bad Boy were not there to see my deerlike speed and agility as I sprang up that trail.

Whenever I heard the zing of a bullet, I silently rejoiced because some rebel had stopped to fire and I had gained ground—and of course I was still alive. As far as I could tell, we had not lost a trooper; and at the finish line was Major Gillette's welcoming party of riflemen. I stumbled through them, and they sprayed lead to stifle our pursuers. There was no time to rest. I jogged to the crestline of the summit and looked down, trying to assess the scope of the battle. Obregón must have seen our retreat because his men were scrambling back up the rockface. Behind him on the other side of the river were chaos, crossfire, flame and ash, and a giant curling tongue of lava stretching down to snatch unwary peasants.

Then I looked behind me and saw an extraordinary sight: Billy Jack had retrieved the golden bell and the glorious statue of El Cid and was now leading the muleskinners on a pell-mell charge up the slope, the bell and El Cid rocking dangerously in their carts. The carts swung into position—towards me—but too fast. El Cid stayed majestically aboard his steed, but the golden bell teetered violently against its restraining ropes, and then burst free. It bounced off the top of the cliff with a deafening clang, and then ringing louder and more erratically than any church bell, it bounded down the rocky face of the plateau. Captain

Obregón's men scattered, the enormous bell skipping past them, tolling doom and crushing rock before it shot out and crashed into Wakesmith's boat like the world's largest cannonball. The impact was terrific. The boat's timbers blew apart in all directions, and the bell hammered the hull into the depths like a nail.

El Cid sat his horse at the summit—like an avenging bronze knight. Under his steady gaze, the rebels screamed like banshees—and their footrace into the jungle was like the fleeing of ants from a broom. The crash and thunder of the bell had apparently unnerved the rebels on the jungle path as well, because our riflemen were cheering; and a new flood of white smocks joined the flight west.

Billy Jack came alongside and said, "The bell is now sunken treasure."

"We need to sink the remaining rebels. Where's Bierce?"

"He follows. Should be crossing Santiago bridge."

I looked down the hill. Bierce's troops were not in view, but he was— his horse tearing up the turf. He pulled up and said, "What in Sam Hill's name was that? It sounded like the last judgment."

"It might be," I said. "We haven't much time. We've engaged the enemy—and that volcano is about to engage everyone. All hell's broken loose, Bierce; you should feel at home."

"It certainly smells like Hades—smoke and sulfur."

"The enemy is on the run; let's charge and scatter him."

"I'm coming with you," said Bierce. "Five minutes and I'll have my army."

Major Gillette arrived aboard Edward. He saluted Bierce and said, "I do hope you brought us some troops, General."

Billy Jack pointed to the river. "Ironclad," he said. "Warship. Have read of them."

"Father Gonçalves," said Bierce.

It was the most stunning sight yet: the spitting image of the USS *Monitor* recreated in blue-black steel. Long, low-slung, with a knob turret, it sailed up the channel like a calm, well-armed monarch of the sea.

Its sight alone affrighted the rebels, and when it fired a cannon shot, flame licked from the turret, and the volcano's thunder was matched from the river.

"That's our rescue ship," I said.

Another explosion from the volcano. I ducked. Charcoal flew past us.

"Yankee General, sir," said Major Gillette, "that volcano's getting our range."

"We've got to get Bad Boy, our horses, and the women to that ship and safety."

"Marshal," said Bierce, "your priorities continue to amaze me."

I saw Bierce's men marching up the slope. I turned to him and said, "Take your troops, and follow Billy Jack to that land bridge over the river. The enemy is running, but we need to ensure our path is clear."

"As you say, Generalissimo."

"And you, Major Gillette, come with me: we'll fetch the women."

The volcano exploded again. We galloped our horses through a shower of charcoal and ash. Though I may have looked like a chimney sweep, Rachel didn't hesitate when I reached down to lift her onto the saddle. Her arms were around my waist like a taut rope. "Thank goodness, you're here," she said. We watched Major Gillette perch Victoria behind him, and Rachel added: "And thank you for making the right choice—dear husband of mine."

"Hang on!" I spurred Marshal Ney up the hill. Bad Boy hurtled after us.

I waved my kepi at Bierce's column. They cheered, and I heard Bierce shout, "All right, boys, on the double!"

I couldn't resist but command "Follow me!" and pointed to the crestline. Major Gillette and I reached it nearly in tandem. Rachel gasped at the sight of la Montaña que Eructa glowing red. Captain Obregón's men were reforming at the jungle trail to the land bridge, and I rode to give him instructions. "Captain, get your men down that trail swift as lightning. Bierce and his column are right behind us. Victory awaits!"

His troopers fired a volley to clear any rebel malingerers, and then charged. Bierce's men poured in after them. It was gratifying, watching from the crestline, as our men pooled out on the valley floor—the enemy in headlong retreat, our troops in pursuit.

A shout behind me: "Generalissimo!" Captain Royce was on horseback. He had a rope tied onto his pommel. Tethered at the other end was a staggering Matteo Rodríguez. The rope bound Rodríguez's wrists together. "As your aide, I thought you might need me as we go into action. I brought the prisoner. What should I do with him?"

"Bring him along—and your horse."

The jungle trail over the land bridge was cleared, and now it was our turn. The volcano bade us hurry, but our battle-tested horses knew better, and as we walked them down the path they stepped carefully over roots and rocks and shied away from the trail's edge and a precipitous fall. When we emerged on the other side of the river, the volcanic heat was searing, and with that and my endless exertion, sweat leaked into my uniform and dripped down my brow.

Rebel bodies littered the ground, but we cut a path through the enemy dead to the shoreline—and there was the ironclad. A welcoming sight stood on its prow: Father Gonçalves, in full naval regalia, sword at his hip, naval revolver pulled from its holster.

"Ah, it's you, Generalissimo. I've been trying to get my bearings. Fired a few shots from my cannon but wasn't sure whether I missed most of the battle or ended it."

"Father, our main enemy now is that volcano. Unless you brought the entire Navy with you…"

"Be not afraid, my son. Thanks to Matteo Rodríguez's foresight," he nodded to our prisoner, "the Navy was confined to quarters. I gave them immediate orders. Marines are evacuating the island." He turned to Victoria. "Your father, Consuela, is safe; I sent a ship to fetch him at the port of Alto Nido de Pájaro."

"Oh, gracias, Father."

To me he said, "Generalissimo, order your men to El Pueblo del Pelicano Sagrado; our Navy is concentrated there."

"Captain Royce," I said, "see to it. You can leave your prisoner here." He untied the rope that bound Matteo Rodríguez to his saddle, saluted me, and rode down the beach. I never saw him again. To Father Gonçalves I said, "How many of us can you take aboard?"

"You Americans, Consuela, the animals—all will fit. But no more. I already have passengers."

A hatch opened from the turret. A man in resplendent uniform—grey tunic, blue epaulets, a red sash, a Cavalry dress helmet on his head—strode up the deck. I saluted. It was El Claudio.

"You know, Generalissimo, I am really glad to see you again. You've done a great job, a really great job—and, of course, I have done a really great job too. I gave you great tools, didn't I: the best soldiers, innovative ships, the finest fighting priests in the world! This ship is his design, you know. Someday, he tells me, it will be submersible. It will travel beneath the seas and be a great benefit to science. But he's still working out the kinks on that part, and he doesn't want to take risks with it now—and I appreciate that. But, again, Generalissimo, let me just say: I did a really great job choosing you, didn't I?"

"Yes, Your Majesty."

"Yes, it's all great, really great, we win—but now we have to go. The island's going to explode—biggest explosion you've ever seen; bigger than the volcano that sank Atlantis, bigger than the volcano that covered Pompeii; bigger than anything. But that's okay, we'll find a new home; a great, big, beautiful home for my family—who are all on board, by the way. We'll make a new life, a great new life; I work hard, you know, and I have plenty of cash to get us started again. We will make do. Anyway, Generalissimo, I just came out to congratulate you on your really great job and my great job of appointing you. *Vaya con Dios.*"

"Excuse me, Your Majesty," Father Gonçalves said, "but the Generalissimo is going to join us."

"Ah, that's even better! No fiery death under molten lava! That's really good news. And your wife? That's great. And Bierce, you're coming aboard, aren't you? Consuela, good to see you; and your escort—that man with the eye patch—how are you? And Indian man, good to see you too. And—what is *he* doing here? Matteo Rodríguez? He should be locked up—the man's a traitor! He tried to overthrow our country! It was corruption like you've never seen; asked me for favors, appointments, then undermined me, worked with the rebels, organized my own government against me. He even fired up that volcano. Can you imagine? He's not coming aboard this boat."

Matteo Rodríguez stepped forward. "Your Majesty, that cleric fills your head with lies. These Americans—they're mercenaries and should be executed; they're the ones working against you."

"Didn't you hire Bierce?"

"Yes, but..."

"That's the one good decision you made. And now I've made one: I'm leaving you here." He turned to Father Gonçalves and said, "Let's get these other people aboard and push off."

"As you say, Your Majesty."

"But, Your Majesty, what about me?" said Matteo Rodríguez.

"You stole the cathedral's golden bell, didn't you?" said El Claudio.

"To keep it safe."

"Well, then you can stay here with it." El Claudio turned to us and said, "I will see you aboard, Generalissimo, Mrs. Generalissimo, Bierce, Consuela, Escort Man, Indian Man." He strode to the turret, ignoring Rodríguez's frantic pleas of "Your Majesty! Your Majesty!"

Bierce took the initiative, leaned from his horse, grabbed the rope that bound Matteo Rodríguez, and led him away. I dismounted and helped load the ladies and horses aboard the ship. There were two hatches at the turret. Father Gonçalves had me take the animals through one that led down below decks and aft to a stable in the hold, complete with stalls and straw, provisioned with water barrels and stacks of hay, and with curry combs fastened to the wall.

At the fore end of the hold there was another hatch. I opened this and stepped into the engine room. Before me was a vast array of levers and bellows and pipes and cogs and glistening steel that rotated and hummed and left me wide-eyed with astonishment, but no more so than the sight of the engineers who kept this machine working: two young priests holding breviaries and looking at engine dials. They nodded shyly at me, and I marveled at the sort of men produced by Neustraguano's seminaries. They pointed to another door, at the opposite end, and I passed into the gun room, which had steel stairs rising to the turret. I went through yet another door and there were my companions gathered in a room resembling an English gentleman's study: bookshelves, chairs, a couch, tables. The women were rejoicing over their accommodations (apparently there were cabins ahead), and Major Gillette was sipping tea and holding a couple of biscuits. I asked him to toss one to Bad Boy. Then I said, "Let's get above deck and wait for Bierce."

Billy Jack and Father Gonçalves were there keeping watch. The sky was black and red and flashed with yellow explosions from the volcano; all around us was a thick muffler of smoke; and then, like a horseman from the apocalypse, Bierce burst through the noxious fog. He jumped his horse onto the deck and said, "All right, Father, say your benedictions and let's get the hell out of here."

"But where is Matteo Rodríguez?"

"Look up there." Through the roiling black and red clouds, we saw the towering statue of El Cid. Dangling from his lance was a rope—and at the end of it was Matteo Rodríguez, hanging by his wrists. "One way or another," Bierce said, "he won't last long."

"*Sic semper tyrannis*, if you'll excuse the expression," said Major Gillette.

I gave Bierce a hard look; he gave me an equally hard look in reply: "That man tried to kill us. He conspired to assassinate the king."

"But Bierce," I said and glanced up at Rodríguez, "that's torture."

"It was a matter of convenience. He didn't merit a bullet, Marshal. And anyway, your statue got the last laugh. He's the victor. That's his laurel."

The volcano erupted again, the ground shook, the river foamed and splashed aboard the deck. And then there was a scream. El Cid rolled back and forth like a rocking horse and then broke free from the cart and went plunging down the rockface, horse and rider diving violently into the river. A giant wave smashed into us and sent us skittering across the deck with Bierce's horse.

"Come on, Father," growled Bierce, regaining his footing. "Say a prayer for his damned soul and let's get out of here."

I grabbed the reins to Bierce's horse and led him down to the stables. I secured him, checked on Marshal Ney and Edward, and paused a moment to catch my breath in their company. "Well, noble steeds, our work here is done."

I passed through the engine room, acknowledged the shy seminarian engineers, went through the gun room, and stepped into the study and a celebration. Father Gonçalves circled with a bottle, pouring out doses of sangria. Somewhat to my surprise, Billy Jack accepted a glass, raised it in toast, and said, "El Cid Campeador: *Sic transit gloria mundi.*"

Rachel sidled up to me, slid her arm over mine, and asked, "What did he say?"

"A prayer to Saint Gloria Mundi, for the peaceful repose of El Cid's statue."

Victoria raised her glass and said, "To Generalissimo Armstrong!"

I declined a proffered glass and said, "Thank you, Victoria. It was my great honor to serve your country. For there is no greater honor than this: to lay down one's statue for another. My only regret is that I have but one statue to give for your country."

Rachel sat me on the sofa, and said, "Enough speeches for you, Armstrong."

I don't believe I had closed my eyes for several days, and with my back sinking into the luxuriously padded settee, I found my eyelids unstoppably sliding down. The last thing I remember was Bierce saying, "And the moral of the story is, there are no morals beyond general expediency." I was too tired to refute him and entrusted that task to Father Gonçalves.

And so, my dear, ended our adventure in Neustraguano, an island now sunk beneath the sea. Most of the king's loyal subjects were evacuated to Mexico, but the king and his family are residents of San Francisco. They live under a pseudonym, which I cannot reveal, and El Claudio intends to establish himself as a hotelier, building the most luxurious hotel in the city. Father Gonçalves has drafted the design and is supervising the construction. Billy Jack is working as a tutor for Captain Briggs's children; and Rachel and Victoria are with me here, along with Bierce who sends his love—and so do I, by the way.

So, let me end, dearest one, by asking: Did you ever find my staghounds Bleuch and Tuck? If so, can you return them with Major Gillette after he delivers you this letter? I do so miss them—and you, of course, my darling.

Your devoted Antie